WINDFALL

By Marilinne Cooper

Names, characters, and incidents are either the product of the author's imagination or are used fictitiously for the purpose of storytelling only. However, real life does inspire fiction, and while resemblances to actual persons, business establishments or events may not be entirely coincidental, they have been used solely to evoke atmosphere, a sense of place, and local color.

PART ONE

CHAPTER ONE

JANUARY 2017

"Tyler? Hello – are you in there?"

With a guilty start, Tyler looked up from the glowing computer screen. He had not realized that the early dusk of winter had already descended on the room, leaving him in solitary confinement in an island of light shed by his laptop and heartsafire.com.

"Sorry, I didn't realize how late it had become. Who's there?" He stood up stiffly and took a few blind steps to flick the switch on the wall of his home office.

A young woman stood in the hallway. The colorful earflap hat pulled low over her forehead was wet with freshly melted snow, as were the shoulders of the heavy wool sweater she wore in lieu of a coat. A long hand-knit scarf was wrapped several times around her neck; her cheeks were ruddy from the cold and her dark eyes appeared wide and fearful.

"It's me. Chloe."

So unexpected was her appearance, that for a second he almost asked, "Chloe who?" The Chloe he knew was his son's girlfriend, who was currently sailing blithely around the Aegean Sea in only a bikini, soaking up the Greek sunshine, somewhere off the coast of Skyros. Not in West Jordan, Vermont, wearing mukluks and mittens, and standing in a growing puddle of freezing water.

The last that Tyler had seen of Chloe had been a brief glimpse via Skype months earlier, when she and Tucker had called to wish him a happy birthday before the video portion of the app had frozen and the call had dropped. He had a fleeting memory of glowing tanned faces against a background of brilliant aquatic blue; he called this image to mind now and then to remind himself that Chloe and

Tucker were happy and safe in their world travels and that Tucker's newfound calling as a Mediterranean sailor-in-training was a great idea.

"Chloe? My Chloe? Holy shit, what are you doing here?"

He could see the tears spill over as he crossed the room and folded his arms around the awkward bulk of her multi-layered body. And around the bulging pack on her back. And the front pack that she seemed to be wearing beneath her many sweaters. Still stunned, he instinctively reached for the padded straps to relieve her of the heavy weight she was carrying. She slipped gratefully out of them, moving away from him and into the lamplight.

"Oh, sorry, I'm getting snow all over the floor. Let me take these boots off." She stepped out of her ill-fitting winter footwear and carried it back through the still dark hallway to the outside door. But she had been illuminated long enough for Tyler to get a better look at her. As she padded back into the room, tripping a little on the oversized rag-wool socks that hung off the ends of her feet, he slowly lowered the backpack to the floor, mesmerized by the profile of her passing silhouette.

"Chloe..." He came forward, his gaze still fixed a few feet below her face. Even the multiple layers of heavy pullovers could not hide the roundness of her belly protruding beyond the swell of her breasts. "Oh, my god. What the..."

Her cheeks flushed an even deeper shade of crimson accompanied by a fresh flood of tears as her hands moved protectively to rest on her stomach. "I know, I know, I'm sorry," she sobbed.

Although Tyler had grown accustomed to Chloe's emotionality during the six months she lived in his household with Tucker, he was still taken aback and confused by it. She took his abashed silence as a cue to continue.

"We should have told you – I was going to last time we talked but then the connection was so bad." She wiped her nose on the back of one fuzzy mitten and sank into Tyler's desk chair. “And then when I left Greece...” she sniffed deeply before the next onslaught of crying began, “I wasn’t so big then but it just started growing and growing...”

He felt as helpless as he ever had in his life, not knowing what to do for a weeping pregnant woman. At the same time he tried to grasp the concept that he was going to be a grandfather. There was no way he was old enough for that.

“It was all the changing countries and time zones,” she went on. “I lost track of when I was supposed to take the pills and then I couldn’t get the prescription refilled.”

She pulled off the earflap hat and tossed it on the floor, looking at it reproachfully as though the colorful Peruvian pattern was mocking her remorse. Tyler noted that she had cut her hair – the dreadlocks she had so carefully cultivated were now cropped to a short spiky style, longer on one side than the other. She saw him staring at it and ran her fingers through the dark minimalist tresses. “Yeah, it had to go. It was time.” Something about this statement caused the tears to start up again.

“Chloe, honey...” He wanted to say something comforting but he found himself distracted with wondering how she had ended up here alone. And where was his son?

She stood up abruptly. “I have to pee. I always have to pee now.” Before he could say anything else she had disappeared down the hallway and slammed the bathroom door.

He shook his head, still having trouble comprehending the whirlwind that had just come out of nowhere and rocked his peaceful existence. He had been having a quiet afternoon, surfing the netherworld of online dating, a private sport into which hours of his life could disappear until he was forced back into the reality of the dark days of winter in northern Vermont. By the looks of Chloe’s clothing and his wet floor, it must have started snowing again; he turned on the outdoor light to confirm the swirling of the flakes outside his window.

How did she get here? He could see no other car in the driveway besides his own rusted Subaru, now covered with two inches of fresh powder. She couldn't have walked. Could she?

The squeak of the bathroom door hinges announced her return. She had washed her face and removed her two outer sweaters, now wearing only a soft-looking gray turtleneck that was thin enough for him to see the outline of her inverted bellybutton pressing against it. She looked enormous to him – but she had been so slim last time he saw her and he had no idea how to gauge a pregnancy.

Chloe sat down heavily again in the desk chair, her eyes straying over at the laptop screen. "Tyler, you hound dog!" A ghost of a grin passed over her face. "Doing a little e-dating?"

In two swift strides he was across the room, slamming the computer shut with a gesture that conveyed all the guilt and embarrassment he didn't think he should feel. "Are you hungry? Come into the kitchen and I'll make us some dinner."

"I'm never not hungry now. So have you gone out with any women you met online?" She asked as she followed him down the hall.

"A few. It gets me out of the house." He turned his back on her and stared into the refrigerator so she could not see his face. "Some leftover Pad Thai?"

"Thai?" Her voice quavered a little again. "Um, I get heartburn from spicy food these days."

"Here – this is what you should be drinking, right?" He handed her a half gallon container of milk and a glass.

She grimaced. "Yeah, strangely I crave it."

"Chloe – how did you get here today?"

"I got dropped off in town and walked from there." She was suddenly paying a lot of attention to gulping down her milk.

"Where did you come from?" Tyler began pulling ingredients off shelves, purposely not looking at her.

"New Hampshire. I met some people on the plane who offered me a place to stay with them and I've been there for a while."

"A while?"

"Like since before Christmas."

He turned to stare at her, a bag of lettuce held in mid-air. "You've been in the states for a month and didn't call me? Where is Tucker?"

She wiped her mouth with the back of her hand before replying. "He's still in Greece. Working on the SS Knossos."

"Have–" he almost couldn't ask the question – "have you guys split up?"

"Not really." She rubbed her belly self-consciously. "I just couldn't be there anymore and he didn't want to leave."

Tyler knew something was off here and he could not zero in on it. "So he's okay with the whole baby thing?" His hands trembled a little as he threw the lettuce into a wooden bowl.

The pause that preceded her answer told him all he needed to know. "Not really."

"Oh, Chloe." They were so young – only eighteen and nineteen, Chloe being the older of the two. Of course, Tucker wasn't ready.

"We got married, you know. No, of course, you don't know. We didn't tell you." The tears began flowing again. "On the beach, in Thailand. Last spring."

He leaned back against the counter, speechless. "Last spring," he repeated in disbelief.

"I'm sorry, we should have told you. It was impulsive. It didn't really change anything. We just thought it would make us more committed to each other." She sobbed quietly for a few seconds and then said, "So, yeah, I'm a Mackenzie now."

The fact that she actually had taken Tucker's last name for her own was the least of the evening's surprises. He straightened up and reached for a tomato. "Well, then. Welcome to the family."

He wished he kept some alcohol in the house; it had been a few years since he had wanted a drink so badly. Maybe he would go over to the West Jordan Inn after they ate, share this unexpected news with Sarah and Hunter. He needed to bounce it off somebody.

He handed Chloe a knife and a cucumber. They worked in awkward silence, side by side, both of them unsure of what would happen next.

"So when are you due?" His inquiry immediately sounded cliché and impersonal.

"Um, maybe in May. I'm not sure."

"I can't do that math – how many weeks along are you?" He didn't know how to talk about a pregnancy, but he thought he was asking the right questions.

"Twenty, maybe. Or twenty-two. I don't know, I'm not exactly positive. I haven't seen a doctor."

Tyler knew little about prenatal care, but he knew that was not the right answer. "Well, we'll make an appointment first thing in the morning then. You ought to see someone."

He sensed that she seemed relieved by these words. "Actually I hope I'm farther along – it's gotten so big in the last few weeks."

Tyler definitely agreed with that statement. "I'll ask Sarah tonight for the name of a good obstetrician; she'll know someone."

After dinner, as he got Chloe settled into the guest bedroom, more and more questions kept popping into his mind. "Where'd you score all the winter clothes?" he asked as he brought her heavy outer sweaters in from the office. He noted the Eileen Fisher label on one and Garnet Hill on the other. The scarf she had been wearing was a finely woven cashmere from Scotland. These were not brands that Chloe the vagabond could normally afford.

"Thrift store, of course," was her casual reply and he decided the answer made more sense than any other thing she had told him all night.

He went out to start his car and clean the snow off the windshield and by the time he had come back inside she had already turned out the lights and was under the down comforter.

"Good night," he called softly and she mumbled a sleepy reply.

On his drive to the West Jordan Inn, he went over all the things she had told him and tried to make a list in his head of which pieces of information seemed suspicious, from her surprise appearance on his doorstep in a blizzard to her unwillingness to talk about what had happened between her and Tucker. All of it was questionable, he decided.

Even on a snowy evening with slippery roads and temperatures near zero, the Night Heron Lounge was half full. Sarah was behind the bar as usual, as she had been for most of the last twenty-five years. Her long hair had been a lustrous near-black shade when Tyler first met her, but now it was dramatically more salt than pepper. The lean, angular lines of her body had softened only a little over the years and she still seemed to move as quickly and gracefully as when he had fallen in love with her.

Their time together had been passionate and full of conflict; when it had eventually grown too rocky to continue, Sarah had left him for Hunter, an easygoing family-oriented man, who was almost the diametrical opposite of Tyler, as well as being fifteen years younger than her. Together they had raised, and were still raising, five children, two of their own and three adopted, the most recent being a pair of orphaned Chinese girls.

"Hey, amigo. What can I get for you?" Sarah asked affectionately. Since his return to West Jordan twelve years earlier, they had buried the hatchet, and along with Lucy, Tucker's mother, had become one extended, if not always functional, family.

"A beer and a crystal ball, so I can figure out what the hell is going on." He slipped out of his parka and tossed it on an empty chair at a table behind his barstool.

"Why – what's up?"

"Chloe showed up tonight, alone in the snowstorm, without Tucker." He took a satisfying swig of the amber ale she placed in front of him.

Sarah's eyebrows went up. "Really. What's up with that?"

"It gets worse. She's pregnant. Like out-to-here pregnant." He demonstrated in front of his stomach. "But she says she's not due until May."

"Oh, wow. I see why you need a drink."

"But wait – there's more." He laughed now, finally seeing the absurd humor in the outrageousness of it all. "They got married nine months ago in Thailand but never told us."

Sarah's expression reflected his own reaction. "Anything else?"

"Well, she cut off her dreads, I'm not sure what that means."

"Oh, Myles did that too a few months ago – maybe that stage of their lives is finally over." As she mentioned her son's name, she frowned a little. "I'm kind of worried – we haven't heard from him in a while now."

"Kids." Tyler shook his head. "I wouldn't let it bother you. He probably just lost his cell phone or something."

"I hope so. He's been acting kind of strange ever since he got back from traveling last summer." She moved to the other end of the bar to ring up a tab for some departing customers.

Tyler had forgotten that, after graduating from high school, Myles had traveled for a few months with Chloe and Tucker. Myles was the closest thing that Tucker had ever had to a brother; and now he wondered if Sarah's son might have any clue as to what was going on with his own.

"Where's Myles living these days?" he asked when she returned.

"Somewhere over the river in New Hampshire. Windfall I think." Doing a quick assessment of the remaining patrons, she began closing down parts of the bar. "He was caretaking a place for a widowed woman there."

"Windfall?" It was an odd coincidence. "That's where I've been taking a tango class once a week."

"You're learning how to tango?" Sarah could not conceal the amusement in her voice. "Must be a woman that brought that on."

Tyler flushed a little and grinned. "Actually I'm pretty good at it. And it's fun." He did not share the story behind how he had gotten involved with tango and what had transpired as a result.

"Sarah, there's a call for you on the landline." Hunter appeared in the doorway, carrying a small girl in fleecy footed pajamas. "Hey, Tyler. We haven't seen you for a while. What's happening?"

In the two decades that Tyler had known him, Hunter had changed very little. He had arrived at the West Jordan Inn as a drifter who had financed his world travels with his horticultural pot-growing skills and who had found himself suddenly solely responsible for a Nigerian baby whose adopted father had been murdered. His ability to rise to the parental challenge had won him Sarah and a new life, one which he had totally embraced. He became a loving stay-at-home dad and caretaker for a family that never seemed to stop growing. He still wore his hair in a long ponytail, he still grew pot, and he still rolled with whatever punches fell his way.

Tyler filled him in on the unusual developments of the day and Hunter, who loved babies and children more than any other man Tyler knew, was touchingly excited by Chloe's news.

"We know a great ob-gyn man. I'll give you his number. He was awesome during Dylan's birth." Hunter put a straw in a glass of ice water and held it up for the child on his arm. "Can you say good night to Tyler, Mai Li?"

The little girl looked at Tyler and then buried her face in Hunter's shoulder. "She's still shy with strangers, especially men. But we're working on it. Maybe I'll see you in a bit."

Watching him go, Tyler thought what a lot of effort it must take to help an adopted child from a foreign orphanage adjust to a new family and culture. Almost as much work as assimilating a pregnant daughter-in-law into your home life.

When Sarah returned a moment later, she wore a distracted frown. "Did Hunter go up already?"

"He did – what's going on?" Tyler slid his empty bottle across the counter and Sarah absentmindedly replaced it with a new one.

"That was the Windfall police department on the phone. They wanted to know if I had seen Myles today." Sarah looked around the bar, decided the other two remaining customers were absorbed in their own conversation, and then discreetly poured herself a stiff shot of tequila. "Apparently he's disappeared."

"Disappeared?"

"Well, they're looking for him and they can't find him."

This didn't sound good and the look on Sarah's face confirmed it. "And they're looking for him because..."

"Because the woman he works for in Windfall was found dead in her driveway and Myles is wanted for questioning." Sarah upended the tequila in one swift gulp.

Tyler hadn't realized he was slumping in his seat until Sarah's words made him sit up straight. "You mean like murdered? Or just like dropped dead?"

"I don't know – they didn't give me any details!" Visibly stressed, she began washing dirty glasses almost violently. "They just said they couldn't find him and that if he showed up here, that I should send him there."

"Well, where does he live there?" Tyler also felt a little nervous, knowing he was probably about to have to come out about his secret online dating life that had led him to Windfall.

"That's just it – I thought he lived at this Sloane woman's house where he worked. But evidently not anymore. So...he doesn't answer his phone and we don't know where he lives. AND the police are looking for him."

The soapy water sloshed over onto her dress and she grabbed a hand towel, pressing it to the wet stain. "So now am I allowed to worry about him?"

Sloane – how many Sloanes could there be in a village the size of Windfall? It had to be the same woman he had gone out with a few times, a wealthy widow with a healthy tan and a well-groomed appearance whose main passions in life were golf and gardening. They had attempted to prove the theory that their personalities would be compatible because they had matched up online; it had been pleasant but there had not been enough chemistry to go much farther than a few dates. They had remained casual friends as Tyler continued looking for other potential partners. Sloane had been a good person to consult for local history or gossip since she had been summering in Windfall since she was a child and living there permanently for the last twenty years.

"Tyler?"

"I – I knew Sloane. I didn't realize that was who Myles was working for."

"You knew her?" But at the moment Sarah couldn't care less about Tyler's love life; her main concern was for her son. "Maybe you can go over there and see what you can find out. See if you can track down Myles."

"I could," he said carefully, about to make his excuses, but when her face flooded with grateful relief he immediately caved. "I'll call a few people tomorrow. After I get a doctor's appointment for Chloe."

"Oh, right, sorry. I got so caught up in my own drama, I'd already forgotten about yours. Good luck with that." She hit a few keys on the cash register and as it spit out the totals for the day, her eyes suddenly filled with tears.

"Sarah..."

"I'm sorry," she apologized again. "I just feel like this is all our fault. After we adopted the girls we didn't have enough money to pay tuition for Myles to go to music college in Boston or even enough credit to qualify for a loan and he couldn't borrow as much as he needed and his grades weren't good enough for merit scholarships and he didn't apply for financial aid soon enough because we didn't think he would need it." She was rambling, almost as though she were speaking the words aloud for the first time. "It totally derailed his future when he got back from Europe. We never have enough money; you know what we have to do to get by."

Although they rarely had spoken about it, Tyler was aware that the supplemental income stream that kept the inn afloat came from Hunter's lucrative pot-growing business. He had tried not to be judgmental, but when Tucker had told him once that his best friend, Myles, had been cleaning bud every fall since he was eleven or twelve to help out during the family's busiest time of the year, he could not help but feel disapproval.

"It really put a strain on our family relationships. Goodbye, drive carefully!" Sarah followed the last two patrons to the door and locked it behind them. Back at the bar she poured herself another hefty shot of top shelf tequila. "Myles seemed to take the bad news well, too well really. I realize now that he kept it all inside, tried to act like everything was fine, that it didn't matter. But things have felt strange since then. And then after he took the job in Windfall, we grew even farther apart. Hunter's been particularly upset – they were so close."

Tyler was surprised he hadn't heard any of this before – but, then again, other than working on stories for his newspaper, he had been putting some space between himself and West Jordan in the last few months.

"When he refused to come home at harvest time, Hunter was devastated. He felt like it was a father/son tradition, something they had done together for years. Even the promise of some decent cash in his pocket, didn't change his mind. He said he was doing fine, that he didn't need the money, but I know that can't possibly be true." She sat down heavily on the bar stool beside Tyler's. "So how do you know – how *did* you know - this woman he was working for?"

"Oh, well, I meet a lot of people covering local news stories for the paper..." She gave him a look that told him she wasn't buying his evasive answer. "Okay, I went out with her a couple of times. It was nothing serious and it didn't work out."

The exhaustion on her face softened a little into amusement. "And how do you meet someone in Windfall? That's over the river and on the other side of the mountain from here."

"Online. I met her online, okay?" His prickly defensiveness seemed to break the tension in the air and they both laughed a little. "It's totally legit, nothing creepy. It's what us single old people have to do nowadays to meet each other if we don't want to go pub crawling."

"And you didn't know Myles was her handy boy?"

Tyler shrugged. "She never mentioned it. I never went to her house. We met at a local restaurant for lunch and then another time for dinner." Sloane had been his first awkward foray back into the dating world after a fiasco of an affair with a woman named Elle on a tropical island a year and a half earlier.

"That sounds pretty civilized for you."

"Well, I am a very civilized guy. Who just happens to have bad judgment sometimes when it comes to women." Elle had not been his only train wreck of a relationship in the last twenty years.

"Hey, I could resent that remark." Sarah stood up, tossing back the rest of her drink. " And now I'm going to have to throw you out – I need to go talk to Hunter; tell him about the call from the police."

After promising to see what he could learn from his Windfall connections regarding Myles's whereabouts, Tyler headed out to clean the snow off his car again. Hearing about Sarah's troubles had helped him forget for a few moments the magnitude of his own family issues. He was going to have to confront Chloe in the morning – get a straight answer out of her about what the hell was going on.

CHAPTER TWO

October 2016

Myles climbed out of the open dining room window and silently closed it behind him. Walking casually down the driveway, he patted the front of his jacket to make sure his cargo was secure. Four sets of silver forks, knives and spoons were stashed snuggly in the inside pockets, along with a pair of scissors, a potato peeler and a stainless steel spatula. In his backpack was a pair of crystal wine goblets wrapped in some Italian linen napkins and a couple of cut glass cereal bowls. There was no reason not to eat his morning granola out of the best and the Emersons would never miss them. They had more dishes for their summer house than the entire West Jordan Inn dining room. And Myles knew how many dishes the inn had, because there had been nights when he'd had to wash them all.

The sun was already pretty low in the sky; he probably didn't have enough time to hike all the way up the trail to his cabin, but he didn't want to haul this stash to town with him. Then he swore, remembering that he had to go home anyway to get his fiddle for the gig tonight. It would be dark by the time he came back down the mountain. Good thing he'd acquired the great flashlight from the Franchettis. That family certainly enjoyed buying LL Bean gear; some of their Christmas presents to each other were still in the original packaging.

He turned up the road towards Sloane Winslow's place and then veered off onto an old logging pass that led into the woods. In a few hundred feet the two lane track became a steep incline of hard-packed mud and rocks. Now it was slippery with leaves, after a heavy rainstorm a few days earlier had knocked down the remaining foliage and finished off the colorful fall season. He nearly lost his footing a few times as he sprinted quickly upwards to where the landscape leveled off for easier travel. He could do the trip in fifteen minutes if he was in high gear like he was now, but if he was loaded down with food or other equipment, it took longer to get home.

Through the trees, the abandoned sugar house came into view. If you weren't looking for it, you could miss it – the weathered wood of the outer walls worn to the color of tree bark, the shingled roof covered in years' worth of moss and lichen. The two windows were on the opposite side of the building, so no reflection of the glass or light within could be seen as you approached. It was a perfect hideaway and part of the Winslow property so stray hikers rarely wandered by.

Sloane had mentioned the sugar house to him when he was working for her during the summer and sleeping on a cot in her gardening cottage; she thought he might enjoy going up that way – if you kept walking there was a view from the top of the mountain. Her husband or her father or some Winslow had tried to keep the maple sugaring operation going, but it was an endless task, and if you weren't in residence in March when the sap started running, you had to hire other people to do the work and it was just a losing proposition.

Myles knew a few people in Vermont who still tapped their maple groves and boiled the sap down, but they did it for the love of the tradition, not for the money. Their sugar houses were funky, functional structures, meant for real work, not as a rich man's hobby. This one had been built as a little miniature jewel of a building to match the rest of the Winslow estate, with a fieldstone foundation and finished woodwork. The woodstove was high quality and had only needed a little bit of renovation to make it usable again. There was a little spring nearby that was low but still running, even in September. Myles had seen all the possibilities of the place and embraced it as his own. He told Sloane that he had found a place to live in town and didn't need to stay in her cottage anymore. She offered him a few pieces of old furniture and he asked to borrow the four-wheel-drive truck to transport it. It was a little touch-and-go but the well-maintained vehicle made it up the logging road without too much trouble, not like driving the ancient piece-of-shit pickup his father used to get back and forth to his dope patch.

Through the autumn, he had still done some work for Sloane, including trips to the dump, which gave him access to the truck. With careful planning, it had not been hard to use it for his own purposes as well. And his new home was pretty comfortable now, thanks to all the obscenely wealthy people he worked for in Windfall.

As he headed for the door, he grabbed his solar lantern from where he had left it on a stump in the sun earlier that day. It was an expensive piece of camping equipment; when fully powered up and hung from a hook in the ceiling it could pretty much light the whole cabin. Unloading his pockets and his backpack, he picked up his fiddle case, slapped some peanut butter and jam onto two pieces of whole grain bread, and shoved a hoodie into his bag because the temperature was sure to drop by midnight. At the last minute he remembered the flashlight and then he was on his way back down the hill, eating his sandwich as he made his way swiftly through the dying light.

The band was part of what made living in Windfall seem like the right thing for him to be doing right now. He had refused to admit to anyone, let alone himself, how destroyed he had been when it turned out he couldn't go to college this fall. He had already been feeling totally down and out when he had to leave Greece because his money had run out, and also for other reasons he couldn't let himself think about even now. He told his parents it was fine, not to worry, he'd be okay, but he so wasn't okay. The prospect of being stuck in West Jordan indefinitely, while all his friends were off to great intellectual and social pursuits, was so depressing that he sometimes slept until way past noon, unable to face life with his cheerful, socially-conscious and totally disorganized family. His two new little sisters didn't deserve the resentment he started to feel towards them, and the fact that his college fund had gone towards their adoption expenses became a sore spot that festered more and more as the days went on.

When he'd seen the ad for "Handyman/Yardworker needed in Windfall, lodging provided" he had jumped on it, anxious for any opportunity that would take him out of the funk he had fallen into and away from his childhood status quo.

When he had his first week's paycheck in his pocket, he took himself out to the local bar where Sloane had told him there was usually live music on Friday and Saturday nights. She hadn't considered the fact that he wasn't actually old enough to drink. He stood outside, discretely smoking a joint until the band started playing, and then made his way inside to join the small crowd on the dance floor, which had been hastily created by pushing the pool table aside.

Before the first set was over, he knew he had come home. The music was an original mash-up of blues, reggae, folk, bluegrass and country rock played by four musicians, (three with wild unkempt beards, one with a clean shaven face and scalp) who covered songs on guitar, mandolin, banjo, keyboard and drums. Their local fans pulsed enthusiastically to the funky beat, a handful of women in tight jeans and buckled boots danced uninhibitedly to the faster tunes. At the break, Myles approached the band, asked if they ever considered adding a fiddler and before he realized what was happening, someone had put a beautiful old violin into his hands and he was jamming with them on a few tunes in the second set. By the time the night was over, he had been accepted into their tribe, and asked to join them the following week.

They were regular working class guys, who just loved making music. By day, Aidan hung sheetrock, Daniel taught second grade, George worked construction and Liam was a disc jockey at a local radio station. They didn't have aspirations to sail around the world or discover a new planet – they looked forward to getting high after work and playing some tunes. Myles enjoyed hanging with them; it didn't require a lot of deep thinking or soul searching, just an open mind and a laid-back attitude. He knew how to manage both of those qualities really well.

Because the band got to drink for free, Myles was usually able to slip in a few beers or down a couple shots of Jack without anyone really noticing. It was always with a sense of profound contentment that he staggered up the mountain on those weekend nights and fell into bed at three in the morning

Now, after wolfing down his hastily made sandwich, he fished the remainder of a joint out of the breast pocket of his jacket and finished it off before he reached the main street that ran through town. Windfall was not much more than a village, but its buildings were New England picture-perfect, all white clapboards and green shutters, without the reality of laundry lines or vehicles up on cinder blocks to ruin the effect. At the far end of town, past the regulated historic zoning, Martin's Mountainview Bar and Restaurant defied the local laws with its yellow paint, red trim and neon sign. The décor faux pas continued inside with a plaid carpet, plastic wall ornamentations and ugly low-budget stools, tables and chairs. The atmosphere at Martin's wasn't entirely created by the tacky furnishings; it was also the result of an eclectic variety of patrons that ran the range from lawyer to logger, and pothead to Patriots' fan.

"Hey, Mya," the bartender greeted him with his local nickname, a combo of his first name, Myles, and his last name, Adams, that someone had dubbed him with after his premier performance with the Why Mo Boys, which, in the same sort of shorthand, was derived from "White Mountains." She wiped a space on the bar clean for him and slapped down a paper placemat and some silverware.

"Hey, Babs." Five nights a week for the last thirty years, the wiry white-haired woman had taken care of the local drunks and diners at Martin's. She was one of the town's treasured characters, always dressing garishly in honor of whatever holiday was coming up next. Currently she was in her Halloween phase, which was, for obvious reasons, easier than many other holidays. Tonight she wore a necklace of bats with red eyes that flashed on and off and sequined pumpkin earrings.

"Clam chowder special tonight – get you a bowl?"

Myles appreciated how Babs always took care of him; actually he appreciated how all the older women in Windfall looked out for his welfare in various ways. "Hmmm, please. Thank you, ma'am."

He put the fiddle in the corner where the rest of the band members had already set up their equipment and scanned the bar for familiar faces. In the short time he had lived here, he'd acquired a few acquaintances with whom he enjoyed casual conversation, but he hadn't developed any deep relationships with anyone yet. He tried to remember the name of the old guy on the stool next to him; he was an odd fellow with wild smoky eyes and a thick bristle of gray hair that stood up straight on his head like a vegetable brush. His grease-stained quilted vest hung open, revealing a heavy belly that spilled over his belt buckle to rest on his lap. He scrutinized Myles now, looking him over from his long golden dreadlocks to his well-worn canvas hiking sneakers.

"You're gonna need some bettah footwear come wintah, boy," he remarked in the kind of classic New Hampshire accent that was rarely heard anymore except among the more elderly and entrenched locals. "Supposed to get some real snow heeyuh soon enough now."

"Want another, Butch?" Babs asked.

"Sure, I'll have one mo-wuh."

Myles marveled at how he turned the word "more" into two syllables; locals like Butch were a dying breed.

"What you starin' at?" Butch demanded, sucking the foam off his Budweiser draft.

Myles shook his head, grinning. "Nothing. Just enjoying the mountain view." He laughed at his own pun, not thinking that Butch would get it, but the geezer caught right on to it.

"Get it, Babs? The boy's makin' a joke heeyuh. He's just enjoying Martin's Mountain View. Where you from anyway?"

"Across the river. Small town in the Northeast Kingdom." Myles took a spoonful of the soup that Babs had put in front of him, savoring the flavor, the warmth flooding through him. He suddenly felt very welcome in his new community.

"Really? I grew up over they-uh. Whereabouts?" Butch looked as surprised as Myles was that they had even this much in common.

"West Jordan. My family runs the inn there. You know it?

A momentary shadow seemed to cross Butch's face; he blinked and then it was gone. "Uh, yeah, of course I know it. I used to drink there back in the day, when Woody used to own it."

"Oh, well, he died a while ago and left it to my mom. And we've been poor ever since." That last sentence had just slipped out; he didn't know why he would have revealed that much to a stranger like Butch. Myles concentrated on eating the chowder in front of him.

"Zat right? Who's your mom? Maybe I knew her."

"You probably did; she's been there like twenty-five years. Sarah Scupper-Adams."

Butch's eyes seemed to momentarily flash. Like he was a character in a zombie movie or something, Myles thought. "That's who your mom is. Huh." Butch stared at him. "Yeah, I do remember her. But I don't think she'd know who I was." He continued to train a narrowed gaze on Myles. "So you're her son. Huh."

"Not her only one. I have a younger brother. AND three adopted sisters, one older from Nigeria and two younger from China." Across the room he saw Aidan and Liam coming in from the parking lot and he held his spoon up in a greeting.

"So where you living over hee-yuh?"

"What? Oh – uh, up by Sloane Winslow's. I work for her and a few other rich people around here."

"Yeah, I know Sloane's. I've done some logging up that way. Not an easy place to get a skidder into." Butch was still scrutinizing him and Myles was beginning to feel uncomfortable. He was glad when the band members approached and crowded around, blocking him from Butch's view.

"Mya, man. What's happening." Liam clapped him on the back. "We were looking for you earlier before we went out to get high. Wanted to run that middle riff on Living in the Shire Blues one more time."

Myles was happy to give up his seat at the bar and put some distance between him and Butch. The man was giving him the creeps now.

A few hours later, when they took a break after the first set, Myles saw that Butch was still there on his same barstool, more slumped over than upright now, but still keeping one eye on the band. Joining a crowd that was headed for the front door, he slipped out of sight into the cool night air. Leaning against the side of the building, he closed his eyes and breathed deeply, unsure of why he felt so unnerved. He could lose himself in the music, disappear into the sweet sounds that came from the strings beneath his bow, but there was always the reality to face when the melody ended.

"Hey, you sounded great in there."

He straightened up, startled by the close presence of another human. A few inches away, a woman was resting her elbow on the wall beside him, gazing at him with the rapt attention of a fan. His first impression was that she was a brawny babe, wide in the shoulders and solidly built right on down through her hips and thighs; in the semi-darkness he couldn't see the color of her wide-set eyes or of the straight thick hair that was chopped just below the chin line. She wore a fleece pullover and knee length shorts, like a park ranger or something, he thought.

"I'm Randy," she said bluntly. "What's your name, beautiful boy?"

"Myles," he stammered, feeling somewhat intimidated by her forwardness. "You live around here? I don't think I've seen you at one of our gigs before."

"No, actually I just blew into town today in that rig over there." She indicated a square ungainly-looking RV with big tires and the appearance of a vehicle that was more suited to fighting Desert Storm than camping in the White Mountains. "Me and Sitka, my husky pup." She looked around at the lights of the village and then up at the stars. "But I might stay a few days. I kind of like it here, especially since there's a bar with excellent music."

"So you live in that thing?" Myles peered at the boxy camper curiously.

"I do. It's outfitted really nice inside, super comfortable. You'd be surprised. Want to see it?"

It was as open an invitation as he'd ever been given and he laughed aloud at her sheer boldness. "Maybe later. I have to get back for the next set in a few minutes."

Randy reached out and stroked a few strands of his hair. "You know, I've never really been a fan of this dreadlock style, but it looks kinda cute on you."

Up close he could see now that she was pretty, in a rugged tomboyish way. He guessed she was a woman who regularly got what she wanted, whatever that might be. "Okay," he said. "Maybe catch you later then, Randy."

"Oh, you will, for sure." To his untrained ear, her accent sounded Canadian or Midwestern or something. "I gotta go check on my dog, but then I'll be back inside. I wanna dance to your music."

He didn't know how to respond; he had not had that much experience with direct come-ons from strong females. Her flattery made him grin foolishly to himself as he headed for the door.

Safely entrenched with his fiddle under his chin, he watched her on the dance floor. She had stripped off her fleece and was now wearing only a tight sleeveless shirt that showed off the strength of her muscular arms and the solidness of her pecs. He noted that her breasts and her butt bounced only a little as she moved rhythmically in time to the music. Every now and then she caught his eye and winked, the thrusting motion of her hips leaving little to the imagination. In another venue, Myles would have been embarrassed, but this was Friday night at Martin's and letting it show was what it was all about.

At one point between songs, there was the sound of breaking glass when Lyle knocked his beer bottle over as he fell face first into a drunken doze at the bar. Abruptly he stood up, slapped some money down and staggered out. Nobody stopped him; this was a fairly usual state of affairs. The local police would be watching his departure.

When the second set was over, Myles lingered longer than usual over his fiddle case, packing up his instrument and then helping to wind up the cords and stow the amps. Somebody brought him a shot of Jack, and then passed him another, and with the warm dizzy rush of the liquor buzzing in his head, he finally allowed himself to look up to where he knew Randy was leaning against a post keeping an eye on him. She blew him an air kiss, cocking her head towards the door questioningly. He gave a nearly imperceptible nod as he approached, feeling a responsive quiver in his pants. He hadn't been with a woman since Greece. Crazy or not, this was happening, he realized. He almost forgot his backpack, scooping it up at the last second as he followed her out into the parking lot.

Inside the industrial strength camper, the light was soft and warm, infusing the wood paneled interior with an unexpected coziness. But before he had time to appreciate the ambience, her mouth was on his, hot and searching, one hand sliding up under his shirt, the other snaking down inside his jeans, and then she pulled him down onto a mattress that was as hard as he was. He groaned as he gave into the power of the passion she was unleashing on him.

At some point in the night, after the cops had rapped on the door and shouted that she couldn't camp in the parking lot, they had gotten into the front seats stark naked and he'd had her drive up to the trail that led to his cabin and then directed her into a clearing a short distance into the woods. She'd let the dog out to pee and the crisp briskness of the air flooding the small space had felt so invigorating that they'd had sex again, standing up outside, his back pressed against the icy metal of the camper, his organ on fire with the heat of her intensity, then hustled back inside to cuddle under a comforter and laugh at how cold their skin was, shrieking as they touched each other with their freezing feet and marveling at the erect sharpness of her frosty nipples against his warm tongue. He liked it when she moaned with pleasure beneath his mouth and fingers, enjoying his momentary control of her vulnerability as she gave into orgasm, and then again and yet again, melting into soft helplessness under his touch.

"Oh, my god, you beautiful boy," she gasped. Loosening her grasp on his hair and falling back onto the pillows, she shivered with the after effects as he continued to stroke and lick, unwilling to give up command of her responses until she came once more, erupting with a volcanic finality that echoed in the small space and left no room for further discourse.

When they finally awoke mid-morning with cold faces and sticky crevices, Myles climbed into the driver's seat and navigated the camper up the steep hill to the yard of the sugar house, where he heated water on the woodstove so they could wash up. Then he made them pancakes doused in maple syrup, which Randy consumed with an appetite as lusty as his own.

"So what's on for today?" she asked him, running a finger through the remaining syrup on her plate and then sticking it in his mouth.

"Well, I was going to split firewood..." he began.

"Sounds good to me. Let's do it. Point me to the axe and splitting maul." She leapt up to put her dish in the wash basin and he was happy she could not see the relief that flooded his face. He was glad she was not leaving yet; he wanted more. He craved it.

They worked side-by-side all afternoon, her strength and endurance was clearly greater than his but he was merely impressed, not intimidated. She didn't stop when it started to rain, finally quitting when the drops came down so hard that the water running off her hair began to blur her vision.

Dropping their wet clothes in a pile on the floor, they climbed the ladder to the loft and made love again, only leaving the bed to grab some snacks and get a bottle of whiskey she had in the RV, and to help Sitka up into the loft so she wouldn't feel lonely.

"These are super nice sheets, dude." Randy ran her fingers over the silky surface. "I fear we're wrecking them."

"500 thread count. Only the best. And please, feel free to do your worst. There's more where these came from." He laughed and took another hit from the bottle. He felt more relaxed than he had in months.

When she raised an eyebrow questioningly, he threw back the covers and pressed his face into the tight muscles of her abdomen, his body forcing her legs to open wide as his lips began the trip downward to the warmth between her thighs, distracting her from further discussion.

By midnight, when he was too spent to keep his eyes open, she seemed to just be hitting her stride again. "The more I get it, the more I want it." She rubbed against him but exhaustion was stronger than his desire now. He did not remember falling asleep but woke several hours later, his arm numb and without feeling, the fingers that were still deep inside her tingling from lack of circulation.

He sat up, his head ringing from too much whiskey and too little nourishment. He squinted to look over at Randy in the pale gray light of predawn. She looked at him lazily, with half-open eyes, and her voice was hoarse when she spoke. "I have to go soon."

"What? Oh, no, you don't." He rolled over on top of her, trying to keep the panic from rising. Although his forehead pounded precariously from his hangover, he pressed his dry lips against hers, forcing her mouth open, kissing her persuasively. Before he realized what was happening, she had rolled him over on his back without breaking their lip-lock, so that now she was the one straddling him. "Yeah, I do," she said. "So give me one more for the road to remember you by."

Even another earth-shaking orgasm couldn't change her mind. Wrapped in a red plaid Pendleton wool blanket, he dragged himself down the ladder and out into the yard to say goodbye, with one last-ditch attempt to change her mind.

"You can stay, you know. I want you to."

"I could, sweetheart, but I'm not going to. It was a great weekend; you way exceeded my expectations, lover boy." She reached beneath the blanket to give his junk an affectionate squeeze and he pulled her close.

"When are you coming back this way?" His voice revealed more desperation than he wanted it to.

"I don't know. Maybe someday. Hey, I know where you live. If I ever come back, I'll look you up."

"How about I come with you?"

For a half second she seemed to consider this idea, and then grinned wryly. "Nah, I don't think so. Sitka, come!" She opened the door and the dog bounded inside and then she swung up after it. "See you round, sailor."

Before the sound of the camper bumping down the rough road had stopped ringing in his ears, Myles was back in bed, with the comforter pulled over his head. He did not get up for three days except to stumble to the outhouse occasionally and then drink some water. On the second day he awoke to the rumble of an engine somewhere nearby and leaped to peer out the window, expecting to see the graceless RV rolling back into view but he saw nothing and decided it must have been wishful thinking. By the time he emerged from his funk, he was no longer mourning the absence of Randy (whose last name he didn't even know), but feeling the painful loss of the girl he'd loved the most in his life and whom he could not have for his own.

His heart felt raw and his mind was dull when he finally stepped out onto his doorstep the third morning and tripped over a plastic grocery bag that he did not remember leaving there. Inside he found a large container of clam chowder from Martin's and a six pack of Budweiser. It was clearly a care package and he could not imagine who had left it or why.

Nobody knew he was living up here. But apparently somebody did now. He cursed himself for having brought Randy to the sugar house – who knew whom she might have told. With a cry of rage, he picked up the container of soup and prepared to chuck it into the woods; then he realized how hungry he was. Instead he dumped it into a pot and turned the propane camp stove on. There was no point in wasting good food.

CHAPTER THREE

January 2017

By the time he got into the car to drive to Windfall, it was late afternoon. Tyler was already exhausted, at least mentally. He had edited a couple of articles for the paper, one detailing the latest town meeting about the illegal landfill expansion and another on a three car accident that had shut down Main Street for several hours during the snowstorm. It seemed as though the breaking news in Jordan, Vermont, was less thrilling than his real life at the moment. He'd had a conference call with his three part-time employees (a young stringer reporter, his ad saleswoman and his graphic designer). He'd set up an appointment for Chloe with a local obstetrician for two days from now and tried to have a conversation with her about Tucker, and also about Myles. However he learned very little; Chloe was all too familiar with Tyler's means of casually ferreting out information and she had all the right defenses in place.

When he told her about the phone call Sarah had received the previous night about Myles being wanted for questioning in a murder, she gasped a little, her large eyes widening a bit. The she blinked a couple of times, and said, "Wow, really. That's crazy," in a rather disconnected way, stirring a large teaspoon of sugar into her mint tea.

"Didn't he meet up with you guys when he was traveling this summer?" Tyler asked, covertly watching her over the edge of his coffee mug. "I thought I remembered something about that."

"Yeah, he did. Twice actually. Once in Instabul and then again in the Cyclades before he came home."

"And did you hear from him after that? Because you know what happened, right?"

She hesitated for a second. “Something happened to him?”

“He ended up losing his place at the music school because his family couldn’t pay for it. He didn’t email you guys about that?” Tyler couldn’t believe that Tucker and his best friend wouldn’t be in touch somehow about something this major.

Chloe smirked a little. “We don’t really do email the way you grownups do. We use Messenger usually.” She hadn’t answered the question and when Tyler didn’t respond to her snarky comment, she went on. “But once we were out on the boat, we didn’t really have any kind of regular access to the internet anyway. And then I went back to the island...so I don’t know if Tucker was in contact with him.” She got to her feet. “Sorry, bathroom call.”

It was her most convenient excuse to avoid any topic, Tyler was realizing. “So you’re saying you haven’t heard from Myles since the summer?” he called loudly after her.

“Guess not,” she called back.

“And how about my son,” he said when she returned. “Your *husband*.” The word seemed to be such an inappropriate description of Tucker that he couldn’t believe he had even used it. “When was the last time you heard from him?”

At the mention of Tucker, Chloe’s eyes filled with tears and she fled back to the guest room. The conversation was clearly over, almost before it had begun, and Tyler had learned virtually nothing. Except that something was seriously up with the “newlyweds” relationship.

Frustrated he went back to his computer and, defying Chloe’s declaration, sent Tucker an email, asking him to get in touch as soon as possible. He assumed that at some point his son would check his account. He called Sarah to find out if there had been any news on Myles. Hunter told him that the police had not only called but paid them a visit that morning. No one had seen or heard from Myles and his disappearance was now considered suspicious.

Finally, a few hours later, Tyler took a shower, put on some clean clothes, and knocked on Chloe's door. "Chloe, I'm headed over to Windfall and probably won't be back until late. Are you all set here?"

The door flew open as suddenly as if she had been standing on the other side waiting for him. "Why are you going there?"

Taken aback by her unexpected response, he stammered a little. "I – I take a tango class on Tuesday nights over there."

Like Sarah, Chloe had trouble hiding her amusement at this piece of information and her grin lightened the tension between them. "I didn't know you tangoed."

"I just started a few weeks ago. I'm enjoying it." He didn't go on to reveal how much he liked holding a female partner, attuning his rhythm to hers, guiding their bodies as a one unit across the floor.

"So you do this at a dance studio?" She leaned against the doorframe, observing him wryly.

"No, at a bar. It goes much better with a Margarita or a beer." For some reason, she stiffened a little at this remark and the tension returned. "So will you be okay here alone? There's plenty of food in the fridge – help yourself to whatever."

"Of course, I'll be fine. You go have a good time. Don't worry about me." She made a half-hearted attempt at a smile. "Maybe I'll watch some television – I haven't done that in months. Maybe even years..."

His concern had merely been a pretense; he had never intended not to go – he had been looking forward to this evening all week. And now it would also be good to get a little perspective on his new uncomfortable situation at home.

On the drive to New Hampshire, he tried to get a bead on what was going on with Chloe. If she and Tucker were on the outs, why wouldn't she have gone someplace else besides Tucker's childhood home? Tyler reminded himself that she really had nowhere else to go; to his knowledge, her crazy mother, Elle, was still locked up in a facility in Puerto Rico and Chloe's father had thrown her out of his house before she was even out of high school.

Tucker had met Chloe on the island of Culebra while he and Tyler had been on a beach camping trip that had gone seriously off-track. When Tucker and Chloe had run away, Tyler ended up getting deeply involved with Chloe's insane mother; his male ego was still recovering from the repercussions of that relationship. Chloe had come back to Vermont after that near deadly excursion; it had been an unconventional arrangement for a sixteen-year-old boy and his seventeen-year-old girlfriend, but it had satisfied all their needs. Tucker and Chloe both got their high school diplomas, earned some money and made a new life together, nesting in a tree house in the yard, under Tyler's vigilant eye but out of his way. He had watched her blossom from a skittish, unfocused girl to a strong-minded young woman with a sense of purpose. He couldn't quite say the same for his son, but he'd seen him go from reticent and rebellious to a self-assured adventurer, willing to do anything for his sexy girlfriend.

But from what he could glean, Tucker had abandoned Chloe for the life of a sailor-in-training...or maybe it was the other way around? Or had it been the pregnancy that had cleaved their relationship in two? By the time he came over the hill into Windfall, he was determined that he was going to get the truth out of her. Tomorrow.

But right now he had two other missions. One was to see if he could find out anything about Myles; the other was to connect with Eva, his tango teacher.

After his first awkward attempt at online dating with Sloane, Tyler's next venture was radically more successful – at least it had seemed so at first. Fern was the librarian for Windfall's quaint and well-endowed library, built in the classic Carnegie style of gray granite with vaulted ceilings, tiled fireplaces and stained glass. Tyler had fallen in love with the building the first time he had walked in to meet

Fern, especially compared to the Jordan Center Public Library, which was housed in an unused storefront and had a budget that barely covered a handful of new books per year.

In person, Fern had not been what he had expected from her online profile, but he realized that should come as no surprise. For starters, she was about fifty pounds heavier than the photo she had posted, her cheeks much plumper, her chin less defined, her chest nearly as well-endowed as the library. Her hair was also a different color, now a very yellow blonde as opposed to the soft coppery curls she had depicted. But her green eyes sparkled and her smile was quick and warm and he had felt instantly relaxed in her company, a feeling he had never achieved with Sloane.

"I know, I've gained some weight since that picture was taken," she apologized almost immediately, and he guessed she'd had this conversation before. "But I did mention that food is my enemy as well as my best friend. If you don't want to stay, that's okay, I get it. But otherwise, I need to close up here before we go."

"Don't be ridiculous, of course, I'll stay." He figured that the visit to the library alone had been worth the drive over.

He watched her as she closed the blinds, her black pants stretched taut across her behind, her red cabled cardigan gapping as its buttons strained to meet across her chest. She was definitely not the type of woman he usually fell for, and right now that made her perfect.

As it turned out, Fern had a sharp quick wit and was an entertaining dinner companion. She not only knew everybody in town, but all their children and some of their grandchildren, whom she entertained at story hour twice a week. She was so upbeat that he suspected she could be equally melancholy. He'd been the unsuspecting victim of this kind of behavior too many times in his lifetime to not be suspicious. When she invited him back to her house for a drink after the meal, she made it clear that she would be happy to have sex on the first date with him if he was interested.

He backed off politely, saying he wasn't ready for that yet, knowing that a younger version of himself would have accepted the challenge without a second thought. But he was intrigued when she invited him to accompany her to Tuesday night tango class and could not resist agreeing to return a few nights later.

"If I can tango, you can tango," she assured him. "The teacher is very good. And it's a great physical release after a day of mental exercise at the library."

Tyler had been surprised by everything about that first session – the students, the venue and most of all how much he liked it. The ten adults ranged from dowager to ski bum and included experienced dancers in high-heeled shoes as well as matronly Fern in her leather-soled flats, who was actually quite light on her feet for someone her size. Martin's Mountainview, the local bar welcomed the "tangueros" and didn't even bother to move the pool table they danced around, they just embraced the dancers as another eclectic source of patronage. And then there was Eva, who taught the class, and patiently spent time with each of the students, going over ganchos and ochos and boleos or basic holds. It was the first time in a long while that a woman had taken his breath away.

It wasn't that she was exotically beautiful or striking, although her features could easily be called pleasing. It was the way she gracefully moved, exuding confidence in not only her own abilities but whatever clumsy person she happened to be guiding across the floor, and the obvious joy she received from sharing her love of tango. How when her smile lit up at someone's success it seemed almost too large for her face, creating deep dimples in her angular cheekbones, and bringing a brightness to her rich brown eyes. And how her dark, shiny chin-length hair bounced and swung around her head as she danced.

He knew he was falling hard from the first moment she had taught him how to place one hand on her back and the other raised in her own, and then instructed him to gently use the pressure against her shoulder blade to let her know when to move and where. Suddenly they were moving as one being, her slim body a weightless accompaniment to his own tentative one. An unseen energy ran through his fingers as they came into contact with the soft ribbed fabric of her sweater.

He was disappointed when she moved to another student and he had to switch back to dancing with Fern, who now felt solid and a little sweaty to him, and who did not read his signals as intuitively as the very experienced Eva did. Everyone changed partners again, and soon he began to learn the differences between dancers he connected with and those who stumbled over their own feet no matter who their partner was. Between rounds, he drank a strong Margarita and then another, trying to keep his focus on Fern, who was his date for the evening, while attempting to hide his fascination with their lithe and captivating teacher.

After the lesson, the class all sat together and ordered pizzas and more drinks. By the time he started his third Margarita, he knew he was not going to be able to drive home and prepared himself for the fact that he would have to accept the inevitable invitation to stay over. He had managed to get himself a seat between Eva and Fern, so that despite the well-padded thigh that pressed suggestively against his own on one side, he was able to hold an uninhibited conversation on the other. Pleasantly drunk on alcohol and dancing, he found himself laughing and flirting with both women in a way he had not done for a very long time.

"How lucky am I to land such a handsome old man in my bed tonight," Fern had commented as they tumbled onto her patchwork quilt, intoxicated way beyond the limits of a weekday work night. By this time Tyler had given himself up to the sensations of the moment, letting himself be carried along by whatever the evening brought next. Fern's lovemaking style was an aggressive contrast to what her country-kitsch Americana décor would have led him to expect. The mattress springs squeaked in appreciative harmony with her vocal accompaniment and Tyler just closed his eyes and went along for the ride, trying not to think, just to feel.

When he woke before dawn with a head-banging hangover and the sex started to seem weird and kinky, he made as quick an escape as possible with the usual morning-after excuses. He had not really been interested in going this far this quickly, if ever, with Fern. But he had not even crossed the river back into Vermont when he received a text from her and he knew he was already in over his head.

"Sorry if I freaked you out with Fifty Shades of Fern this morning. Hope to see you again on the weekend if not before. XXOO."

He managed to beg off until the following Tuesday, claiming prior weekend plans. This didn't prevent Fern from sending countless texts and emails, sharing everything from funny kitten videos to political cartoons to websites for men's tango shoes. After years of being alone, the overload of her attention felt suffocating and overwhelming, especially given the fact that he didn't really want to get deeply involved with her. But he did really want to continue tango lessons.

As he had anticipated, her cheery public persona was balanced with intense periods of self-deprecating depression which he found out-and-out scary. He had no interest in being involved with unstable women anymore and a month of Tuesdays later, he had to break it to her that he didn't want to be her "boyfriend." She took the news more stoically than he expected, squaring her jaw and asking quietly through her teeth if they could still be just friends.

"Of course," he said to her immense relief. "I enjoy our conversations."

So then, although they no longer had sex, his Inbox still overflowed on a daily basis with communications of all sorts from Fern and there was always an unnecessary message or two on his voice mail. He tried to send her a message of his own by telling her he was dating Sloane again, even though this was far from the truth. It was Eva he was aching to get closer with, and she was more than half the reason he continued coming to Windfall each week.

Eva was very private, trying to not mix the rest of her personal social life with the public persona she displayed during Tuesday night tango. He managed to learn that by day she taught Spanish at a nearby regional high school, that she lived alone in an apartment in a farmhouse on the "back side of the hill" as the locals referred to the poorer section of Windfall. It was the only area in town where most of the descendants of the original village residents could still afford to live. Tyler schemed ways he could get her alone without upsetting the equilibrium of the dance class, which really meant keeping Fern from finding out.

Finally, after the holidays, he asked her to meet him for coffee on Saturday morning so that he could interview her for an article he was doing on tango for his newspaper. He congratulated himself on coming up with a brilliant justification for some one-on-one time with her, away from other distractions. Unfortunately, it turned out that Eva was from Miami and did not drive in snow and a blizzard had forced a postponement of their meeting until the upcoming weekend.

Now, as Tyler entered the outskirts of Windfall village, he wondered how it was that he could have been coming here weekly for months without knowing that Myles was living here somewhere. Then again, he was always amazed by the new acquaintances he made every day in the West Jordan area, where he had now lived for years. In rural communities, where people resided in forests on country roads, it was totally possible to never see the other folks in your neighborhood, especially if they were in a different age bracket. But certain inhabitants knew more about the local residents than others – the town clerk, the school secretary, the village bartender. And the librarian.

He hesitated in the library parking lot – he had not visited this building since he had officially broken it off with Fern, but if anyone would know who and what was going on in this town, she would. And it would be better to talk with her now rather than during tango class. Taking a deep breath of the frosty air, he went up the granite steps and pulled open the heavy wood and glass door.

Fern was helping an elderly woman check out a stack of mystery novels and load them into a shopping bag with wheels. Tyler hung back, reading the bulletin board until she was done. As he came forward, he watched her face register a range of unreadable emotions, finally settling into a surprised and bemused expression.

"Tyler! What brings you to this esteemed establishment today?" She straightened the piles of bookmarks and flyers on the desk, not meeting his eyes. "I guess the news about Sloane must have reached all the way to West Jordan."

"It did actually. I thought you might have the inside scoop." He leaned on the counter, closing the space between them, creating a sense of intimacy that he didn't feel. "What happened – do you know?"

She took a step back, removing her reading glasses to stare at a point over his head. "I guess she was found frozen in her driveway – they said it looked like she had been run-over but they aren't releasing the details. I'm sorry – it must be a shock to you."

He looked at her questioningly. "It must be a shock to everybody, especially her family. Do her kids know?"

"No, I meant, you going out with her again and all."

He understood her uneasiness now. "Well, we weren't really that close, but, it is upsetting. Did you ever meet the young man who worked for her?"

"Mya? The one who is a suspect? Such a sweet boy, hard to believe. He did yard work and odd jobs for several people in town on Sloane's glowing recommendation."

Tyler felt as though the tile floor beneath his feet was suddenly slightly tilted. "What did you call him?"

"Mya. I think that must be a nickname - short for something, like Jeremiah." She frowned."Why – what do you know about him?"

"Myles. His name is Myles. He's the son of my close friends and my son's best pal; I've known him since he was young. Do you have any idea where he might be living?"

Fern gave an uncomfortable laugh. "That's an odd coincidence, isn't it? The world is always smaller than we think. No, apparently he had been staying at Sloane's house when he first arrived but moved out to somewhere. The police are looking for him."

Tyler hoped he could get to Myles first; there was something very wrong here. "So how do you know him?"

"He came in here a couple of times to use a computer. Brought his girlfriend a few times last month." She hesitated. "Actually they pet-sat for me over the holidays but we didn't actually intersect. You know, I left before they came, they were gone when I got home."

His girlfriend. This was news that Sarah had not known. "So maybe he could be staying with her?"

"It's possible. I got the sense that she was from out of town. I think they've been trying to find her but nobody seems to even know her name. Also he plays with the Why Mo Boys down at Martin's on the weekends; that's what most people in town would identify him with. He's a real pro – really gave them a boost when he joined."

"The who? What kind of team is that – pool players?" Tyler felt very confused and this time Fern giggled for real.

"No, silly. It's a band – he's their fiddler. But you must know that if you've known him for so long." She eyed him suspiciously.

Tyler did remember now; Myles had an uncanny musical ability, playing the piano by ear when he was just a small child, entertaining guests in the bar at the inn. Despite his talent, over the years he'd had trouble playing with the school orchestra because he didn't read music or just wouldn't, as the case might have been.

"So maybe somebody in the band might know where he lives? Do you know the names of any of the people he plays with?"

Fern shrugged. "I don't really – Aidan Beaulieu is one of them, I believe. His family owns the lumber yard out on the river road."

Tyler checked the time– it was almost five o'clock; that would give him a couple of hours to do a little scouting around before class started. And to stop at Martin's and ask a few questions also.

"Thanks, Fern. Gotta run – I'll see you at tango." Before she could protest or suggest accompanying him, he hurried out of the library. Not until he had started up his car did he look up "Lumberyard in Windfall NH" on his phone browser.

Five miles of snow-packed dirt roads later, he pulled into the parking lot of Beaulieu's and stared glumly at the "Closed" sign on the office door. On a hill above the business building, he could see the lights on in a two story house and drove his car slowly up the steep driveway to park behind an old pick-up truck.

His footsteps on the porch set off a clamor of barking from somewhere deep inside and within seconds the overhead light had clicked on and a woman's face was peeking out from behind a curtained window. Tyler gave a friendly wave and did his best to look unintimidating. A minute later the door opened.

"What can I do for you? Lumberyard closed an hour ago." The smell of cheap wine rolled out of her mouth with the words.

"I'm looking for Aidan actually. Is he around?"

Her eyes seemed to grow smaller in her puffy face as she scrutinized him. "No, he ain't. He don't live here no more. Whatchoo want with him anyway?"

"I'm trying to find a friend of his, one of the band members." Tyler couldn't remember what Fern had said the name of the group was. "Do you know where I can find him?"

"Yer not the first person here today askin', you know. I'll tell you the same thing I told them – once my boys are eighteen, if they ain't workin' the yard, then they's out on their ass and on their own."

Tyler nodded sympathetically as though he agreed with her and she seemed to soften a bit.

"He's got an apartment over to Littleton now somewhere with a friend, can't afford nothin' here in friggin' Windfall. I've never been there so I can't tell you nothn' more." She sniffed and scratched her neck. "But if you find him, tell him he better get his shit out of the back shed or it's going to the dump next week. I need that space for some baby pigs I'm gettin'."

Tyler thanked her for her time and backed his car down the slippery hill, only slightly more informed than he he'd been when he'd arrived. It had probably been the police who had preceded him looking for Aidan, and with their resources they had probably already located him.

Tyler's best bet was to head to the bar; Babs and the other regulars would be the most helpful choice for proceeding in his search for Myles. As well as the best place to get some dinner.

There was one seat left at the far end of the bar that he squeezed into. Behind a post and near the emergency exit, it was not the best vantage point for conversation or observation and he leaned forward, craning his neck sharply right to see who else might be there. It was a very different crowd from the tangueros who would show up in an hour or so and although he recognized a few faces, he didn't really know them.

Babs acknowledged his presence with a smile and he was glad he was memorable to at least somebody in Windfall.

"What can I get for you tonight, dear? Our specials are chicken enchiladas or shepherd's pie and we're out of Sam on tap." With her usual efficiency, she already had a place setting and a glass of water in front of him.

He ordered the enchiladas and a Corona and when she brought his beer, he quickly asked, "Babs, you know a young guy called Mya who plays music here sometimes?"

"Course, I do. He's a sweetheart. Terrible what happened up to Sloane's the other night." No explanation was necessary – she had easily transitioned the topic to the town's biggest news.

"Any idea where he lives? I need to get a hold of him."

"You and everybody else in Windfall. Turns out nobody has a clue. But if you can wait until Friday night, he'll probably show. Always does."

"You a cop?" The question came from somewhere out of right field and Tyler bent backwards in his seat to see the speaker. A heavy-set older man with spiky white hair was slouched over the bar, his unfocused eyes like two dark wells. Tyler reminded himself that he should no longer be thinking of people as older - the guy was probably his own age.

"No, just a family friend."

The unsettling gaze squinted at him, piercing the short distance between them like parallel arrows. Tyler couldn't decide if there was something familiar about him or if he just had the appearance of every other North Country drunk. "From West Jordan?"

Now he felt decidedly uneasy. Taking a deep swig of his beer, he asked, "How'd you know that?"

"Just figured, if you knew his family you musta been." The man shrugged and sunk down on his left elbow, looking the opposite direction so that all Tyler had was a view of the sweat-stained armpit of his flannel shirt and the back of his square head.

"So you know Myles then?"

"Yeah, I know him. Well enough to know that when he wants to be found, he will be."

There was truth in that statement, although Tyler hated to admit the man was right. "You know him well enough to know where he was living?"

"Oh, I'm guessin' some cabin in the woods somewhere, like every other young hippie round here does."

"Do you know his girlfriend by any chance?"

"Nah. She was a looker but kinda chubby, if you know what I mean. Only saw her once. She didn't come to the bar with him much. What'd you say your name was again?"

"Tyler Mackenzie. And yours?"

The grizzled jaw slackened for a moment, registering something like recognition or emotion. "Butch." He spat the name out like a belch in a harsh, unpleasant way.

"Got a last name, Butch?"

He snorted. "That's all I go by. It's nuff. Everybody knows me. Not like there's anybody else named Butch in Windfall."

Over Butch's shoulder, Tyler saw a tall young woman coming in through the outside door. Again he had a sense of déjà vu, like he knew this person from somewhere else. She had a "well-bred" appearance about her, tanned and blonde, wearing a lightweight state-of-the-art ski jacket and expensive-looking boots. Babs leaned over the bar and spoke quietly but distinctly. "That's Sloane's daughter, Laurel. Come in from Colorado to take care of the arrangements."

He was relieved to realize that what he had recognized was the family resemblance – it was like seeing a much younger version of Sloane herself. "I should offer my condolences."

He introduced himself to Laurel, who was clearly suffering from a combination of jet lag and emotional exhaustion. "It's just all too much, and so sudden. The whole police inquiry into her death is just putting me over the top." Suddenly she was speaking rapidly, spilling a days' worth of pent-up feelings. "Plus I've been finding odd things missing all over the house which makes me question whether she was experiencing early onset dementia."

"Really – like what kind of things?" Tyler did not think Sloane had been absent-minded but he didn't know her that intimately.

"Well, the down comforter off the guest room bed where I always sleep, for starters. It's pretty hard to misplace something as big as that. Some of the clothes I keep here are gone. And some dumb basic things, like I can't find this really nice corkscrew I gave her for Christmas. Which is why I'm here." She laughed ruefully. "I need a glass of wine."

"Maybe she was just decluttering. Parents eventually do get rid of their kids' possessions." He had an unfounded pang of guilt, remembering the bag of old sneakers and ripped T-shirts he himself had taken to the dump last month.

"They also keep asking about that boy who worked for her but I don't know anything about him. Some kind of drifter she hired. Another reason I think she might have been losing her mind – why would she do such a thing? What does it take to get a glass of Pinot around here?" She raised her hand to get Babs' attention, her nerves stripped raw enough now to display a wealthy sense of entitlement and impatience.

He was about to make a comment, when he saw Eva come into the bar with one of the tango students. Ben was probably the youngest man in the class, a quick learner, dark and wiry with a lean face and a prominent nose. And sticky hands, at least that was what he had heard from the women dancers. Tyler could not suppress the twinge of jealousy he felt at seeing how something Ben said made Eva's face shine with merriment as she touched his arm in an intimate reaction to the sharing of a joke.

"Excuse me," he apologized to Laurel as he pushed pass her, leaving her halfway through a sentence that he hadn't even heard the beginning of.

"Your food is served, Tyler!" Babs shouted after him.

He was gratified that Eva's eyes lit up with responsiveness of some sort when she saw him. "You're here early tonight, Señor Mackenzie. Ben and I were just going to run a few steps before class. Do you want to join us?"

Regretfully he returned to his seat at the bar to eat his enchiladas and nurse his bruised ego, watching them from afar, feeling as though opportunity has been snatched from him yet again. His phone vibrated in his pocket and he looked at it as he put a forkful of spicy chicken and tortillas into his mouth.

It was a message from a woman named Caroline who had contacted him through heartsafire.com charmed by his online profile, asking him to check hers out. Behind him he could hear the first strains of tango music starting up. With a shudder of self-pity, he clicked on the message and began determinedly typing a reply.

CHAPTER FOUR

November 2016

A thin crust of snow crunched rhythmically beneath his feet in time to the music still playing in his head. The late night climbs up the mountain could be pleasant as long as he was not too tired, but tonight all Myles could think about was the cozy bed that awaited him at the end of his uphill hike. It had been a long day, stacking firewood for ninety-year-old Mrs. Hall who still wanted to heat her house with a woodstove this winter, the way she always had. Then he spent an equally long, but more pleasurable evening, playing a couple of extended sets with the band down at Martin's. He was glad he would not have to leave home again until late tomorrow afternoon when he would head back to town for the Why Mos' usual Saturday night gig.

The light of his solar headlamp was getting dimmer and dimmer but even in the darkness the white swath of the path was easy to follow. The snow had not fallen until after sunset and then had turned to a sleety rain for a short while; it was not enough to turn the surface to ice, although he feared that could happen by morning. Might be a good time to try out that nice wooden toboggan that he'd found collecting dust in the rafters of the Chevaliers' garage when he helped them close up their "cottage" for the season.

He stumbled up onto the porch and then instinctively stopped short. Next to the door there appeared to be a huge bulky shadow obstructing most of the space. Fear filled his lungs and for a moment he could barely breathe before he decided his exhausted eyes had to be playing tricks on him. Feeling for the door latch, he let himself inside, grabbing his powerful lantern from where he had left it on a shelf by the door. Turning it on to full brightness, he quickly surveyed the inside of the sugar house.

Everything was as he had left it that morning; his cereal bowl was still in the sink, the book he had been reading was still face down on the table, his dirty clothes from the previous day remained in a discarded heap on the floor next to the now stone-cold wood stove. Steeling himself, he whirled swiftly, wielding the lantern like a weapon, as he moved back out on the porch to dispel whatever monster he might have imagined.

He had not imagined it. A sheet of dirty black plastic covered something enormous, maybe six feet long and four feet high. Tentatively he stretched out a gloved hand – whatever was underneath seemed hard and solid, made of wood and resonating with a strangely musical echo when he rapped on it.

Placing the light carefully on the floorboards, he grabbed the piece of plastic firmly and, with a dramatic gesture, pulled it away, flinging it to the ground below. He stared at the apparition in front of him, more stunned than he had been a minute earlier.

A beautiful upright piano had somehow materialized on his porch. Myles closed his eyes and then opened them again – he had to be dreaming. How could it possibly have gotten here? Was it real?

In an effort to catch this apparition before it slipped away, he swiftly used his teeth to pull off one of his gloves, and then cautiously ran his fingers over the polished surface of the curved keyboard cover. The wood was cold beneath his fingertips; he lifted the lid and gazed at the pristine white and black ivory keyboard below. This was clearly not a neglected instrument. s he reflexively did whenever he saw a piano, he could not keep himself from playing a couple of one-handed chords. The sound rang out through the frosty woods, rich and melodious. He ran a quick scale – amazingly it was only slightly out of tune.

He looked around nervously. Even though it was the middle of the night and he was sure he was alone, he wondered if somebody was watching him. Nobody knew where he was living. Nobody, he reassured himself. Then he remembered the day he had found the beer and soup in a bag on his steps. He had convinced himself that Randy had come back and left it. Had she brought him a piano too?

The whole situation was so improbable that he could not think clearly. He was cold and tired. If the piano was real, it would still be here in the morning. He went inside and closed the door, and began the mechanical process of making a fire in the stove to at least take the chill out of the air before he went to bed.

But as he knelt down to feed some more kindling into the flames, his mind continued to whir and then the musician in him began to rise to the surface – who would be so insane as to leave a good instrument like that outside in the winter?

Before he even realized what he was doing, he was outside again, examining the base of the piano.

"Holy fuck," he exclaimed aloud. "The freakin' thing has wheels."

A light freezing drizzle was starting to fall; there was no wind, but it would take only the slightest breeze to send raindrops onto the porch and the piano. It didn't matter if it was past midnight. There were some tasks in life that couldn't wait until morning.

When he finally woke it was nearly noon although the sky was so overcast he would never have been able to guess the time of day by glancing out of the small circular window in the eave at the end of his sleeping loft. He was pissed to see how late it was; it meant he only had a few hours of November daylight left. He stumbled down the ladder to step outside for a pee and almost banged his body into the piano.

It was standing in the middle of the room where he had left it after finally maneuvering its unwieldy bulk through the door. To angle it into the small space, he'd had to muscle the kitchen cupboard out of the way and shove the couch up against the sink. It had already taken over his life, like an adopted puppy might. He squeezed by and slipped outside to relieve himself.

The black plastic covering that had been protecting the piano on the porch had blown up against a tree in the dooryard and wound itself around the trunk. He folded it up carefully, looking for a clue that he knew he would not find. It was standard issue, heavy duty, garden-variety hardware store plastic, infinitely useful, and he stashed it carefully in a box under the house.

Most of the snow had washed away and now he could see the tire tracks in the mud, a few deep ruts on either side of the steps where somebody had skillfully backed up. He was no forensic scientist – one tread looked like another to him. Shaking his head, he shivered and went back inside. He needed some coffee and a fire before he could contemplate the what, how and why of the elephant in his living room.

Nobody in Windfall had even known Myles played piano until a few weeks earlier during an impromptu performance at Martin's Mountainview Halloween party. In Windfall they celebrated Halloween in a way he had not experienced during all his years growing up in the bar at West Jordan. Here people took the opportunity to put on a costume and become the uninhibited personalities they wanted to be the other 364 days a year.

"Actually we do this at Mardi Gras too," Daniel informed him. "People like having another chance to not be their boring usual selves, I guess." Daniel was dressed as Marilyn Monroe in a white halter dress and a platinum blonde wig, which seemed like a blatant signal that he was either secretly gay or was secure enough in his masculinity to enjoy his feminine side. Myles didn't care which it was, he liked the fact that Daniel felt comfortable enough to perform like this.

Myles himself hadn't had much available to make a costume, but Aidan's girlfriend had done a great paint job on his face in classic man-eating vampire style. Some glow-in-the-dark spider webs strategically sprayed on his dreads and several ketchup packets smeared down the front of a ripped T-shirt had been enough to classify him as Halloween-worthy, although he worried about getting the gooey green shit out of his hair afterwards.

Liam had dressed as a boy scout in his own too-small childhood uniform, cutting off the sleeves and ripping open the sides to squeeze into it, the neckerchief sitting atop his bare hairy chest. But the best part of his get-up was the water canteen full of Maker's Mark that the band shared around while they played. Myles's tolerance for whiskey was still way lower than the rest of them and he tried to pace himself.

The party at Martin's had just begun when a previous band member of the Why Mo Boys showed up, bringing his electric keyboard with him, ready to jam. His piano skills were mediocre and during the first break, Myles sat down to run a few tunes. He was already feeling pretty ripped and when his fingers touched the keyboard they seemed to fly of their own accord.

He didn't realize the bar had grown quiet until he'd finished the reggae riff on Fig Leaf Rag and looked up to see if it was time to start playing again. A wide-eyed crowd had gathered on the other side of the piano and, after a few seconds of silence, wild hoots and deafening applause filled the low-ceilinged room with shouts for more. He could see Aidan shaking his head in stunned admiration and nodding his approval. Myles broke into his own version of Dr. John's Boxcar Boogie combined with a Jerry Lee Lewis jam and by then it was time for the band to start up again.

As he stood up and got ready to resume his fiddling, he saw the owner of the electric keyboard glowering at him and Myles thought maybe he had overstepped his welcome.

"Well, happy birthday, Mr. President," Daniel murmured under his breath as Myles passed him. "That was a fucking awesome surprise." He blew him a lipsticked kiss and winked, not breaking character. "I love a multi-talented man."

Myles laughed, feeling stoned from the pleasure of making music. During the second set, a group of girls danced purposefully in front of him. One of them was a tiny sprite in a sequined turquoise bodysuit and matching wig who smiled seductively and adoringly at him as she shook her little bootie in time to the beat. He still could not get used to the way women acted towards him onstage, like he was some real rock star instead of a poor punk in a local band, but he was learning to roll with it.

When he stepped off the stage for a few songs to give the guest keyboard player some limelight space, the girl approached him. "You are so gifted," she said, standing on her toes to give him a kiss on a grease-painted cheek. "Can I buy you a drink?"

"Um, sure." It was a bad way to start, not admitting to her that he wasn't legally old enough, but hell, it was not like anybody was paying attention to the rules tonight. "I'm kinda lit up already but a beer is fine."

"I'll say you're lit – you're on fire." She pulled him along with her as she crowded into the line at the bar. "I'm Madison. And I know who you are." Deep dimples formed in cheeks that glistened beneath spangled eye makeup. "How long have you been in the band, anyway? I come home from college for the weekend and it's like the whole vibe has changed because of you."

"About that long. So you're from here?"

She made a face. "Sort of. Born and raised outside of Boston, but my family spent all our weekends and summers here. Except for the part where I got sent away to prep school and camp. How about you? What galaxy of handsome men are you visiting our planet from?" She took a deep sip from the glass of white wine she was waving around in her other hand, the one that wasn't clutching his arm. "Oh, and oops, I am well-bred enough to know I ended that question with a proposition. I mean preposition." She giggled drunkenly.

"Yeah, well I am none of that. I grew up on the other side of the tracks in Vermont." He recognized that the familiar heat rising in his chest was caused by a feeling other than the easy sexual attraction he felt for this Madison person. "Where do you go to school?"

"Dartmouth. But not because I am brilliant, only because everyone in my family has gone there since the beginning of time. I don't know; I might be flunking out this semester. I broke up with my boyfriend and it's been, you know. Stressful. Affecting my grades."

No, he didn't know, and chances were he would never know, but he successfully suppressed the jealous anger and outrage that were threatening to surface now. "Who's your family?" he asked with careful casualness. "Maybe I've done some work for them."

He looked over her head at the costumed characters of his new hometown, wondering how many of them were more like her than like him. Between the rhinestone cowboys and wanton witches, he saw Butch watching him from his usual bar-side sprawl. Something about Madison had already brought out the most rebellious in-your-face side of Myles's personality and before she replied, he said, "Excuse me for a minute. I need to go check in with my buddy Butch over there."

"Butch is your friend?" Her mix of disbelief and mirth were evident.

But before Myles could push his way through the mob of party-goers, Butch had somehow slid out of his seat and slithered his way to the emergency exit door, which stood open to allow some cool air into the overheated building. Myles could see only the top of Butch's grease-stained cap bobbing unsteadily out into the night and towards the parking lot.

"Oh, guess I missed him. So who'd you say your family is?" He turned back to Madison who had finally made her way to the front of the line and was pulling a credit card out of some dark recess of her stretchy spandex costume. In a moment she was at his side again, pressing a cold beer into his hand and clinking a fresh glass of wine against it.

"Here's to hometown Halloweens. Because you just never know." She took a big sip of wine and then said, "Carter. My dad is the Carter of Paine Carter."

He didn't have a clue what she was referring to, maybe a law firm or a medical center. "Really?" He hoped his voice didn't sound as smirky as his thoughts.

"We have that big white Victorian up on Maple Hill. Full of old-school antiques. Nothing sexy about it." She waved to one of her girlfriends on the other side of the bar and made some uninterpretable hand sign. "How about you – where do you stay over here?"

"Oh, Sloane Winslow gave me a place when I came over to work for her," he answered obliquely.

"Oh, the Winslows and my family go way back."

"Oh, I bet they do."

"What kind of snarky remark is that?" Her head tipped quizzically, a turquoise strand of polyester hair falling over one eye.

"Nothing. Sorry. I'm just an uncouth yahoo fiddler who's already had too much to drink." He saw the piano player rise, apparently finished with his guest set. "Thanks for the beer. I gotta get back up there now."

"See you later, love." She squeezed his arm as he moved away, grateful to have a reason to extricate himself from the direction of their conversation.

"You always get the good ones," Liam commented as Myles picked up his fiddle. "Even when you look like a fuckin' zombie."

"Eye of the beholder, dude." He was happy for the familiarity of his chin rest and bow and to be able to disappear into the comfortable abyss of music again for a while. At the insistence of the crowd, he played a few more tunes on the keyboard, but was relieved when the final chords of the last set resounded and the party was over. However, seconds later, Madison materialized at his side, looking as bedraggled as she was bedazzled.

"Can I offer you a ride? I'm going right by your place."

For a moment a chill went through him, but then he realized she meant Sloane's house.

"Of course, he wants a ride, darling," Daniel answered for him. "Go with the girl, boy."

He was not surprised when she led him to a late model Mercedes with a keyless entry system. "You sure you're okay to drive?" he asked as she fumbled with her door handle.

"I could drive these roads in my sleep. I'm fine. But I need my sweater." Her sequined-covered butt glinted in the parking lot lights as she dove into the back seat, emerging finally with a long soft cardigan.

Myles had to admit that she was cute and hot and that he was willing to go wherever this ride took him. She started up the engine and then looked over at him and grinned. "Oh, I want to kiss you but not with that shit on your face. Want to come see my house?"

They took their shoes off and tiptoed through a kitchen that was more than forty feet long with no less than twenty copper pots hanging above a wide center island. "We're going up to the third floor," she whispered and he followed her up a wide curving staircase and then another narrow straight one, down a long hallway and then over a door jamb into what appeared to be a separate wing of the house.

"Now we can make noise," she breathed, flicking a switch that illuminated an open expanse of wood paneling and exposed beams. There was a stone fireplace at one end and a large king bed at the other. "My parents won't be able to hear us up here."

The whole thing was so beyond his expectations of what the night might bring, that he almost felt dizzy with anticipation. Pulling her towards him, he ran his fingers down the length of her body, feeling the response of her well-toned muscles as she leaned into the embrace.

"I don't know even know what your real hair color is," he laughed.

"You'll know soon enough. I'm a natural blonde. Everywhere. Come." She pulled him farther into the room, past the fireplace to a bathroom twice the size of the bedroom he'd grown up in. "I think some make-up remover and a shower are in order."

He could not keep his hands from stroking the thick fluffy towels that were neatly rolled in a giant basket next to a shower big enough to hold his entire family at one time. The sink was a large free-standing glass bowl on a marble pedestal; water seemed to fall magically like a mountain stream from a curved brass tap.

"Is this your room and bathroom?" He sat on the toilet lid and closed his eyes as she ran some kind of moist towelette over his face.

"No, this is just the den-slash-guest room. You wouldn't want to see my room – it's all pink and purple and lace. It's kind of a…sexual turn-off, to say the least."

It was weird but it felt good to have her cleaning his face, wiping it down with a warm washcloth, drying it with a super-soft hand towel. He felt sleepy and well-cared for, ready to be tucked into bed.

"There. Oh, you are beautiful." He opened his eyes and for one second saw her, all naked and white except for the shiny blue wig and then, she was straddling his lap and kissing him on the mouth.

When he woke in the morning, he could not remember where he was or how he'd gotten there. All he knew was that he was feeling sooo comfortable, enveloped by somebody's warm body in the most luxurious sheets he'd ever slept in. As his consciousness slowly floated to the surface, he began to see his surroundings – the handcrafted wooden beams above his head, the enormous abstract oil painting over the fireplace, the facets of mullioned window panes that transformed the morning sunlight into hundreds of rainbows around the room.

What was he doing here, soaking up the pleasures of wealth that he despised so much? He threw back the covers and saw the graceful hand that rested on his hip, the trio of tiny gold rings on one finger, the impeccably manicured and painted nails. He sat up abruptly and took in the pale pink nipples of the perfect little breasts, the expensive haircut still matted down after being crammed for hours beneath a wig. Even her dark blonde pubes were flawlessly shaped and trimmed.

He had been sleeping with the enemy – and even though he hated her casual entitlement to an existence of privilege and promise, he hated himself more because he had enjoyed the experience. She could have whatever she wanted, a fancy college education, an expensive car, even a night of slumming with a local musician. It seemed so unfair that for a moment his stomach cramped violently and he had to pull his knees up to his chest until the pain subsided.

Then he slid silently out of the silky sheets and quietly crossed the room to where his battered backpack lay unzipped on the polished wooden floor. His phone said it was almost eleven; time to slip away back to his cold crude cabin, make a fire, feel comfortable with himself again.

When he went into the bathroom to pee, he saw the hand-woven basket overflowing with plush white towels. Removing two of them, he stuffed them into his bag and then fluffed up the remaining dozen to fill the space. They would never be missed. Who needed that many towels anyway.

Madison was still sleeping peacefully as he moved stealthily down the stairs, his dirty hiking boots in one hand, fiddle case in the other. He stopped motionless on the last step and listened for any sounds of life, remembering that her parents might be around. On the second floor landing he could see a narrow Oriental carpet in a deep burgundy shade running the length of a long hallway that ended at an elaborate pair of carved wooden doors that stood open. The master bedroom, no doubt. He suppressed his urge to peek inside and continued his stealthy descent, trying to remember if the kitchen was to the right or left of the grand staircase.

He froze again, listening for noises, hearing only the loud continuous ticking of a massive grandfather clock that hovered menacingly in the front hall. He could not shake the feeling that he was an intruder, even though he had been invited here. He was a freakin' guest, for Christ sake, what was his problem. He'd already been in most of their neighbors' houses as a laborer or caretaker, and had learned to at least appear comfortable with it.

The kitchen was impossibly light and sunny and for a brief instant he wondered why he wanted to go back to his dark cave of a cottage in the woods. There was a note propped up on the counter – "*Off to church and then back to Wellesley. Chocolate croissants in the basket. Safe trip back to Hanover and see you for Thanksgiving in a few weeks. Love, Mom and Dad. P.S. Don't forget to lock up and set the alarm.*"

"Sweet," he said aloud and was surprised to hear how sarcastic one simple word could sound. He helped himself to one of the croissants, so light and flaky it barely took the edge off his growing hunger. He opened the refrigerator and whistled softly. "Oh, yeah, baby. Bring it on."

Half a dozen cloth shopping bags hung on a row of hooks by the back door. Choosing an older one that was slightly ragged on the edges, he began to fill it from the refrigerator and the cupboards. It had been a long time since he'd had a brie and smoked duck sandwich. Like maybe never.

He'd stayed home for several days after his night at the Carters, leaving only on Tuesday afternoon to do the weekly dump run for Sloane and a few other elderly women. The days were growing shorter and the weather was bleak in that November way that could so easily bring him down if he wasn't careful. Life began to settle into a steady rhythm; he got high a lot, listened to music and tryed not to think. He had forgotten to recharge his phone when he was taking the trash to the landfill in Sloane's truck, so it had been dead for a while by the time he plugged it in at Martin's on Friday night. He listened to a message from his mother and actually felt a little homesick for the first time. He called her back and hid his emotions, begrudgingly agreeing to come for a few days at Thanksgiving.

He was moody and quiet during the weekend gigs, constantly scanning the bar for any signs of Madison, fearful that she might make the drive up from Dartmouth and come looking for him. He was relieved when she never showed but also a bit hurt, wondering if it meant he had been a bad lover, but knowing in his heart that it had been just another one-night diversion in her spoiled rich girl life.

And then, a week later, the piano had shown up on his porch.

It took the better part of a day to rearrange the furniture in the sugar house to accommodate the piano. Eventually he moved the kitchen cupboard outside, creating a not-quite-big-enough spot against the wall, but by dropping the side leaf of his dining table, he made it work. Then he banged some nails into the wall above the stove to hang the pots and pans, put a row of books on top of the piano and used the bookshelf for the dishes and silverware. He was somewhat concerned about all the mouse poop he found in the drawers and cabinets when he cleaned. Now that it was getting cold the mice would be looking for warm places to survive the winter and he hoped his cabin wasn't one of them. Finally satisfied with his accomplishments, he sat down to bang out a couple of tunes before it was time to head out to work again.

Myles still felt a bit skittish as he headed back down the mountain. Would there be something else on his porch when he returned late tonight? Should he feel guilty about the fact that the piano was now part of his house? But who was he going to tell – the police? The truth was people unloaded upright pianos all the time – "free to a good home." He assured himself that somebody was probably just getting rid of it, but that did not answer the question of who knew where he was actually living.

Myles was spooked again when the cat showed up on his doorstep a week later. He supposed he was really not that far from civilization; somebody's pet could have wandered into the woods and found its way here. When the cat came to him immediately, meowing a few times and then rubbing against his legs, he knew this was no feral creature. It looked like a half-starved stray, bony with long legs, tiger-striped except for one white paw.

He picked it up and it curled against his chest, and with the sound of a motor that hadn't been started in a while, the little body rumbled with a rusty uneven purr. Peeking between its back legs, he ascertained that the cat was a girl.

"Okay, you can stay." He didn't have much a cat could eat but she happily consumed the remains of the smoked duck from the Carter's refrigerator and a few pieces of cheddar cheese. He would have to go to town and get some cat food, but hopefully she also liked the taste of wild mice. Moments after arriving, she was stretched out on the rug in front of the woodstove as though she had lived there all her life.

He found himself talking aloud to the cat most of the time. He named her Diva and she followed him around, as happy for his companionship as he was for hers. After he found her scratching in the kindling box, he took a pane out of one of the windows and made her a cat door with a magnetic flap so she could do her business outside. He had a hard time convincing her she should stay put when he went to town; on Friday night he found her waiting for him at the bottom of the trail, cold and wet, and she happily rode inside his jacket against his chest for the hike back home. Eventually she came to trust that he would return and was happy to keep his pillow warm for him instead.

Myles wondered again, had it really been "divine providence" that had brought Diva to him? Had he casually mentioned in conversation somewhere that he had a mouse problem? He tried to rethink where he had been the week before she arrived and with whom he might have spoken; he'd gone to the library, the grocery store, rehearsal at Aidan's, the bar. He'd had tea with old Mrs. Hall after moving some wood indoors for her, he might have talked about mice then, but he didn't think she remembered or even heard half of what he said. It didn't matter – he tried to convince himself that nobody knew where he lived, but clearly somebody did or there wouldn't be a polished piano sitting in his house.

And then it was time to go home for Thanksgiving and suddenly he didn't like the idea of leaving Diva alone for three days. But Hunter was so happy to see him waiting in front of the village grocery that he didn't care that Myles was bringing a cat for the weekend.

"We have missed you so much, buddy!" His father squeezed him in a big man hug. "And now we've got a whole forty-five minutes alone before we get back to the inn, so tell me all."

He talked a lot, there was plenty to tell, but he couldn't tell all. It made Myles feel kind of sad, his dad was open to anything and had never judged him, but he couldn't share everything now.

His mom was so happy to see him that she could barely speak and he couldn't have brought a better gift for his new sisters than the company of a playful cat. His younger brother, Dylan, seemed a bit resentful about having to share his room again for a few days, but after they got high together he loosened up.

Thanksgiving dinner was a bit tenser than usual. The presidential election results had left everyone depressed and anxious about the future. Myles, living his life in the woods, had barely been aware of it happening and the adults chastised him about not exercising his right to vote now that he was of age. Kashi, his older sister who was a dance teacher in Burlington, had brought her new boyfriend home and it was obvious to everyone that he was not comfortable in their loosy-goosy unruly household. Both of Tucker's parents, Tyler and Lucy, had been invited as always, but without Tucker there it felt kind of weird for all of them. They both questioned him intensively about his travels with Tucker and Chloe, and were surprised that he had not heard from them. He was relieved when they started arguing with each other and the spotlight was off of him.

"What is this hard green stuff in your hair?" Sarah asked as he was helping her put the leftovers away.

"Some cobwebs I sprayed in at Halloween. I haven't been able to get it all out." He hated confessing to his mother that maintaining his dreadlocks was a problem; it had been a bone of contention between them for years. "Maybe I can try soaking in a hot bath while I am here." He didn't want to admit to her that he didn't even have a real shower where he was living.

It was harder to say goodbye at the end of the weekend than he thought it would be. He got out of the car at the bottom of Sloane's driveway and waved until they were out of sight, and then, loaded down with leftovers from his mother and a big bag of weed from his father, he headed up the trail. Diva ran ahead, happy to be in the woods again after three days of smothering attention.

His life had barely returned to its weekly pattern of winter repetitiveness, when one evening the sameness of his new existence was abruptly overturned. He had just settled down at the piano to entertain himself for an hour while his dinner cooked, when he felt the vibration of his phone in his pants pocket. He didn't recognize the number flashing on his screen.

"Hello?"

"I'm here."

"Wow! This a nice surprise! So you're where? In Vermont?"

"No, here. In your town."

"What?" He stood up, Diva falling abruptly off his lap and onto the floor. "In Windfall?"

"Yes. I'm at the restaurant in town. Can you come get me?"

"It's just you alone?" His heart was suddenly pounding so hard, he could barely hear anything else.

"Um, yeah." He didn't understand the hesitation in her answer but it didn't matter.

"I'm on my way." He was already putting his boots on, the phone tucked between his ear and shoulder. "Have a drink or something, it will take me about half an hour to get there."

"Okay, I'm not drinking but..."

He grabbed his head lamp and headed for the door, at the last minute remembering to turn the fire off under the beef stew. "Chloe, this is so amazing. I can't believe you're really here."

CHAPTER FIVE

January 2017

Tyler fidgeted restlessly in the uncomfortable molded plastic chair. He would have thought that a doctor's waiting room that was frequented by so many pregnant women would have seats that were more accommodating. The magazines on the side table were all about mothering and parenthood, but he finally found an old issue of National Geographic with which he distracted himself. He was engrossed in an article about the "Blue Zones," which were five places in the world where people regularly lived to be over a hundred years old, when he realized Chloe was standing over him, looking pale and nauseous. The doctor hovered behind her, carrying an open laptop computer, which Tyler recognized as the replacement for the old-fashioned folder and clipboard of earlier eras.

"Everything okay?" he asked anxiously.

"Mr. Mackenzie? I'm Dr. Willard. Everything's fine, but with Chloe's permission, I'd like you to join us for a conversation. I understand you are the father-in-law." Exceptionally tall and silver-haired, Dr. Willard exuded the sense of calm and experience that was expected from those in his profession. Without waiting for an answer, he held open the door to his office.

Magazine in hand, Tyler was still thinking about extending his life by moving to Sardinia or Okinawa as he followed them. He looked quizzically at Chloe who bit her lip and shook her head.

"Will somebody please clue me in? What is going on?"

At least the leather chairs across from Dr. Willard's desk were well-padded. Chloe sat down heavily, looking at her protruding abdomen which, to Tyler's eyes, seemed to have grown even bigger in the last hour.

"Nothing terrible, just a double helping of babies. Congratulations. Chloe is expecting twins." Dr. Willard seemed to enjoy the pleasure of delivering the news as much as he probably enjoyed delivering newborns.

"Twins. Like in – two babies at once." His classic response elicited a ripple of laughter from the doctor and a wide-eyed affirmation from Chloe.

"That's right. We're not sure exactly how far along she is or how the babies are positioned, so we need to do a sonogram and run some tests over at the hospital. I've let them know you are coming. Whatever the results, she is going to have to pay attention to what she eats and how she is feeling. And she is going to need your help, especially during and after the birth."

He felt a flush of embarrassment at the feelings that flooded his chest – incredulity and surprise were quickly replaced by anger and indignation. Why wasn't Tucker sitting in this seat instead of him? How could he abandon Chloe at a time like this?

Suck it up, he admonished himself. And step up to the plate.

"Well. That is amazing news." He reached over and squeezed Chloe's hand, which was tightly clenching the leather-covered armrest. "I guess we have some planning to do. And some calls to make."

He was actually glad that Chloe was sobbing uncontrollably by the time they got to the car. It gave him something to focus on besides his own gut feelings of distress and helplessness. "What am I going to do?" she moaned, banging her forehead against the passenger door window as she waited for him to find his keys. "I have no home, no income, I have nothing. Nothing! It isn't fair. Life is so unfair!"

Reassuring her that he was there for her, Tyler held her until she had calmed down and then helped her get inside. "We'll figure this out. Together." But he felt as desperate as she did. He'd never had to deal with one baby, let alone two.

It was dusk by the time they left the hospital knowing that Chloe was carrying two healthy babies, sexes unofficial but potentially girls. Seeing the sonogram of the small beating hearts, tiny growing brains and the tangle of little arms and legs had made them realize how real the situation was – and how totally awesome. The technicians thought she was about 25 weeks pregnant, which made her due date sometime in mid-April, although she had been warned that twins often came early and that she should be ready for the "event" any time from the beginning of March onwards. They had signed her up immediately to join a Monday night childbirth class, even though it had started two weeks earlier.

When she had been told that "You'll need to bring a birthing partner," her expression had become so despondent that Tyler had immediately promised that he would go with her and learn how to be her support person.

"So what do you think - should we tell Lucy on the phone or in person?" he asked on the ride home. It was the million dollar question; Tucker's mother had been sternly disapproving of the "older woman" in his life and the vagabond existence the two of them had pursued. Despite the inevitable acceptance of the young couple's lifestyle, Lucy and Chloe were oil and water; in fact, Lucy was still unaware that Chloe was back in West Jordan.

"You know she's going to go ape shit."

For a few seconds they sat in silence and then both burst out laughing.

"It would be easier to just hold the phone away and let her rant, but she is less likely to rant if we are there in person." Tyler spoke from years of experience.

"Yeah, I think the phone, for sure."

"And what about Tucker?" Now that the tension had been broken, he thought it was a good time to bring up the most obviously missing element in the equation. "How are we going to contact him? There has to be some way to reach him on that boat. I would consider this an emergency."

It was no surprise that Chloe clammed up again. "He doesn't want to be reached."

"Chloe, look. You can either help me or not. Don't underestimate my power to find someone." In his mind, he was already weighing the various means he might use to locate his son.

She sighed heavily. "I know, I know. There's really nothing else I can tell you. If you want to call out the Greek coast guard and embarrass the shit out of him, that's up to you."

"I don't fucking care if I embarrass his irresponsible teenage ass! This is his problem as much as yours." He hadn't meant to use the word "problem," but it was too late now. "Does he even know you're pregnant?"

"Yes, he knows!" she shouted back at him. It was just like old times, only then it had been he and Tucker fighting in the car on the way home from school about some adolescent issue that felt trite compared to this. "And he doesn't care. It was just a big inconvenience to him and his precious future. He blamed me and he was right. It WAS my fault for not paying attention better and remembering to take my pills. He didn't love me enough to forgive me. He DIDN'T WANT A BABY. AND HE CERTAINLY DIDN'T WANT TWO!!!" She was beyond distraught now and he was instantly worried that her anxiety might be bad for the fetuses in some way. "Stop the car."

"Calm down, it's okay. We're almost home." He didn't know what to say.

"STOP THE CAR. I'm going to be sick."

Sloane's memorial service was scheduled for the next afternoon and Tyler felt he probably ought to go. Besides, a room full of local Windfall residents would be the most fertile ground for digging up clues to Myles's possible whereabouts.

"I know it's a depressing event, but do you want to go with me?" he asked Chloe. "You could get out of the house for a bit." Now that he had accepted the fact that this was a long-term arrangement, he was worried about what the isolation of winter could do to her already fragile mental state.

"Hmm, I don't think so. But maybe I could drop you off and take the car into Littleton to do some shopping?" She gave him her most big-eyed winsome look.

"I'd say fine, but when was the last time you drove?" he asked suspiciously. "I'm guessing not Thailand or India or Instanbul or Greece...maybe a year and a half ago when I taught you that summer?"

"Well, yeah. But it's the same car and it's like riding a bike, isn't it?"

He gave in, knowing she would need to hone her beginner's driving skills if she was going to stay for a while. To reassure himself that she actually knew what she was doing, he let her drive the two of them to New Hampshire that afternoon. He did not mention he could see that in a few weeks' time it might become physically impossible for her to even get behind the wheel.

She dropped him at the Windfall town meetinghouse, where a steady stream of serious-looking people were making their way along a path of packed snow from the parking lot to the large double doors, their bright parkas and colorful scarves covering their somber funeral attire.

"I'll see you in a few hours; you have the directions to Sloane's, where the reception is, right? And get yourself a cell phone while you're out!"

"I will. I'll just wait in the car for you outside. I don't want to come in; I'm not ready to talk to people about this." She touched her belly. "I'll be there by five."

Tyler shook his head as he watched her drive off, but before he could start stressing about his car and his life, someone touched him on the arm. He looked up to see Fern, her round cheeks rosy with the effort of walking up the road in the cold.

"Who was that?" she asked, nodding her head towards where his Subaru had been. There was an odd expression on her face, which he might have called jealousy if the idea wasn't so ridiculous.

"My daughter-in-law. Who lives with me now. AND will be giving birth to twins soon."

"What?" Fern's amazed laughter was so genuine that he had to join in, enjoying the absurdity of the situation. "Sounds like we have some catching up to do. A lot has happened in Windfall in the last few days."

But they had joined a line of people who were entering the building in a hushed silence and he could not ask her what the news was. As he sat on the cold metal folding chair listening to a minister eulogize about Sloane's philanthropic accomplishments, his mind wandered. Fern's presence at his side reminded him of his latest online dating failure – he had arranged to meet the woman from heartsafire.com named Caroline for dinner at a restaurant in St. Johnsbury the night before and she had never showed. When he tried to contact her again, she would not even respond to his messages. It was another frustrating blow to his dwindling self-confidence in his ability to start and sustain relationships with women.

Across the room he saw Eva sitting solemnly with Ben and a couple of women he recognized from tango class. He was pretty sure Ben was gay, but Tyler still felt threatened by his ability to dance well and his outgoing personality, both of which Eva seemed to find very appealing. He was gratified when he caught Eva's eye and a smile briefly replaced her somber expression. He hoped she would be going to the reception afterwards.

As with most memorial events, once the service was over and people got some food and liquor into their systems, the atmosphere relaxed a bit. Sloane's house had a large, open floor plan, easily accommodating more than a hundred people, at least standing up. Laurel had hired a local catering service to take care of everything, but there was still the usual surfeit of neighborly casseroles and salads. Tyler had positioned himself on the arm of the couch onto which Eva and a few other women had squeezed themselves, precariously balancing plates on their laps while holding drinks aloft in their hands. He was having a hard time following their conversation but they seemed to be excitedly discussing some local topic of interest that they all felt strongly about.

"Tyler, you run a newspaper, right? You should do a story on this." Eva brushed his arm with hers and nodded towards her seat mates.

"Sure. What's that?" He felt like he would agree to anything if she paid attention to him.

"There's been a weird epidemic of thefts in town in the last few months," a plump, gray-haired woman on Eva's right informed him. Her face was strangely flushed, either from the heat of all the bodies in the room or from the red wine she had been consuming in copious quantities.

"What's weird about it?"

"Well, they're not stealing money or valuables. More like food out of the refrigerators and clothes out of drawers." She accepted a little hotdog wrapped in croissant dough from a tray offered by one of the servers and popped it into her mouth.

"It's more than that – there are other things," a woman on the opposite end of the couch piped up." Some fine crystal goblets and bowls went missing from the Emersons and the Franchettis thought their maid was stealing the silver."

"You sure people aren't just misplacing these things?" Tyler's curiosity was already lapsing; he was more interested in the fresh scent of Eva's shampoo and where her iridescent dangling earrings might have come from.

"How do you misplace a piano?" the plump woman giggled, putting a self-conscious hand over her mouthful of dough-covered wienies and they all laughed with her.

"Someone's piano went missing?"

"The Clarks discovered it gone when they came up over Christmas vacation. It was a valuable antique – not just to their family but it had belonged to some famous musician as well." The other woman reached across the laps between them to extend her hand to Tyler. "I'm Mandy, by the way. This is Jean, this is Connie and you know Eva."

"Right, wasn't it somebody like Stephen Foster or George M. Cohan? Some American icon," Jeanne added. She towered above the others, peering down out of round wire-rimmed glasses beneath a headful of carrot-colored pin-curls.

"Of course now everybody is blaming anything they've misplaced on our serial bandits."

"You think it is a gang of some sort?" Tyler was interested now.

"Well, my lord, how could just one person steal a piano?" The group dissolved into laughter again.

Despite a resolve not to mix personal life with work, Tyler pulled his notebook out of the inside pocket of his jacket.

"In a community like this, it's hard to even know when there's been a break-in," Eva explained. "So many people are only here half the time or on weekends and those are the people who have been burglarized."

"So basically the wealthier residents." Tyler hoped he wasn't offending any of them but a round of nods confirmed his statement. "And do the police have any suspects?"

"They checked up on a couple of local kids who were known for dealing and doing drugs but didn't find anything," said Connie.

"So maybe the piano is just a coincidence and not related to the other thefts. But tell me all the things that you ladies know have disappeared."

"You're going to do a story on this?" Mandy's voice almost squeaked with excitement.

"It's just a small Vermont paper, nothing to get worked up about," he assured her with amusement.

"There are some that think Sloane's death might be related," Jean informed him importantly now. She had the strongest New Hampshire accent of the three.

"Really. How so?"

"I guess the door to her house was standing wide open and Laurel has noticed a few missing items. And then there was the thing with the dog..." Her voice drifted off with dramatic significance, waiting for Tyler to ask for more info.

"Sloane's dog?" He remembered a little terrier, the small yappy sort that always jumped on your legs, eager for attention.

"We're not supposed to know this, but..." Connie gave Jean a meaningful look and then lowered her voice. "They say it was on its walking leash but tied up outside to a fence post with a bowl of food and a dish of water."

"He was even wearing his little fleece vest."

These were definitely details that had been kept from the public; they could mean everything or nothing at all. "How do you know this?" he asked curiously.

"Oh, my son is on the life squad that was called out that night." Jean's tone indicated the importance of this position. "But don't put that in your story."

"So how did they get the call?" This was a point that Tyler had been wondering about – how long Sloane had been dead before the police were notified.

The women glanced at each other and then almost as a group, they all shrugged. "We don't know that. Either they're not saying who phoned it in or they don't know."

Tyler was actually glad that at least some information was considered confidential in this community.

"Do any of you know Myles, the kid who worked for Sloane?" he asked almost casually as he put his notebook away.

"The suspect you mean?" Mandy's high-pitched voice seemed to echo off the walls. Across the room, Tyler saw Fern look up from the food table where she was trying to covertly consume a large piece of chocolate cake.

"I know him." In surprise, he turned to Eva, who had contributed very little up till now. "He helped me out one night when my back tire had gone flat. He was super nice."

"Consider yourself lucky then that you weren't his first victim."

Mandy's snide remark made Tyler's stomach lurch a little and he was pleased that Eva quickly defended Myles. "Isn't it innocent until proven guilty in this country?"

"I thought there was nothing to connect him to Sloane's murder," added Tyler as he watched Fern approaching them.

"Except the fact that he just happened to disappear at the exact same time and can't be found. Seems pretty guilty to me," sniffed Connie. "Laurel's ready to press charges."

The couch-full of women went suddenly quiet as Fern came into earshot. There was definitely some tension in the air that Tyler hadn't noticed before.

"How about you, Fern? Anything been stolen from your place?" Tyler asked.

Her features tightened momentarily and then she shook her head. "I – I was just wondering if you needed a ride anywhere, I'm getting ready to go." Fern addressed him with an intimacy that was clearly intentional.

"Thanks, I'm fine. My daughter-in-law is picking me up. It'll be dark soon; hopefully she can find this place."

The words "daughter-in-law" were enough to turn the conversation in a whole new direction and the women digressed into the usual buzz when they heard about the expected twins. As he had hoped, Fern said goodbye and slipped away. Finally he had a moment to speak to Eva alone.

"So I'd still like to reschedule our coffee date, uh, meeting for that story. On tango. That we talked about. " Tyler felt like he was just stringing random words together and not making any sense. He wished he could channel the smooth-talking, charismatic personality of his younger self around Eva, but instead he always felt as though he was either stumbling over his feet or choking on his phrases.

"I'd like that also." The smile she gave him was so surprisingly warm that he wondered if that was the reason his face felt suddenly flushed and radiant. "How about tomorrow afternoon?"

He was so high from this exchange that he had little memory of saying his goodbyes to the other women or of offering his final condolences to Laurel. As he walked down the driveway looking for Chloe and his car, he checked the messages on his phone. Not just one, but two new contacts were interested in connecting with him on heartsafire.com. There was a voice mail from Sarah wondering if he had learned anymore about Myles's whereabouts – they were apparently feeling increasingly desperate about his situation. And there was a text from an unknown number. *"I'm at the end of the driveway waiting for you."*

Apparently Chloe had acquired a phone.

The village of Windfall looked cold and white and inhospitable in the long shadows of twilight. "Can you pull off here?" Tyler asked as they approached Martin's Mountainview. "I want to stop at the bar for a few minutes, see if anyone has any news on Myles. They tell me he usually plays here with a band on the weekends."

Chloe declined his invitation to come inside, saying she would just rest in the car for a few minutes. She was reclining the seat all the way back as he got out, but when he looked back he could see the blue light of her new phone flashing as she rapidly typed a message into it and he reminded himself that she was still technically a teenager.

The Saturday Happy Hour crowd was different than the Tuesday group that Tyler was used to seeing and he recognized no one except for the logger named Butch.

"Ain't no tango dancin' tonight," was Butch's greeting when he saw Tyler.

"Thanks, I know." Tyler felt uncomfortably overdressed in his funeral clothes, particularly in comparison to Butch's usual greasy attire. "Are any of the band here yet – the...uh...Why Mo Boys? I need to talk to them."

"Nah, they won't be hee-yuh for a few mo-uh hours." Butch turned his back and hunched over his beer, their conversation apparently finished.

Tyler could not bring himself to leave without at least trying to find out something. "Were you here last night? Any sign of Myles?"

"Ayuh. And nope." Butch appeared irritated by having to give even the most abrupt of answers. Tyler thanked him and looked around fruitlessly for someone else who might be more helpful.

As he headed for the door, it was pushed open by a bearded young man in a Peruvian earflap hat carrying what appeared to be an electric keyboard. Tyler pulled back a few chairs so he could get into the room more easily and got a sullen nod in response for his help.

"Are you with the band?" he asked.

"Yeah, I am now," was the surly reply. The man unzipped his jacket and stuffed his hat into a pocket, sweating from the effort of hauling his instrument in from the parking lot. "Now that Mya has gone MIA."

"What do you mean?" Tyler acted ignorant, thinking he might learn more that way.

"The fiddle player that evaporated into thin air. Poof." There was a finger clicking gesture as demonstration. "The one they say killed that woman. The band says they'll take me back now that he's not showing up anymore." There was clearly some bad blood here and Tyler wondered if it was significant to Myles's disappearance.

"So nobody has any idea where to find him?"

The keyboard player snorted as he tossed his coat into a corner behind the small stage area. "Believe me, I wouldn't be here if they did. That dude was wicked popular. Too bad for them that he turned out to be badass. I need a beer."

Tyler trailed him to the bar, unsatisfied with the conversation. "So nobody in the group knew where he was living? Or are they just not telling."

"I have no idea. Why should I care. And really..." A pair of steely eyes turned to stare at him coldly. "Why do you care?"

There was something so frigid in his response that Tyler decided it was inappropriate to share any personal information or continue the conversation. The guy definitely held some kind of grudge against Myles, that was for certain.

He trudged back across the parking lot and opened the passenger door to the car. "Well, that was useless," he said as he slid inside. But Chloe was not in the driver's seat. He looked over his shoulder to see if maybe she had decided to lie down in the back, but silence greeted him again. "What the..."

A tightness gripped his chest and he started to get out of the car when suddenly the other door opened and there she was, breathing hard, her purple wool scarf hanging haphazardly long on one side. The ends of her fingers exposed by her fingerless gloves appeared to be stiff with cold as she pulled the handle shut behind her and turned the key in the ignition.

"Where were you?"

"I had to pee. When you gotta go, you gotta go." Without looking at him, she put the car in reverse and began to back out.

"Oh, I didn't see you come inside." He peered at her curiously.

"I couldn't wait – I peed in the woods over there. What? You have no idea what it feels like having thirty pounds of babies sitting on your bladder." Her voice quavered a little and he put his hand on her shoulder.

"Stop the car – let me drive. You must be exhausted." He shouldn't have made her wait for him.

"Okay." She pulled off onto the snow-covered shoulder of the road and opened her door again. This time in the dim illumination given off by the overhead light, he could see that her face was covered in a fine sheen of sweat, like she had been running. When she hauled her bulky body out into the night, she held a hand beneath her abdomen as though she had a cramp.

"Chloe?"

"I'm fine. I just shouldn't have run back to the car is all."

They switched seats and she reclined hers for the ride back, turning on her side so she faced away. Her behavior seemed as peculiar as ever to him, but he was trying to learn how to accept it.

In the close quarters of the car, he was aware of the strong aroma of wood smoke that filled the space; it seemed to be emanating off of Chloe's many layers of sweaters. It was one of the side effects of living in a wood-heated house; you didn't realize how much your clothes could reek of smoke until you were out of your own environment. He would have to check the stove when they got home, see if the dampers weren't closing well enough or if the gaskets needed replacing. Or maybe Chloe just needed a lesson in how to run it.

CHAPTER SIX

December 2016

Myles ran his fingers lightly back and forth over the round curve of Chloe's bare belly. "I think it's grown since yesterday, don't you?"

"It's getting bigger every day. Does that bother you?" She stroked the soft skin on the inside of his arm.

"Not at all. I find you sexier all the time. Do you think these girls are going to keep growing too?" He cupped one of her heavy breasts in his hand as though he were weighing and measuring it.

"God I hope not. I already feel like I need to start wearing a bra. I hate that thought."

"Well, you don't have to wear anything at all around here. And it's cool how sensitive they've gotten." He liked how the most feathery of touches to her darkened nipples made her twitch and shiver.

"But that's not really what I meant." She gasped a little and then grabbed his wrist to stop the erotic motion. "I mean, does it bother you that it's not yours."

"No, it does not." He leaned forward to kiss the swell in her abdomen. "I love everything that's a part of you. And I love that you are here. I cannot even begin to tell you how much."

He laid his cheek against her stomach, breathing the earthy smells that arose from her skin, the musk of recent sexual activity combined with coconut soap and wood smoke. A week ago it would have been beyond his wildest dreams that Chloe would be here in his bed, living in the sugar house with him, sharing his oatmeal with a silver spoon, drinking spring water out of his crystal goblets. He had not been able to let himself even think about what had transpired between them in Turkey and Greece this past summer; at times the loss of what might have been felt heavier than the groceries he hauled on his back up the trail. He went through periods of hating Tucker for having found her first and no longer appreciating his fortune, of anger at Chloe for the choices she had made, but mostly of loathing himself for allowing it all to happen.

When he had moved to Windfall, he had been recovering from not only the pain of not being able to go to college; he had also ruined the best friendship of his life and lost the girl he loved. He could not smoke enough weed to make it all go away. He realized now that everything he he'd done since then had been an antidote to keep him from thinking and feeling. He'd finally been doing a pretty good job of it, almost even enjoying his newfound daily reality, until Chloe's surprise arrival had made him understand the big empty hole that existed where his heart used to be.

There was an almost imperceptible flutter against the side of his face and then a cry from Chloe. "Oh, my god, oh my god – did you feel that?"

At the next tiny twinge of movement from inside her, his eyes found her eyes and saw the glowing excitement edged with fear. "There's a little person in there," she whispered. "What now?"

"Time to find a cradle, I guess," he laughed. Sunlight suddenly flooded the loft, meaning that it was probably nearly nine, the mid-December morning having finally dawned.

"Okay. But let's have breakfast first. I'm starving."

Chloe sat in the one comfortable chair, an old overstuffed brocade-covered armchair that had come from the Morrison's screened porch. She was eating a piece of toast as she watched Myles cook their breakfast on the woodstove – a skill she hadn't quite mastered yet.

"That looks beautiful on you," he said, nodding at the long red cashmere sweater robe she was wrapped up in.

Mrs. Fletcher hadn't even taken it out of the box yet, which had included a card with it that read "*Christmas 2014.*"

"Thanks. It feels good too." As she caressed the soft knit surface that stretched over her belly, Diva hopped into her lap and began kneading her paws into the coziness. "And Diva likes it too. And so does Algernon." She patted her baby bump.

"I thought we agreed on Bartholomew." He was glad she was joking about it; she had given him some very cross, judgmental looks when he asked her not to question where all the nice things in the cabin had come from. When she had arrived, shivering in only a thin denim jacket over a gauzy Greek cotton shirt, he had been delighted to outfit her grandly – although in just a short time, Madison Carter's clothes were starting to get a little tight on Chloe. He made a mental note to check out Laurel Winslow's sweater drawer next time he went down to Sloane's house.

The only thing he had been up-front about was the mysterious arrival of the piano, but it seemed she had marveled more about his playing than about the improbability of the piano itself. He didn't care – there was nothing he wanted to do more than impress Chloe.

They had spent most of their waking hours during the last week either in bed or eating. He had been as gentle as she asked him to be with her female parts that were now more tender than previously. She came with him to the bar that first Friday night to hear him play, but it was too long a stretch for her and she was seriously exhausted by the time they got back. After that she had been content to hole up at home, paying attention to what she called her "nesting instincts," which seemed to mean sleeping a lot and reading a book he had found on the Emerson's bookshelf called "What to Expect When You're Expecting." He liked that the cabin was warm when he got home, even if it meant he was going to have to cut more wood to get through the winter and he loved crawling under the comforter and curling up next to her warm naked body and having her sleepily turn towards him and nuzzle her face into his neck.

But neither of them ever brought up Instanbul or what had led both of them to this point in space and time from which there was no turning back.

They had started the night in a hookah lounge down the street from the hostel where the three of them had bunks in a four-person room. Tucker and Myles had been talking nonstop for hours by the time they got there and were already so wired on their reconnection that the shisha they smoked did little to relax them, even as they sprawled on an orange silk couch with tufted cushions under low lights with harem music playing.

"I wonder if we can score something real here," Myles had mused aloud as the novelty of the water pipe began to wear thin. Chloe had slipped away and returned in a short while, a small piece of hashish concealed in her palm.

"I don't want to know what you had to do to get that," Tucker had commented wryly.

"Oh, please. A little tit flash goes a long way in a country like this," had been her teasing comeback and Myles hadn't known if she was joking or not.

Chloe looked hotter than ever to him, wearing a gauzy white dress decorated with delicate embroidery in all the essential places, creating a dramatic contrast to the deep color of her skin, evenly bronzed from months spent living on beaches in tropical countries, her dreads tinged blonde from the sun. Sliding onto the sofa between the two of them, she laid a slim tanned hand on his thigh and boldly left it there, the heat of it burning into his leg and running like a live electric line into his crotch.

After the three of them smoked the hash, they wandered out into the street, buying stuffed baked potatoes called kumpir and trying to eat them with their fingers while walking. Myles didn't remember much about this part of the night except that it was really noisy and the air seemed hot on his face and they were laughing really hard about something all the way back to the hostel. They could barely contain themselves as they tried to make their way quietly up two flights of stairs to their room where they locked the door behind them, and threw themselves onto one of the bottom bunks, hysterical with the restrained hilarity of the moment, relieved that no one else had arrived to occupy the remaining bed in the small space.

"Oh, my god, it's so hot in here." Chloe whipped her long-sleeve dress over her head and then stretched out again between them, wearing only a tiny strip of lace underpants. It wasn't like Myles hadn't seen her naked before; the summer she and Tucker had lived in the tree house in West Jordan they had rarely put any clothes on, pretty much reveling in their uninhibited nudity whenever he came to visit. But tonight there was something so charged in their combined energy, he could barely contain himself as her damp body grazed his own.

As if reading his thoughts, Tucker proprietarily put a hand over Chloe's breasts, reflexively rubbing one of her nipples with his thumb, as he lay back with his eyes closed. "T, this isn't fair to Myles," Chloe murmured, and then her fingers found Myles' fingers and brought them to her other breast.

He held his breath, unable to believe that this was happening, realizing that Tucker, in his stoned and sleepy state, was not even aware of what Chloe had just done. She had already hardened beneath his tentative touch, pressing against his fingertips and sighing with pleasure, her own hand sliding provocatively down to rest on the growing bulge in his jeans. Then suddenly he was kissing her, their tongues wrapping and wrestling around each other and he heard Tucker say, "What the fuck?" and Chloe pulled away from Myles and rolled over to put her mouth on Tucker's.

The rest of the night was a blur of passion and emotion – he remembered there was a brief, breathy discussion in which Tucker laid down the rules ("Okay, but no actual intercourse except between Chloe and me") and then a struggle to put the two bottom bunk mattresses on the floor together and then the hasty stripping off of clothes and then the urgency and newness of three bodies finding each other.

At times it seemed like a contest of who could get Chloe off more and it was definitely weighted in Tucker's favor since he held the trump card, but they found a rhythm, unbalanced as it was, eventually falling asleep in a jumble of sweaty arms and legs. At some point Myles awoke to find Chloe holding a finger over his lips and whispering, "Shhh" as she straddled his body. And then he slid silently and deeply inside her, instantly aroused by the amazing warm wetness that surrounded him. The effort of holding back their groans intensified the experience beyond anything previously between them and the unified shudder they shared rocked his world permanently.

When she slipped off of him and returned to her place in the middle, she curled against him, her ragged breaths becoming soft and even as she drifted back to sleep. But Myles lay awake for a long time, his arms around her, his lips pressed to the top of her head, still dazed by the night's events and wanting the present to go on forever.

A few hours later he awoke, stiff and sticky, with a seriously big headache. Untangling the bed sheet from his ankles, he sat up and took in the aftermath of the night's events. His naked butt felt irritated by the exposed surface of the scratchy ticking-striped mattress on the gray tile floor. Pale daylight leaked in through the barred window, partially blocked by the iron frame of one of the bunk beds. It was enough illumination for him to see that Chloe was not in the room and that a few feet away Tucker was still sleeping soundly, one long arm covering his eyes, one bare leg wedged up against a concrete wall.

Shit, this had really happened. He felt around for his pants or his pack, but he was completely disoriented, not even sure which bed had originally been his. Finally he grabbed the loose bottom sheet, wrapped it around his waist like a towel and stumbled to the door. It had been held open with a shoe and he was thankful for Chloe's resourcefulness because it had not occurred to his dulled brain that he might lock himself out by going to the bathroom.

Taking a leak was a relief but not enough; he ducked into the shower room and, hanging the sheet on the towel bar, let a torrent of tepid water run over his body for a few minutes. At least the pressure was decent. He dried off with the sheet and stepped out into the hall, almost colliding with Chloe.

Although she was balancing three small cups of strong Turkish coffee and a pile of bread, Chloe managed to gracefully sidestep around him as he stopped short. She had a colorful batiked sarong twisted around her body and tied behind her neck, her wild hair swept up with a woven straw clip. Her face flushed as he gazed at her, noting how soft and swollen her lips looked and how soulful and loving her eyes seemed to be.

"They call this 'continental breakfast.' Although technically this is not really the continent. Or at least not that one." It was nervous chatter, and he realized he'd never seen her unsure of herself before. "Take one, please, before I drop it."

He hurriedly reached for the uppermost coffee cup and relieved her of the bread as well and then they walked back to the room together, the feeling between them so strong that neither was able to speak.

They sat crosslegged on one of the mattresses, their knees touching, their backs against the cold metal slat of a bunk as they sipped the strong hot liquid and ate the dry bread and watched Tucker sleep. Eventually he stirred and rolled onto his back, opening his eyes, and they could see him trying to figure out the where, when and why of his situation. When his focus settled on them, he sat up abruptly, rubbing his forehead as he experienced a wave of physical and mental dizziness, before throwing himself back down onto the thin pillow and groaning.

"Tell me that didn't really happen."

When neither of them responded, he propped himself up on his elbows and glared at them through narrowed eyes. Myles cleared his throat and Chloe pushed the last cup of Turkish coffee towards Tucker.

"Drink this. You'll feel better afterwards."

"I don't think so." With another dark look at her, he upturned it quickly, drinking it like a shot of tequila in one long mouthful. "Nope. I still feel the same way."

"Tucker..." Chloe reached out a hand to him but he didn't move.

"What?"

"You agreed to it. We all did this together. It's nobody's fault."

'"Really? Because I don't think I'm the one who seduced my husband's former best friend."

Chloe let out a sob as she stood and fled from the room, letting the heavy metal door clang shut behind her. Myles felt overcome with emotion, his own eyes filling with tears, unsure of what he could say to make things right.

"I'm sorry, bro. I thought you were cool with it last night."

"I know. I thought I was too. I guess I'm just not that cool of a guy." Tucker rested his forehead on his knees, the fingers of one hand running nervously through his hair.

"So what happens now?" In the awkward silence that followed, Myles's question seemed to hang above their heads, like a cloud of shisha smoke, before dissipating into the stale air surrounding them.

"You have to go." Tucker did not lift his head as he spoke. "You can't travel with us anymore."

"What?" Myles could not believe what he was hearing.

"You heard me. You need to leave." Tucker sat up, his expression hard and distant.

"Tucker..."

"Now. I don't want to talk about it. Just go."

The two old friends stared at each other, Myles dumbfounded, Tucker defiant, but neither of them stirred. Finally Tucker spoke again softly. "Please. Just go."

Myles did not pretend that he wasn't crying as he dressed and packed his things. Tucker continued to sit motionless, his eyes the only part of him that moved as he watched Myles's shaking hands stuff possessions haphazardly into his bag.

By the time he paused at the door, the tension between them was so overwhelming that he could not even bring himself to say goodbye. Blindly he threw his gear and his boots into the hallway. He leaned against the wall, wiping his nose with the hem of his T-shirt, trying to get calm enough to walk down the stairs to the lobby where he would have to see other people, retrieve his passport from the desk and move on.

But when he got to the top of the stairwell, there was Chloe sitting on the top step, her arms wrapped around herself in a classic self-comforting position. She looked up at him and frowned, at first not comprehending the significance of the pack slung over his shoulder, before fear and sadness flooded her face and she leaped to her feet, grabbing his arm.

"No, no. What is happening? Where are you going?"

Myles shook his head, unable to speak. "I don't know," he finally said. "Somewhere else, I guess."

She pressed her own wet face into his shirt and he folded himself around her. They stood that way for several minutes, until a group of young British travelers came noisily up the narrow stairwell and they had to move aside to let them by.

"You have the number of our international phone, right?" she asked.

"Yeah, but I'm probably not going to text you. He doesn't want to hear from me."

"I need to know you're okay." She looked distraught and desperate. "Message me on Facebook. I'll try to check it regularly. Let me know where you are." Her eyes filled with tears again. "Shit, I'm so sorry. I wanted you to come to Greece with us."

"Hey, don't worry. I'll be fine." Reassuring her actually helped him feel more confident himself. "I'm a gregarious guy. I'll be out partying with new friends in no time at all."

"Good use of the word gregarious in a sentence." She smiled weakly and then stood on her toes to graze his lips with her own. "I guess I better go back in there."

He stumbled down the stairs and out into the street, walking several blocks before he remembered that he had forgotten to pick up his passport at the hostel office. At that moment, as he retraced his steps through the hot alleyways of Instanbul, he felt his life couldn't have sucked more.

"I think the pancakes are burning. Earth to Myles." Chloe's voice brought him back to the present. Black smoke was rising from the cast iron frying pan in front of him; yes, he had burned the breakfast. He opened the cabin door and flipped the charred contents out into the snow.

"Sorry, I'll start over."

"No, let me. You go get dressed. You'll be late." She dumped the cat off of her lap as she moved to take his place at the woodstove.

"Aren't we just the picture of domesticity?" He kissed her and climbed up to the loft to prepare for his day, feeling lucky and ready for anything.

His good fortune continued throughout the morning. When he filled Sloane's truck with the week's garbage, she came out and gave him an early Christmas cash bonus, making sure he was on board for watching the house while she went to Colorado to visit her daughter. Then he headed over to the Emersons where there was a note on the door for him to please call them because they too needed a house sitter for the holidays. When he was done with his chores, he headed over to the library to use the high speed internet for a few minutes to download a couple of songs into his ipod and that was when things got a little weird. The librarian, a heavy woman whose name he couldn't remember, asked him if he would pet-sit for a few days between Christmas and New Year's.

"Well, I've already got a couple of other places to take care of around then. Where's your place and what kind of animals?" he asked. She had come over to where he was sitting and was standing really close to him, or maybe it was just because her breasts stuck out so far in front of her it made her seem close, and because he was sitting and she was standing, they were right at eye level, in fact like right in his face.

"It's out on the Burke's Farm Road. Not far. Could you do it just over the New Year's weekend? I think I can find someone to feed them for Christmas and then I will be back for a couple of days." She was close enough now that he could smell some fruity fragrance that she was wearing, perfume or deodorant or hand cream. It made him feel like gagging.

Why don't you come over this weekend so you can meet my cats and I can show you where things are." Her words were so blatantly provocative that Myles felt himself actually blushing. He could not believe the librarian was coming on to him; she seriously had to be twice his age and maybe twice his weight as well.

"Um, I don't know. I'm kind of busy. And I don't have a car."

"Oh, you're so cute. Do you need a lift? You can meet me here on Saturday morning and I'll give you a ride." She winked at him and there was no misinterpreting her intentions this time.

"Well, it would be my girlfriend and me," he said quickly. "You good with both of us staying there?"

He could see her stiffen and back away a little. "Oh, you always come here by yourself, I thought..."

He liked making her as uncomfortable as she had made him and he suddenly wanted to see her house, make himself at home there, explore her drawers and closets and refrigerator and to feel as entitled to her possessions as she seemed to think she was to him.

"I'll bring her by tomorrow so you can meet her. But, yeah, I think I'd like to take care of your...stuff." He wasn't used to this kind of banter, but he thought he delivered that line pretty well. She visibly relaxed and then purposely brushed against him as she squeezed by on her way back to the desk.

"That sounds good. And if she doesn't want to come out to the house on Saturday, that's fine too."

Jesus Christ, he was sweating now as he waited for her to retreat, purposely intent on watching the upload icon spin on the little ipod screen, wishing he could walk out right now. What a freakin' cougar. Did she really believe he would do her? Well, she would probably back off when she realized that Chloe actually did exist.

He checked the name plaque on her desk as he left the library. "Okay, so see you, Saturday, Fern." He tipped a couple of fingers in the air towards her and slipped out before she could respond.

Chloe was napping when he returned home late that afternoon, still wearing the red robe. He sat on the edge of the bed, gently brushed a lock of hair off her face and watched her eyes blink lazily open, registering where she was and the hour of the day. His heart had been racing again and he breathed deeply to calm it down; he always feared that he would come back to find that she was gone or that he had been dreaming.

"Oh, I must have fallen asleep. Again." She laughed.

"You lazy thang. You never even got dressed today." He slipped his hand under the soft fabric to stroke her bare thigh.

"Unfortunately there's a reason for that. I couldn't zip my jeans up this morning." She pouted a little. "What am I going to do – I need some pants if I'm ever going to leave the house again."

"Or you could just stay naked beneath this robe until spring. You know you like that idea."

"No, seriously. Do you have any sweat pants or something I can wear?" She sat up and wrapped her arms around him. "So how was your day, dear?"

"It was great – we now have three house-sitting jobs over the holidays. We are going to celebrate Christmas in luxury style – wait until you see a couple of these places."

"Oh, you are so good at your job," she teased. "Did you bring me anything special today?"

"Of course." He unzipped his backpack and revealed two soft and voluminous turtleneck sweaters and three bars of dark chocolate. "Oh, and this. Because you need it." He handed her a half gallon of milk.

"So thoughtful." She opened the plastic container and chugged a few mouthfuls. "I can't believe I crave this stuff."

He tugged on the belt of her robe to loosen it. "And now for my reward, right?" But as he stretched out beside her, his phone began to chime in his pocket.

"Answer it. You don't want them to keep calling you. I'm not going anywhere." She slid the robe off her shoulders and pulled one of his hands to her full ripe breasts.

"You are so distracting." As he caressed her, he also peered at his phone. "Shit, it's my mother. Hi, Sarah."

Chloe reached for the zipper of his jeans and he laughed and rolled away from her.

"Nothing," he said into the phone. "What's up... Fine, everything's fine... Oh, huh, really...well, I'm house-sitting for a few people over Christmas, but I'll try. I guess I could come for the day...Of course...Okay...At the village store, like last time, yeah...Let me get back to you on that...Love you too." He threw the phone onto the floor next to the bed. "Fuck."

"It's okay. I'll be fine."

"I'll only go for a few hours. I don't want to leave you." He flung an arm over his eyes, unable to deal with the collision of his worlds.

"It's just another day. Last year we were in Southeast Asia and it was nothing. Don't worry about me – do what you have to."

"I wish you could come with me."

"You know I can't." She slid out of the robe and climbed on top of him, shivering a little as her skin met the air. It seemed as though her belly now protruded almost more than her breasts. "But I could come with you right now if you cooperate."

When he played his gigs at the bar that weekend, Myles wondered if anyone could tell how much his life had changed in the past few weeks, if they saw the difference in him, if the music he made sounded as full as his heart felt. But the only one who commented was Butch, who eyed him from beneath heavy lids and said brusquely, "Haven't seen you out much."

Myles grinned. "Don't need to go out much anymore."

"Oh, must be a woman in the pick-chuh." Butch snickered to himself, apparently seeing some lewd vision in his odd mind. "Careful you don't get her in the family way now, boy."

"Kinda too late for that, I'm afraid." Hell, what was it that made him feel safe telling this grizzled old man things he wanted to keep secret.

Butch sat up straighter than Myles had ever seen him sit and opened his eyes wide enough for Myles to see the bloodshot corneas. "Well, ain't you just a hound dog. Let me buy you one. What are you drinkin'?"

"Shhh." Myles put a finger to his lips and winked surreptitiously. "First thing, don't tell anyone around here, okay? Might wreck our fan base if the girls know I've got a sweet thing at home with a bun in the oven."

Butch actually looked pleased with the idea of this conspiracy. "Got it. Mum's the word."

"And second, you can't buy me a drink. I'm not old enough." He winked again as he took a sip of Jack Daniels from his Nalgene water bottle.

When he left Butch wheezing with concealed laughter at the bar, Myles realized that the pits of his shirt were drenched with nervous sweat. He was going to have to make an art of keeping his mouth shut; it was much harder to keep a low profile when you were no longer alone.

CHAPTER SEVEN

JANUARY 2017

In a blue funk, Tyler sat outside Martin's Mountainview checking his messages. He could not believe the downward spiral of his luck with women – he couldn't even seem to actually meet them, let alone find out if they might be compatible in person. On Sunday when he'd had another no-show for dinner, he checked his profile to make sure someone hadn't hacked him and made him seem like some sort of predator. Today, after he'd already arrived at the restaurant, his lunch date had begged off, saying she had a really bad cold, could they reschedule for next week some time. Now he was waiting in the parking lot to meet with Eva before tango and he'd just gotten a group email from her asking what people thought about the weather; it was supposed to snow tonight, should they call off class?

NO! he responded in capital letters. *And I hope our meeting is still on for 5 pm.*

If his time with Eva got postponed again, he was just going to give up. Forget heartsafire.com, let go of his dreams about Eva and concentrate on just being Grandpa Tyler. Maybe that was really his fate now.

Thinking about the babies gave him an instant headache. He was trying to accept the idea that that they could be a major part of his household for a while but he was having trouble picturing the future. Even just having Chloe around all the time was making him a little crazy, being accustomed as he was to his privacy. And she was *always* there, it being winter and her having no car, money or social life in West Jordan.

To keep her occupied, he'd given her some of the writing and editing to do on the newspaper – he knew she was really good at it because she'd done it for him before, when she and Tucker had been saving up for their trip around the world.

Chloe was brilliant, but she had derailed her education with some rebellious high school misbehavior, and so far had not pursued any kind of higher education or career. And now with twins on the way...derailment was putting it mildly. But when he saw how gladly she took on the tasks he gave her, he realized that she was probably bored out of her mind and glad to have a distraction from her impending condition. Before she arrived, he had been seriously entertaining thoughts of selling the paper and moving to some place warm and exotic. But now he had begun fantasizing that maybe instead, Chloe could just learn how to run the business and take it over and he could become the vagabond.

It was a valid fantasy, but he reminded himself that it could not become a full-fledged dream once she had two infants in her life. Meanwhile, however, she could get the experience, keep from being bored and make enough money to pay her phone bill.

His phone dinged with an email response from Eva. *Okay, class is still on. See you in a few minutes.*

Tyler pumped his fist silently in the air and then went back to listening to his voice mails. Another desperate message from Sarah, wanting to know if he'd had any more leads on Myles. He'd never known Sarah to cry much, she was a rock, but each of her calls sounded increasingly more tearful and more anxious than the last. He wished he had something to tell her.

After his plans for lunch had gone downhill, he'd finally gone to Littleton and managed to find the apartment of Aidan, lead singer for the Why Mos. Bearded and serious, Aidan had shaken his head sorrowfully. "It's a huge bummer, man. Mya is the best – I can't believe this has happened. And he just dropped off the map. Like sailed over the edge of the horizon. Doesn't answer my calls, nothing. I've left him like a hundred messages, no joke. And some of our fans are so bummed they aren't coming to see us anymore. He was such a draw, for chicks especially."

They exchanged contact info and promised to stay in touch if either of them got any news, but the conversation had just added to Tyler's growing depression. Myles had either fled town or was deep in hiding; either way he had nothing hopeful to share with Sarah. Tyler took the coward's way out and sent her a text message.

But Eva was on her way. Maybe his luck was turning. He leaned over to check his appearance in the rearview mirror. Still old. Damn. Gray curls looking wild and wiry, amber eyes a bit too mournful behind his titanium-rimmed glasses, forehead wrinkled with worry, expression too earnest. Lighten up, he told himself. Be a fun guy.

By the time class began, Tyler felt like a different person. He had charmed and laughed and flirted his way through the previous two hours, interviewing Eva for his tango story and then putting his notebook away and just enjoying her company. When the lesson began, she partnered with him to teach the new steps to the class and he was happy to let the rest of the world disappear around him in a whirling blur. He ignored Fern's resentful glare and Ben's aggrieved presence and reveled in Eva's attention.

The only downer was when he took a break to get a drink at the bar and realized he was standing next to the morose keyboard player who'd replaced Myles in the band. They nodded curtly at each other and Tyler said, "Hey, how you doin'. Sorry, I've forgotten your name." Not that he had ever known it.

"Gray. Yours?"

An appropriate name for a man with such a dark cloud hanging over him all the time, Tyler thought cynically. "Tyler. So you got a permanent position with the band now?"

The comment earned him a sharp stare. "How'd you know about that?"

Tyler shrugged and stepped back, giving Gray the space he apparently needed. "We talked a little about it last time. And I'm still looking for the guy you replaced."

"Replaced? That is definitely not how I would describe it. Not that it's any of your business."

"So how would you describe it then? Can I buy you another one of those?" Tyler signaled to Babs to bring Gray another drink.

"I was one of the founding band members of the Why Mos – that bastard usurped my place with his frickin' talent." Gray fueled his outraged sense of injustice with a big swig of beer. "So too bad for his sorry murdering ass, now I'm back."

Tyler could easily imagine why the group might have been eager to find someone else to take the place of this surly character; it was harder to imagine why they had re-accepted him back into their fold. But old rural friendships could run deep, and loyalty could often supercede common sense.

He glanced over his shoulder to see if the next round of dancing was about to begin, but it seemed the tangueros were more interested in looking at someone's cell phone. Then one older woman ran over to the door to peer out. Tyler apparently still had a few minutes remaining for more stimulating conversation with Gray.

"So do they have any proof yet that Myles – Mya – actually committed this crime?" he asked as casually as possible.

"The guy's frickin' disappeared, what more proof do they need. Plus my sister works as a dispatcher, she heard they've got his fingerprints all over everything there."

On the next barstool down, Butch swiveled around slowly, training a steady evil eye on Gray. "'Course his prints are all ovah the place – he worked fuh huh, dickhead."

"Who asked your opinion, you frickin' weirdo," Gray spat back at him and then picked up his beer and moved to the other end of the bar.

Butch nodded at Tyler and then resumed his usual slouched position, facing the other direction, where he could see the television screen mounted on the wall above the liquor bottles.

Tyler gave an involuntary shudder as he made his way back to the tango dancers on the other side of the room. Windfall weirdos didn't begin to describe it – he definitely needed to learn a little more about this Gray guy.

It turned out that class was cut short – the storm had blown in at full strength and snow was now falling fast and heavy, inches actually accumulating on the roads. Although most of the other bar patrons sat tight, the tangueros were apparently more prudent and agreed that they all should carefully drive home right away.

Disappointed, Tyler stayed to help Eva pack up the sound system. As they carried it out to her car, she laughingly exclaimed at the wet snow seeping into her lightweight high-heeled boots. But as they cleared the snow off their windshields, Tyler could hear something else in her voice. When she stopped to peer into the swirling flakes that obliterated the outlines of familiar shapes in the darkness, her eyes were wide and fearful. He realized she was terrified of driving home in this blizzard.

"Eva?" He touched her arm with his gloved fingers.

"I don't have good tires and my car is terrible in these conditions. But I guess if I just drive really slow in low gear..." She stared bleakly down Main Street into the oblivion of the storm.

"Look, just leave your car here. I'll take you home. My Subaru has all-wheel drive and does great in the snow."

"You sure? You have a long way to go..." Beneath thick dark lashes wet from falling flakes, her eyes expressed visible relief.

"And all night to get there," he assured her. He hated to admit to himself that his mind was already moving ahead to the part where she invited him in for a cup of coffee and then... To stop the fantasizing, he concentrated on the task at hand, reaching past her to turn the key in her ignition to the off position. "Come on, we better get going."

"Thank you, you have no idea how much this means to me." She grabbed her carryall out of the front seat and locked the door. "I owe you one."

What Eva said was usually a ten minute drive took the better part of an hour. Visibility was only a few feet in front of the headlights and gusting winds blasted white clouds of heavy flakes from various directions, making it difficult to see the road. Even Tyler, with years of blizzard experience, had to admit his hands were stiff from gripping the steering wheel by the time he stopped the car in front of a long dark farmhouse.

"I think you better come in for a while." It was the first words either of them had spoken in several minutes.

"I will." Even if it had not been his intention all along, he would have accepted the invitation at this point.

"I must have forgotten to leave a light on." She led the way across a white expanse toward one side of the building. "There is actually a path here, but you would never know it right now."

Tyler held his cell phone over their heads, illuminating the way to a small porch that framed a red wooden door with double-hung windows on either side. Eva reached for a switch on the wall and then said, "Shit."

"No power?" He realized he'd never heard her swear before.

"I don't think so." Stepping inside, she confirmed her suspicion. "Hold on – I have a kerosene lamp somewhere." She disappeared into the darkness.

"Do you have a back-up heat source?" he called after her.

"There's a wood stove, but I don't know how to use it. Shit, and I don't even know where the matches are."

He heard her fumbling in drawers in the next room. Turning on his phone flashlight again, he made his way towards her.

"Welcome to my real world." He could hear some humor in her voice. "To the public she is the organized schoolteacher who never misplaces an accent mark and the tango instructor who keeps everyone in step. At home she is a disorderly hot mess who routinely loses her keys, her checkbook, and frequently her sanity. Once I found my cell phone in the freezer. Oh, there, finally."

A sulfuric smell accompanied a flash of flame and then the room was bathed in the soft golden glow of the gas lamp.

"Well, don't worry, I can't see your disorder at this wattage. Do you have some firewood? Let me make you a fire." He had almost said "light your fire" and he tried to suppress a laugh.

"What?" She turned to him in a warm intuitive way and he could not help but lean in, savoring the intimacy of the situation.

"Light your fire. Set you on fire. Fire you…up." His face was inches from hers as he whispered the last word, hesitant but hopeful. Her eyes closed momentarily, her lips moved towards his and then she stepped abruptly back.

"Yes, please. A fire would be really wonderful right now. And then we can – talk."

Tyler was not sure what had just happened. Had they been on the verge of kissing or what. Then she called from the dark recesses of the kitchen, "The wood is on the porch. Do you want some wine?"

When he awoke many hours later, blinded by sunlight reflected off vast quantities of snow, he was still awed by how adversity had been transformed into opportunity. He shut his eyes, not wanting morning to arrive yet, knowing it would mean that his night at Eva's was over and he would have to face the prospect of shoveling out and then leaving.

It had been a strange evening, even by his standards, not the lustful fantasy of his imagination, but a cozy sharing of stories and circumstances, snuggled together under an afghan on the couch by the woodstove, close and comfortable.

They had revealed their current situations – Tyler talked about the impending birth of his twin grandchildren which seemed nonthreatening compared to Eva's revelation that she was actually still married to a man in Miami.

"Still in love with him?" He tried hard to swallow the lump in his throat.

"No, just not divorced."

"And you moved here why?"

"Because I knew he would never follow me to a place like this."

They had discussed past relationships, Tyler telling her about his disastrous island affair with Chloe's mother, his discovery after six years that he had fathered a child with his friend Lucy, his fire and ice romance with Sarah and his various blunders with femme fatales throughout the last few decades. Her list was way shorter than his but with quite a few missteps, including some abusers and users. He shared his unspoken dream to sell the paper and move some place tropical, his anger with his irresponsible and unreachable son, his past battle with alcohol. She was a good listener, compassionate and not judgmental. When he finally kissed her, she responded and then pulled away, admitting to a fear of intimacy.

"What's there to be afraid of?" He gently guided her head to rest on his shoulder and stroked her soft hair.

"You knowing my vulnerable spots. Mistaking lust for love. Losing a friend if it doesn't work out." Beneath the afghan, she squeezed his hand.

"So you're not a risk taker."

She laughed. "No, I guess not. And I'm guessing you are."

He told her a few stories about his close encounters with death, the time he nearly burned up in an abandoned hotel, his experience of being drugged and set adrift on sailboat for almost fourteen days, of spending a hurricane in a wine cellar on a Caribbean island.

"And remind me why you find *me* interesting?"

"Don't diss yourself. You're totally alluring." He kissed her again, more deeply, feeling her loosen a little and connect more with him.

"I think you have me confused with an exotic fictional character from your past life." She yawned suddenly. "See, I'm even boring to myself. But really, if this snow stops soon, there will be school in the morning and I'll have to get up for work."

"So you're going to make me sleep here on the couch? Even if I promise to behave myself?" He realized he was so enchanted he would take anything she agreed to at this point.

And that was why he had woken up with his head on a bed pillow propped against the arm of the sofa and his bare feet hanging out below the end of a patched eiderdown quilt. He realized that what had woken him was the insistent vibration of his phone on the coffee table.

It was Chloe. "Are you okay? I only just noticed now that you never got home last night."

He was touched that she had actually worried about him. "I'm fine. I stayed at a friend's house. Sorry I didn't let you know."

His phone said it was nearly 8 a.m. and he struggled to a sitting position, feeling a little hung over. Had he drunk a lot of wine the night before? Probably. From the direction of the kitchen he could smell coffee and something else, maybe whole grain toast. Hunger shot through him like a speeding arrow; he could not recall when he had last eaten.

Eva appeared in the doorway, a thick white bathrobe wrapped tightly around her lithe body, damp hair tucked behind her ears, a cup of coffee in each hand. "Lucky for me school's delayed two hours. Ready to do some shoveling? Don't give me that look!"

"You mean the 'I'd rather have sex than shovel because you are so smoking hot in that robe' look?" The coffee and her appearance seemed to have instantly revived his spirits.

"Watch your language, señor, or you will end up in detention!" she warned. "And don't give me that 'I would love to be detained by you' line because I have heard it all before. Now come make yourself some breakfast, because I have to get dressed for work." She winked at him. "Eat hearty - you're going to need your strength – we have two cars to shovel out."

He followed her willingly, realizing he would probably do anything she asked at this point. He had fallen hopelessly over the cliff ...

Tyler's car was not too much of a problem to dig out, but Eva's was another story entirely. The town plow had pushed a pile up against the back of her Toyota and whoever took care of Martin's parking lot had buried the driver's side in a mountain of snow. Tyler was down to his T-shirt after ten minutes of hard labor in the winter sun and it took another twenty to remove enough snow so that the car could actually move.

"I might just make it in time." Eva slipped in behind the wheel and peeked up at him from beneath the curtain of dark hair that closely framed her face below her knitted cap. "Thanks for everything. See you soon, I hope?"

Although he felt both unattractively sweaty and cold at the same time, he still couldn't help but lean over to give her a kiss goodbye. "How soon?"

She laughed and then rolled the window up as she started to drive away. There was an uneven thumping noise and Tyler momentarily thought that maybe too much snow had been packed into the wheel wells of her car. But when she pulled out into the flatness of the plowed road, he saw what was going on.

He shouted at her and waved his arms but she either didn't see him or didn't want to stop. "Shit." He ran back to his own car and leaped inside, veering crazily out of the parking lot and onto the snow-packed surface of Main Street, following in her tracks, flashing his lights at her and honking his horn. Finally Eva slowed, either seeing or sensing that something was wrong, Eventually she stopped in the middle of the road, after realizing there was nowhere to pull off, and she threw open her door.

"Something is wrong –" she started to say at the same time that he shouted, "Your back tires are completely flat!"

But as he approached her car, he realized that it was not just the rear tires that had lost all their air; in fact all four wheels were down to their rims.

Eva stood in the road, staring speechlessly at the damage. "How...did they freeze to the...is this normal?"

A truck was driving towards them in the other lane, and Eva did not even seem to notice, she was still so stunned. Tyler grabbed her quickly, bringing her to the safety of the space between their two vehicles, and then squatted down to examine her tires more closely.

Each of the valve stems had not only been neatly broken off, there were deliberate slash marks in all four tire walls.

"No, this is not normal," he answered finally, desperately trying to imagine who would have a reason to sabotage the property of this sweetest of women. An angry student? A jilted lover? Maybe there was more to Eva's story than she was telling him.

But in the middle of a snowstorm? It would have had to have happened before morning, when the plow trucks came out. "I think I better drive you to school. You're going to be late."

By the time he got back to Eva's abandoned Toyota, the town cop had arrived and was beginning to write up a ticket. Tyler explained the situation to him and the ticket became a police report instead as they waited for a tow truck to arrive. As the two of them circled the car, the cop shook his head in disbelief. “Believe it or not, this ain’t the first time we’ve seen this same thing in the last year.”

“Really? Here in Windfall?”

“Not at liberty to say any more, but last time we was thinkin’ personal vendetta. Now I ain’t so sure. But let me ask you, do you know, does this Ms. Melendez have any enemies?”

“I – I don’t know. I mean I don’t know her that well. I wouldn’t think so, but she does teach at the high school. You can find her there today.” Still trying to process the strangeness of this repeat crime story, Tyler tried to read over the uniformed man’s shoulder but could not decipher his scrawl without being too obvious.

“And what’s your relationship? You her boyfriend?”

“Uh, no. Just a friend. Got stuck here in the storm last night, couldn’t get home.”

“And where’s home?”

“West Jordan, Vermont.” As Tyler reached into his pocket for his license, he realized the man was now peering at him suspiciously.

“Excuse me a moment.” He stepped a few feet away and reached inside his cruiser for the two-way radio receiver, turning his back on Tyler as he spoke, looking over his shoulder a few times.

Tyler had a sick feeling in the pit of his stomach but he was pretty sure he knew what was going on. And it might be just the opportunity he needed.

“Can I see your license and registration please?” Obligingly, Tyler handed them over. He looked at his watch. This was not how he had expected to spend his day. He had not had a shower, was still wearing his same clothes from yesterday, and had a weekly printer’s deadline to meet by late afternoon. And he had loosely promised Eva he would come back for her if she couldn’t get a ride home.

As he waited for the cop to return, he shot a quick text to Chloe. *Could be held up here for a bunch of reasons. Can you do final edits and get paper ready for press check?*

Flashing yellow lights in his periphery vision indicated the tow truck had arrived. "Mr. Mackenzie, would you mind following me to the station?" The tone was polite but much colder now. "We have a few questions to ask you."

Oh, and I have few questions to ask you too, Tyler thought as he watched the burly young cop pull out in front of him and make a U-turn. His phone buzzed and he glanced at it surreptitiously as he trailed the police car.

No prob. Love to. Will you pick up some more milk?

CHAPTER EIGHT

December 2016/January 2017

A few days before Christmas, Chloe sat with the scissors poised above Myles's head. "So we're really doing this."

"Yeah, I'm ready. And what a gift for my mom."

"If I do it to you, you need to do it to me." She grasped one of his dreadlocks and held it between the sharp shiny blades.

"You don't need to cut your dreads just because I am."

"Call it solidarity. Or maybe I just need a good excuse. Whatever. Mostly it reminds me of the last phase of my life and I've left that behind now."

"Yeah, hardly." He put his hand on her abdomen. "Maybe this baby will be born with dreads."

"Oh, my god, that would be so cute!" she giggled. Sometimes she was so girly that he had no idea how to relate to her. "Okay, here goes." Seconds later she handed him a long matted hank of hair. "Numero uno."

He wanted this to be some kind of rite of passage; he'd started growing his locks when he was only twelve, much to the consternation of his public school teachers. They'd sent letters home only to get missives back from his father declaring full support for Myles's decision regarding his own body. He learned how to keep his hair clean and tidy and always kept a cap handy for tucking the dreads away. He knew he'd been the inspiration for several other kids in town, including Chloe and Tucker who had adopted the style during the summer they lived in the treehouse before leaving for Southeast Asia. But he was not that same person anymore – he was not sure who he was, but getting rid of the dreads was a symbolic gesture of moving on.

Besides, he still hadn't been able to get all of the green gooey spider webs out.

An hour later, she stared at him and then burst out laughing. "I don't even know you!"

"Shit, am I just another normal-looking guy now?" He ran his hand over his short stiff hair. "Shit. What was I thinking."

"You are so not normal." She walked around him, looking at her handiwork from all angles. "But you sure look different. Then again, if you wear your hat, no one will even know."

"Oh, so true. And my head is going to be colder now anyway." He reached for his earflap cap and pulled it on. "If I wear this when I play at the bar, nobody will know the difference, right?"

"Not unless they look closely and see that you've got nothing stuffed up inside." She grabbed the tassels of the hat and pulled his face to hers for a kiss. "Okay, now it's my turn."

"I don't know if I can do this."

"Of course you can. It's easier than splitting wood and you do that very well."

"But what if I fuck it up?"

"I'll fix it. I've cut my own hair before. I don't want it even anyway. Try to make it longer on this side." When he still hesitated, she picked up a half-smoked joint from an ashtray on the table and lit it. "Okay, here. Have some of this first."

They were silent for a moment as they held the smoke in their lungs. "Agamemnon looks way bigger today. Are you sure you aren't having this baby for Christmas?"

"Don't even joke about that." Chloe pulled up her sweater and they both gazed at the roundness of her bare belly, the skin stretching tighter by the day.

"A basketball yesterday, a beachball today, and tomorrow..." His joking words expressed the bewilderment they both were feeling but he could see Chloe start to tense up. "Sorry, hand me those scissors and let me make you as beautiful as me."

She closed her eyes as he began snipping. "Think of it as a commitment to each other," she whispered not daring to look at her dark tresses mingling with his golden brown ones on the floor.

"Feels more like a fraternity hazing. Just kidding!" He put a hand out, pressing his palm against her heart and without opening her eyelids, she mirrored the gesture. "Love you, girlfriend."

"Love you too. Left side longer, please."

The next day they filled Diva's bowls with food and water, and put a few things into Myles's daypack. "We aren't going to need much of anything where we're going," he advised. "Don't bother to bring any clothes – there will be plenty. And I'm sure they've left their refrigerators full of food for us."

"Okay, but here's the real question – which house has the most comfortable bed and the biggest bathtub? I would love to take a really long hot bath."

"Well, I think we need to try them all out, doing what we do best. And I don't mean sleep." He was turned on by the idea of having sex in the master bedrooms of the mansions and manor homes where he worked, although he was starting to get worried about it being increasingly uncomfortable for Chloe.

A light snow was falling as they trudged down the hill. The plan was to spend the night at Sloane's and head over to the Emersons in the morning to feed the dogs and hang out, have supper there, maybe watch some TV, before returning to sleep at Sloane's. At least they had the use of the pick-up truck. And then the next day Myles had to go home to West Jordan for Christmas dinner, but planned to be back with Chloe by bedtime. A few days later they would head over to Fern's, where they would housesit through the New Year's weekend.

"So here's what I was thinking," he said after they had shed their wet outer clothing in the mud room and were sitting at the polished granite-topped kitchen island drinking hot cocoa. "This is where she thinks I will sleep." He flung open a door to reveal a well-organized storage room with a neatly made twin bed against one wall.

"Cinderella-style," Chloe commented wryly. "You mean she didn't offer you a pallet on the hearth?"

"Come on, Sloane loves me. Like a son. I think she just doesn't want me tracking dirt all over the house."

"Loves you as a servant is more like it."

"ANYWAY, come up here." She followed him up the stairs to a spacious bedroom with giant picture windows on three sides that framed a view of the entire Presidential Range of the White Mountains. "THIS is where we are going to sleep. AND..." he opened a closet in the hall that contained piles of neatly folded sheets and blankets, "...this is what we are going to sleep ON." He handed her a stack of glossy bed linens that were the color of a full-bodied Italian wine. "Red silk sheets, let's see how it feels to sleep in excessive opulence." He laughed and kissed her. "Merry Christmas, baby."

"Oh, my god, you are so good at being a bad boy." Chloe stretched out on the king-sized bed and gave a sigh of delight. "Come here, Robin Hood."

That night they ate steak and chocolate mousse on the red sheets while watching a giant flat screen television that was recessed into the wall. They took three super-hot showers in the custom-built stone and glass stall and Chloe enthused about being able to flush the toilet every time she peed.

"It's fun being rich," she commented as they ate breakfast in bed the following morning. They were both wearing thick white terry bathrobes with gold monograms and drinking French Bordeaux. "Do you think we would ever get sick of it?"

"Stick with me and you'll probably never get to find out. But it is a bit of an upgrade from sleeping on the beach in Greece, right?"

Three weeks after he'd left her in Instanbul, she'd messaged him from Skyros. He read her words in an internet café on Ikaria, just a few islands away, where he had been camping in the village of Nas, along a river that ran right into one of the most amazingly beautiful beaches he had ever seen.

"Where are you? Are you in Greece? Can you come to Skyros?"

"I'm on Ikaria. Yes, Greece. I'm fine. How is everything?"

"Eh. Okay. Tucker went off to crew on a yacht for two weeks and I didn't want to go with him. I'm alone."

He could actually feel his heart start to beat faster; or maybe it was actually beating for the first time in weeks.

"How about you come here? I only have a week left before I have to fly home."

It seemed like an interminably long minute before her answer came back. ***"Where should I take a ferry to? I'll leave tonight."***

It had been, without a doubt, the best week of his life. The images were burned indelibly into his memory; he didn't need any snapshots to remember them. Meeting her at the ferry, hitchhiking back along the north coast of the island to the beach. Feeding each other fresh figs and feta, her tanned naked body in the impossibly blue sea water, stretched out next to him on her sarong in the hot sand. Making love in the ruins of a Greek temple under the stars. Making love in the tent by the river. Making love in an ancient olive grove under the watchful eyes of sheep.

Chloe was delighted that he'd actually found a beach that nudists frequented. During the days they spent together, she rarely wore more than the thong bottom of her bikini, unless they climbed the steep stairs cut into the high cliff that led to the village, where they drank pitchers full of local red wine, which was ridiculously cheap and delicious. Then she would throw on a sexy crocheted lace dress that barely provided coverage for the parts that needed covering, but that seemed perfectly appropriate as summer fashion in Greece. She seemed to visibly ripen and bloom, no longer the hyper, sharp-edged girl who had copped hash in Istanbul, but a more relaxed and happier version of her former self.

She confessed that things had been strained for months between her and Tucker, long before the fiasco at the hostel. They had been trying desperately to make it work, including their impulsive marriage on the beach in Thailand, hoping that commitment would actually make them more committed.

Then she and Myles agreed that they wouldn't talk about the past anymore and they wouldn't think about the future; they would stay in the present for the rest of the week, no matter how hard it was.

It was idyllic beyond anything he had ever imagined and as the time for him to return home grew closer, he tried to stay in the moment, appreciating every wonderful second. But the last night was difficult for both of them and they broke their promise not to discuss what might happen.

"Don't go back to him. Come home to Vermont with me," Myles whispered in her ear as they lay still for a moment in the middle of having sex, suspended in time in the closest, most intimate way, moving against each other every now and then to remind themselves of how connected they were.

"I can't. Please don't talk about it."

"I love you."

"I love you too."

"Then come with me."

"I'm married to him. I have to go back." But he began to move inside her, more insistently now, clearly trying to convince her otherwise. "You'll be in school. We wouldn't be able to be together anyway. Oh. Oh. Oh, god."

In the early dawn hours, they went together in the taxi to the airport, their hearts full and breaking. She kissed him goodbye when he got in the line to board the small plane that would take him to Athens.

"You'll be okay getting to the ferry by yourself?"

"I've been traveling for almost a year now. I'm a professional vagabond, I'll be fine." She kissed him one more time. "Never been better. Now go have a good life."

Then she turned and ran swiftly away, not looking back and Myles thought he might never see her again.

And now here they were, and it was Christmas morning and he felt seriously depressed, and not just from the effects of the bottle of wine that he had consumed pretty much on his own since Chloe wasn't supposed to be drinking. He hated leaving her to go to West Jordan, hated the fact that he was not going to be able to tell his family that Chloe was with him now in Windfall, hated that he might even have to see Tucker's father and mother as part of it all.

"Don't worry about me. I'm going to hike up to the house and make sure Diva is okay and then I am going to soak in the tub and then get under the covers and watch some holiday chick flicks. Do you know how long it's been since I've been able to watch mindless TV for hours in a language I can understand?"

She sat cross-legged in the middle of Sloane's big bed and watched him pack, purposely not asking any questions about the unusual assortment of small gifts he had acquired in various places for his parents and siblings.

Suddenly he sat down in a chair across the room and stared thoughtfully out the window. "What do you think he's doing today?"

She shrugged. "I have no clue." She knew exactly which "he" Myles was referring to. "Something self-absorbed, no doubt."

"You don't think he misses you. Not even on a holiday."

"He doesn't miss me guilt-tripping him about his lack of responsibility to anyone other than himself. He didn't want anything to do with little Iphigenia here. He suggested I get rid of 'it.' Didn't want anything to take the wind out of his sails." She snorted at her bad pun.

"You don't think he might have changed his mind now that he's figured out that you're actually gone?" As he said it, he wished he hadn't. Cold fingers of fear squeezed his heart at the thought that she might go back.

"Too late for that now, isn't it? Speaking of late, you better scoot. Come on." Without meeting his eyes, she slid off the slippery sheets and started for the stairs. "I'll be waiting at the door to kiss you goodbye."

It was well into the evening when he finally pulled the truck back into the yard. He could see a light on in the living room where he found Chloe asleep on the couch under a fuzzy white blanket, with Diva curled up on top of her.

"Diva, what are you doing here?" he whispered, although the scenario was pretty clear in his mind.

"Mmm, she followed me and wouldn't go back." Chloe rolled over and stretched. "How was it?"

"Good. Hard. This was the best part." He pulled a large bag of weed out of the front pocket of his pack and tossed it onto the coffee table. "Tell me about your day instead."

She blinked at him for a few seconds, trying to assess his mood, but he had spent the day putting barbed-wire fences around his feelings, and he was not able to shed them quite yet.

"Nice. Quiet. Comfortable. Oh, and weird." She reached for his hand to pull herself to a sitting position. "When I got to the cabin there was something on the porch."

He became suddenly quite still. "What do you mean?"

"A big gift basket. Like wrapped up with red cellophane and stuff. I know, creepy, right?"

"What – what was in it?"

"Food. You know, gift food, like cheese and sausage and bonbons. Who would leave something like that on your porch? I mean, who knows you are there?"

Who indeed. Creepy did not begin to describe it.

"Well, this is certainly a step down from our former place in society," Chloe said as she sat down heavily on the soft sofa in Fern's cottage. "But it's cozy and there are cats. So tell me again why you agreed to this job. Because I was loving that lap of luxury we were sitting in at Sloane's."

But he couldn't explain it to her. He hadn't given her the details of the afternoon that Fern had taken him to her place and openly tried to seduce him. He knew he shouldn't have gone but he wanted to check it out, see if there was some way he could undermine her sense of entitlement to his sexuality. He had managed to escape unscathed with a mild amount of flirting and rebuffing, and then she had agreed to a price double what he usually got paid for house and pet sitting. There was something about how she had treated him, like a sexual object, that made him want to stick it to her. He couldn't help himself now - he was looking forward to leaving sex stains on her sheets, to rifling through her dresser and medicine cabinet, to searching the files on her personal computer.

What are you doing?"

"Nothing. Just checking things out." Myles was standing by a wooden desk, looking curiously at a pad of paper set neatly next to the place where a laptop was usually plugged in. Of course it made sense that she would take her computer with her; he had just not been expecting it. There was a list of names neatly printed on the lined yellow legal tablet. Caroline had been crossed out, Magda and Eileen had checks next to their names, Serena and Wendy had question marks. Beneath the list were some dates and times and notes: *"Magda lunch at Extremities, St. J, Monday, Eileen dinner in Littleton, Bailiwicks? Beal House? Which is more expensive?"*

Although it made no sense to him, he took a photo of it with his phone. "You want to go up to the bedroom and fool around?" he asked casually.

"I might want to go up and take a nap. Unless you think you can seduce me."

His head whipped around and he stared at her guiltily over his shoulder for a moment before relaxing. "Seduce? Of course I can. I know just what you like."

He put his face between her legs and eventually she fell into an exhausted sleep, the sheets and blanket satisfyingly damp beneath her. Rolling over onto his back, he opened the nightstand drawer and made a triumphant sound. "Holy shit, Fern," he whispered. "You perv, you."

Retrieving a plastic shopping bag from under the kitchen sink, he filled it with her sex toys. He certainly didn't want them, but it would be somebody's lucky day when they found them at the recycle table at the town dump. And he dared her to confront him about it next time he went to the library.

As he carried the bag downstairs to put it in his backpack, he was startled to catch sight of himself in a mirror, a rawboned naked specter with close cropped hair, crazed eyes and a self-righteous expression. He did not even know who he was anymore, and he didn't care. Until Chloe came along, he hadn't had to answer to anyone for his actions. Now he was involving her in this lifestyle choice he had made for himself and what had seemed so right was starting to feel wrong.

But when he went back up to the bedroom, he could not help but be overcome by the sight of her, so beautiful and so vulnerable, her long dark eyelashes against smooth flushed cheeks, her soft lips, looking a little swollen and bruised from so much lovemaking in the last few days. Her naked breasts spilling over the covers, the Mediterranean tan fading away into blue-veined fullness as the weeks passed, the nipples even darker and larger now than when she had arrived, so sensitive, so erotic, just like the rest of her. Gently he pulled back the blanket for a moment so he could see her whole body, the taut round belly above the dark hair that had grown thicker and longer since she had stopped caring about bikini waxes or shaving. The soft skin on the inside of her thighs that he loved to stroke until she would sigh and open up for him like a spring blossom in the sunshine, the long graceful length of her muscular legs from knees to ankles to the toes that still displayed the chipped remnants of dark purple polish.

She shivered a little in her sleep and instinctively curled up into the fetal position, destroying the relaxed beauty and openness he had been admiring. Reluctantly tucking the blankets back in around her, he added a gray cashmere throw she had grown attached to at Sloane's, slipping it under the sheets so she would awaken to feel its coziness against her skin. He noticed the sparkle of the two tiny diamond earrings she wore in one ear, one of the first gifts he had brought home that had delighted her beyond words, before guilt had set in and he stopped doing risky and impractical things like raiding Madison Carter's jewelry box just to impress Chloe. But despite her unspoken disapproval, she loved the luxurious and elegant things he provided. And he loved making her happy.

There was no way he was going to stop now.

Fern kept lots of food in the house and they feasted like gluttons on New Year's Eve. "Who keeps sixteen quarts of Ben and Jerry's in the freezer?" Chloe marveled. "It's better than going to the village market in West Jordan."

"She has some great French cheeses too." Myles had a variety of bries, chevres and camemberts spread out on the counter.

How do you know about that kind of thing? I think I am not supposed to eat brie." Chloe thumbed through the now dogeared "What to Expect When You're Expecting" book, looking for the reference to ripened cheese.

"My parents are foodies. I may be a small town boy, but I had a world class education in cuisine. Tucker too. We resisted as often as possible. Going to McDonalds was like porn for us." He stood thoughtfully for a moment, still holding a knife in the air. "I'll be right back."

Anyone with a stash of sex toys like Fern's had to have a collection of porno videos also. He took the stairs two at a time, and threw open the cabinet beneath the bedroom television. "Bingo. Gold mine," he murmured. More possessions she would never report to anyone but might miss terribly. He swept them into another plastic bag. The guys at the dump were going to have a field day.

"Yeah, no cheese for me," Chloe said when he returned to the kitchen. "But I'm thinking about thawing one of these steaks in the freezer and grilling it. I have a hankering for red meat today." She opened a cupboard over the stove and revealed a startlingly large assortment of cookbooks. "Maybe I should learn how to cook – which of these would you recommend, connoisseur. Or do I mean concierge..."

"Both, to you, mademoiselle."

"That's madam, I believe, monsieur."

Myles studied the books and chose the most expensive-looking one, hard-covered with glossy photographs of elegant meals from around the world. Brushing a little dust off the top, he cracked it open . " Guess, she doesn't use it very often. Oh, a signed first edition, no less. That Fern has her connections, doesn't she..."

"I'm kind of growing attached to this place." Chloe stroked one of the longhaired cats, who had jumped on the counter and was now licking the butter dish. "And some of her clothes actually work for me in this condition." She opened the long loose sweater she was wearing to model the pink satin and lace nightgown she'd found in the closet. "And it's adjustable." She demonstrated the drawstrings on her shoulder and above the swell of her belly.

"It would have to be to fit her." Myles made a mental note to slip the garment into his backpack before they left the house.

"Don't be mean. She's just a big woman. And right now I am too. And she has some awesome tango shoes in the closet; they're a beautiful shade of fuck-me-red." She laughed. "Totally appropriate for climbing a snowy trail to a cabin in the woods. What's this?" She pulled a slip of paper out of the pocket of the sweater and opened it. "Huh, that's weird."

Still thinking about Chloe hiking up the trail in red high heels, Myles looked over her shoulder. "Oh, that's totally weird. And a little Twilight Zone-ish. Do you think they know each other?"

Myles stared, his mind racing. Written in red ink was the name of Tucker's dad and his phone number. Could Tyler and Fern actually know each other? Of course, they could. There were any number of good reasons; but did it have anything to do with him? It was unsettling; like some sort of cosmic warning that he and Chloe were playing with fire. In so many ways.

"Fuck it. Who cares if they do." For months now he had felt like he was sky-diving without a parachute. He slid his hands beneath her sweater and pulled her towards him, until her nose touched his. "You know what I'd like to do right now?"

"Let me guess. Something to do with me lying on my back wearing nothing but a pair of red tango shoes?" She laughed. "Because there's no way I'm going to be standing up in those things."

"Oh, Chloe, girl. You know me so well."

On Sunday afternoon, it took them three hours to clean up the debauched mess they had made of Fern's house. Myles hauled bags of trash out along with the booty he had lifted from the bedroom. He had declared the upstairs off limits to Chloe, telling her he would take care of straightening it up; he didn't want her to know that he had no plans to strip the sex-stained sheets off the bed or that he was going to bring home the red shoes and the pink nightgown along with a few other nice pieces of clothing she might be able to wear in the coming months.

"You need to empty the cat box," she called up to him. "Apparently I'm not supposed to touch that stuff either while I'm pregnant."

"Yes, dear. Anything for you, dear." He stuffed the clothing into his pack and headed down to the laundry room to deal with the kitty litter.

"What is this cookbook doing with our stuff?" Chloe asked as he passed by her on the way to the truck with a bag of trash. "We shouldn't take this home."

"We'll just borrow it for a little while. She should get the borrowing books thing – she's a librarian, right?" Myles was astounded at his own ability to fabricate an excuse so quickly.

"Maybe we should leave her a note, let her know."

"Sure, but she'll probably not even notice. It looked like she hadn't used it in years." He watched Chloe scratch out a short message on a Post-it note, and decided it was a good thing, almost a decoy to distract from the rest of the "borrowed" items. But he had an uneasy feeling as they locked the door to the cottage behind them. He felt maybe he had gone too far this time, stepped beyond the bounds of his personal code. Fern might be an offensive bitch, but she was a working woman, not a self-entitled wealthy person with more privilege and money that she knew what to do with. He needed to stay in line with his 'non-profit mission' here or there might be guilty retribution to pay.

"You what? Feel like knitting?" Myles put his hand on Chloe's forehead. "Hmm... you don't feel feverish. Is this part of that nesting instinct thing? Do you even know how to knit?"

"Yes and yes. Don't make fun of me. It isn't just old ladies who knit. I feel like making stuff. Can you pick me up some needles and yarn somewhere?" She frowned a little and adjusted her position. "Probably not in Windfall. Maybe need to go to Littleton."

"Not to worry. I know where I can get exactly what you need."

A few days later the outdoor temperatures plummeted, putting the White Mountains into a brilliant sub-zero deep freeze. Myles and Chloe hunkered down inside the sugar house, Mrs. Franchetti's knitting needles and merino yarn clacking away in time to ragtime piano variations on *The New Groundhog Day Blues.* The woodstove needed continual feeding during weather like this and Myles taught Chloe the intricacies of keeping a fire going so that she could stay warm when he went out to play music on Friday and Saturday nights, the occasional backdrafts mingling with the ongoing weed smoke that lingered in the air. They thawed and roasted a turkey that Myles had brought home (Chloe no longer questioned his sources) and made a big pot of turkey soup with the bones and leftovers. Time disappeared into a pleasant haze of short days and long nights in their cocoon of coziness.

The wind picked up on Saturday afternoon and by the time he reached the bar Myles was chilled through. "Something warm, please," he begged Babs, who reached over and put her palms on his cheeks and held them there in a motherly way for a moment.

"Some mulled cider, coming up, and a bowl of fish chowder." She disappeared through the swinging doors to the kitchen.

A few barstools away, Butch smirked. "You'll be whizzin' all night, with all that hot liquid in you."

"No different than drinking beers, Butch." Heating up at last, Myles was about to pull his hat off and then thought better of it. He was not ready to deal with any comments about his shorn hair. The band hadn't played over the holidays and he'd already almost forgotten he'd cut his locks.

"Someone was in hee-yuh lookin' for you a little while ago. That librarian woman."

Myles hid the wave of fear that ran through him behind some playful bar bravado. "Librarian? How would you know that's what she was, Butch? Bet you've never set foot in the town library."

"Well, just because I ain't never died yet, doesn't mean I don't know who the unduh-take-uh is." It took Myles a moment to translate Butch's New Hampshire pronunciation of the word "undertaker" and then he gave the appropriate guffaw.

"So what'd she want?" Myles wrapped his cold hands around the steaming mug of cider and tried to act casual.

"Didn't say. Maybe you got something big that's long and overdue that's she waitin' on." Butch leered at his own innuendo and Myles rolled his eyes. "How's that girlfriend of yours doin'?"

Again he felt a shiver of panic, wondering how Butch knew about Chloe, but then he remembered that he had mentioned her pregnancy. "Uh, good, good. Getting big."

"When's she supposed to pop?"

"Pop? Oh, uh, don't know that really." He realized he was having trouble paying attention, fearful that Fern was going to return and have a confrontation with him.

"Well, be careful. Bad cold going 'round hee-yuh. S'why Babs is workin' on her night off – Pinky's home sick." Pinky was the weekend bartender; Myles hadn't put the disconnect together of Babs and Saturday night, but apparently Butch was all over it.

"Okay, good to know. I'll stay away from people." Any excuse was a good one and Myles moved over to the stage area where Aidan was already setting up.

He had a difficult time losing himself into the music that night. No matter how he concentrated, he found his eyes drifting towards the entrance, watching the customers who blew in from the cold, many unrecognizable until they removed their winter caps and scarves. But Fern never reappeared and by midnight they were calling it a night. He dreaded the walk home, knowing that the temperature was probably somewhere south of ten below zero now, and that he would have to keep moving at a steady pace to keep his body heat up. But there was no alternative – at least he had Chloe at the end of it, keeping the cabin and his bed warm.

Sunday morning was the coldest yet, with gusty winds that found all the places between the logs that had not been well-chinked, sending chilly drafts blasting through the interior. Myles stoked up the fire and then they stayed in bed, under the down comforter until the sun was as high as it was going to get and they were too hungry not to eat.

"We're out of milk again." Chloe drank the last of the gallon straight from the plastic container and tossed it into the recycle box. "Just sayin'."

"You'd think you'd be able to start producin' your own soon with the size those jugs have grown to. Just sayin'."

"Not funny. I'm scared at how big they're probably going to get when I actually start nursing." Chloe stared down at her seemingly mountainous breasts.

"Okay. Well, usually wind like this will die down around sunset. If it does, I'll make a quick run down to the village store. Because you know I will do anything for you." He came up behind her and wrapped his arms around her girth, running his hands over all her sensitive places. "And I think I'm starting to have a thing for really big women."

As he had anticipated, the weather calmed down just before sunset and the temperature even rose to above zero. "I'll be expecting a reward when I get back for going beyond the call of duty." He stepped into a pair of fur-lined boots and pulled on mittens crafted of double-thickness fleece.

"Your prize will be here waiting, barefoot and pregnant and in the kitchen. Well, maybe not barefoot." She kissed him goodbye. "You're the best."

Working out a jazzy upbeat refrain in his head, he made it to town in record time. It was already dark as he turned into the bottom of Sloane's driveway, the gallon jug of milk keeping time against his back with every step. The rhythmic bumping ended abruptly when he stopped short at the sound of voices ahead. He edged forward, keeping to the edge of the plowed area, ready to dive over the snow bank if necessary.

Two heads were silhouetted in the porch light.

"I've been worried sick. Are you okay? You were gone for two hours! I didn't know what I was going to do if you didn't come – Myles? What? What is it?" Chloe came towards him, more quickly than she had moved in a couple of months. “Why are you crying? What happened?”

“I can’t believe it. It’s so awful. I can’t believe it. I think she’s dead.” The frozen tears and snot on his face were joined by a fresh outburst as he threw himself down on the couch and buried his head in his hands. The fresh snow that covered his hat and shoulders melted onto the floor at his feet.

“Who’s dead? What are you talking about? Myles! Tell me!”

“I called 911 and then I ran. But what if they come here? What if they find this place? Oh, my god, oh, my god.” He rocked silently back and forth and shivered, Chloe clawing vainly at his arm trying to get him to stop moving and calm down.

“Myles. Look at me. LOOK AT ME. Tell me who you think is dead.”

And finally he raised his face to her, his red-rimmed eyes as grim as gravestones and told her what happened.

PART TWO

CHAPTER NINE

JANUARY/FEBRUARY 2017

By the time Tyler picked Eva up in front of the high school, he felt as though he had just flown in on a red-eye flight from California. Bleary-eyed, unshaven and hungry, he wished that Eva did not have to witness him in this grumpy and unappealing state, in which he could not predict his own behavior.

"I don't understand – it was my tires that were damaged; why did the police bring you in for questioning?" At the end of her work day, Eva still looked full of energy and Tyler had a momentary flash of resentment at her vivaciousness.

"They're grasping at straws in Sloane's murder. The fact that I was friends with her AND live in the town that their chief suspect is from was enough to get them excited. Their problem is they have no case at all. This is the turn, right? Looks like you're finally getting plowed out now."

He stopped his car on the road to wait for the truck that was making another sweep of the snow on the driveway. The driver halted his vehicle by the entrance to the house and gunned the engine, rolling down his window.

"Oh, he probably wants to be paid. He likes cash." Eva dug in her purse as Tyler moved slowly to a parking spot beside the plow truck. "Oh, I don't have enough; I'll have to run inside. Sorry, Butch!" she called. "I'll be back in a second."

Tyler recognized the old logger who was a regular bar patron at the Mountainview. Pulling up next to him, he put down his own window. Butch moved a toothpick up and down in his mouth and regarded him with mild amusement in his bloodshot eyes.

"Well, well, if it isn't the man from Vuh-mont. You doin' the tango teacher now too?"

Tyler frowned and resisted the urge to put his fist into Butch's jowly face. "'Doin'?" he repeated.

"You know, bangin', screwin'. Don't go denyin' it; I know a Subaru tire track when I see one and they was only goin' one way this morning." Butch leered at him. "She's a nice piece, that one. Nicer than that ole fat library lady."

Despite his efforts to show no reaction, Tyler felt his cheeks burning. How did Butch know so much about his comings and goings? The old drunk was sharper than he appeared.

"Yeah, I do her too." Butch laughed at his expression. "Her driveway, that is. And Sloane's too, for that matter. You're quite the horn dog about town, Mistuh Mackenzie." The slamming of the house door made them both look up. Eva was counting the bills in her hand; she shook her head and then went back inside. Butch made a slurping noise with his tongue. "You can have that big-ass Fern any day; me, I love me some of sweet tits here."

"Shut the fuck up, asshole. You don't know shit about me and I don't want to hear you talking about Eva that way." Tyler could not believe how fast he had sunk to Butch's level.

"Yeah, well, don't think I haven't seen me some. When I come in hee-yuh plowin' on those dark mornings and she's already got the lights on, it's like I'm at the drive-in movie thee-ay-tuh!" Butch wheezed a little, enjoying his joke and the effect it was having on his audience.

With a violent motion, Tyler flung open his door. The scrape of metal on metal and a dull denting thud indicated that he had done some damage to the driver's side of Butch's truck. With one door wedged against the other, Butch could not even get out of his vehicle. As Tyler strode quickly towards the house, he could hear a raging string of expletives behind him. He met Eva at the front steps; her alarm at Butch's angry frenzy was visible.

“He’s a misogynist stalker and I think you need to fire him.” Tyler turned to watch Butch as he struggled to open the passenger door of his truck.

“What?” She stared at him for a moment and then laughed. “Butch? He’s just rough around the edges, that’s all. Besides there is no one else who does plowing in Windfall, at least not for this price.”

“Eva – no, wait…” Exhausted, Tyler leaned against a porch post to observe the exchange between Eva and Butch, who had finally extricated himself from the cab and was now storming about the destruction Tyler had wreaked on his truck.

He heard Eva say, “He’s not my boyfriend,” and saw her put her hand on Butch’s arm to calm him down and then she pressed a wad of bills into his palm. With a triumphant sneer in Tyler’s direction, he got back behind the wheel and spun out of the drive, leaving a cloud of noxious black smoke and fumes behind him.

“You think he’s pissed at me?” Tyler gave her a half-hearted grin, grimacing inwardly at what it might mean to have Butch as an enemy. But he was more upset about the “not my boyfriend” part of the argument than the wrath of the drunken logger.

“You think?” She left him for a moment, returning with a couple of apples and a chunk of cheddar cheese. “For your ride home, you must be starving.”

Gratefully accepting the food, he leaned over to kiss her on the cheek. “Sorry, I know I reek, I need a shower. Can I talk you into coming to my house for dinner on Saturday night? I used to be a chef…”

“You? A tentative yes, depending on my car and the weather obviously.” Her forehead wrinkled at the thought of her tires.

“You okay to get school tomorrow?”

“Yes, Fern will give me a ride. She only lives a mile or so away and she does a reading class on Thursday mornings. My car should be ready by the afternoon and the garage will come get me.”

Something about Fern and Eva commuting together and engaging in carpool chat made him uncomfortable; he didn't really trust what Fern might say about him. "Okay, then, I'll call you. And I'm serious about Butch. At least pull your curtains; the man is watching you."

"That's creepy. Don't even say that!" She scoffed at his worry. "See you soon. Be careful driving back!"

He was too tired to argue about it anymore. As he headed back into Windfall, ravenously consuming the apples and cheese, he noticed that his gas tank was nearly empty. One more thing to deal with. He pulled into the convenience store/gas station on the far edge of the village and as he was swiping his credit card, he recognized Fern's car on the other side of the pumps. Freakin' small towns, he thought. Maybe she wouldn't notice him.

"Hey, Tyler! What are you doing here on a Wednesday?"

"Um, just helping out a friend. No library today?" He didn't need a full tank; a couple of gallons and he could be on his way.

"Closed Wednesdays. And I had to drive down to Manchester to buy a new pair of tango shoes. Mine seem to have disappeared."

"Your red ones?" Despite what he might feel about Fern, her red high heels were definitely the best footwear in the class.

"Yes. And sadly not replaceable. I had to settle for these." She dangled a pair of shiny gold dancing shoes from her one hand and winked. "Want to come over for a glass of wine?"

"Sorry, I'm on the run today. Have to put the paper to bed and I have a meeting tonight. Another time maybe." He should just be straight with her but he didn't have the energy to deal right now.

When she didn't respond, he looked up at her face. Her jaw seemed frozen into a smile but her eyes looked like two blue flames flashing fire at him. "Sure. Whatever." She turned away. "You still doing heartsafire.com?"

It seemed like he hadn't thought about online dating in days, but he realized it had been a little more than twenty-four hours since he had been stood up for his last lunch date with...whatever her name was. "Yeah, well it's not really working out for me." He tightened his gas tank cap and closed the cover.

"Oh, don't give up. Keep trying. Sometimes it takes a while to find the person who's really right for you. You'll know it when it happens." Her tone was oddly bright and cheery in the bipolar Fern sort of way that always weirded him out.

"Well, thanks for your romantic advice. See ya." He didn't care how abrupt his reply had been, he wanted to get away from her quickly.

He was glad he had asked Eva to come to West Jordan. It would be nice to relate to her on home turf instead of in this strange and incestuous-feeling village.

On Saturday morning, Chloe tried not to smile too broadly when Tyler told her the news. "You're having a woman over for dinner - tonight?"

"Don't look at me like I've never done this before, you little twerp! Instead you could offer to bake this flourless chocolate torte recipe for me." Holding his sticky hands in the air, he touched the laptop keypad with his elbow to refresh the screen.

"How about I just take the car and go out for a few hours tonight and give you two some space here?" she suggested, looking at the clock as though it was already time to go.

It was an appealing thought, having his home to himself again for an evening. "But where will you go? I don't want you to have to just drive around."

She shrugged. "I'll go to the movies or something. Don't worry about me. I've got plenty of company." She patted her enormous belly.

"How can I not worry about you...but okay, fine. I would enjoy that. You do know the nearest movie theater is at least half an hour away."

But she had already disappeared into her room. Peaking around the edge of the door, he could see her rapidly typing into her phone. He wanted to believe she was just looking up cinema schedules, but he could recognize texting when he saw it happening. He knew he shouldn't invade her privacy, but...at some point he was going to have to get his hands on her device.

"What time is your date coming?" she called loudly, unaware that he was only a few feet away.

He moved back into the kitchen before shouting his answer. "Five."

"Oh, an early bird special. For the old folks. Maybe I should go to a matinee."

Tyler threw a wooden spoon at her door. "She wanted to get here before it got dark so she could find it easily."

Although he was distracted by trying to create the perfect intimate supper, he still made note of the details of Chloe's departure. After filling her daypack with a huge quantity of snacks, she tromped out the door wearing all the requisite winter gear, promising not to be back before ten.

"If you get tired, come home!" he called after her, feeling a small amount of guilt at turning a hugely pregnant woman out into the cold. But now he had about ten minutes to rifle through her stuff before Eva showed up.

He opened the closet in her room and stared glumly at its contents. Most of the clothes on hangers were Tucker's from years ago, old rugby jerseys and a couple of suit jackets he had outgrown. Chloe had hung up a few tiny gauzy dresses and flimsy blouses that were totally inappropriate for winter in Vermont and that she could not possibly fit into anymore. There was a miniskirt mysteriously made of real fur; he had never seen anything quite like it. On the floor, beneath these odd pieces of apparel, her backpack slumped dejectedly, like the world-weary traveler it was, a well-worn and cherished possession that had now lost its purpose. Just as he reached for it, he heard the ding of his phone in the kitchen.

Thinking it might be Eva, he hurried to check it. The screen informed him that there were two new email messages; the subject lines of which made his stomach lurch a little. *"Thanks, Skank!"* and *"You Pervert"* were not the usual for his Inbox. They had been sent to his *"editor@jordantimes"* address.

"Disgusting pictures. If you think I find this attractive, think again. Don't even bother to reschedule our date!" read the first one, signed by Caroline.

What the hell was she talking about? Quickly he clicked on the second email.

"Glad you're so proud of your enormous dick, you asshole. Keep it away from me." The was no signature but there was an attachment of a photo of the organ that was supposedly his.

Someone had definitely hacked his account. Before he could do anything to fix the situation, there was a knock at his front door. "Tyler?"

He slid the phone into his pocket. What did he care about online dating now anyway.

The furniture was pushed to the walls, the rug was rolled up and they were dancing around the living room in their socks when Chloe slipped quietly in through the kitchen door.

"No, like this, slide your leg between mine and then quickly back," Eva was saying. "This is tangoing, not tangling!" She laughed as Tyler caught her ankle with his and then steadied himself with a hand at her waist. "You'll get it soon, I promise."

"I'd like to get some soon," he whispered into her neck and then suddenly became aware of Chloe standing in the entranceway watching them.

"Don't mind me, kids," she said loudly. "I'm just going into my room now, shutting the door..."

Eva pulled away, self-consciously straightening her sweater and Tyler silently cursed Chloe's untimely arrival. "Eva, meet Chloe. My daughter-in-law."

Chloe waved hello before quickly disappearing into the bathroom.

"Wow, she looks like she's due any day."

"Actually not." Tyler reached for her again but Eva was already moving across the room, looking for her shoes.

"I should get going."

"You could stay," he suggested softly.

"I'm kind of old-fashioned. This is only our first real date."

He wrapped his arms around her. "Okay. If you say so. How soon can our second date be? If you stay until midnight, can we call that a different day, and a different date?" But he wanted her so badly, he knew he would wait.

He walked her out to the driveway and then realized that Chloe had parked his vehicle behind Eva's, probably assuming a sleepover was in the works.

"Oh, I guess you can't go. Wait a sec, while I move this thing." He pulled up next to Eva's car, but when he got out, she was just standing motionless, staring at his back bumper. "What? Is something wrong?"

He followed the direction of her gaze. On the back hatch of his Subaru was a single word, spray-painted in white capital letters: PERVERT.

"Where did you go, where did you park the car?" Tyler purposely took a stance that blocked any chance of escape from Chloe's room, arms out, elbows resting on either side of the door frame.

"I just went to Littleton – to the movie theater and then to Walmart. I parked on Main Street and in the Walmart parking lot. That's all." She was stretched out on the unmade bed, a hand over her eyes, not looking at him.

"I didn't notice anything, I guess I didn't walk around the back of the car."

In the closeness of the space he was aware of the faint odor of pot smoke emanating from the sweaters Chloe had just taken off and tossed on a chair.

Where had she copped weed...there were too many questions here and she was not telling him everything.

"So you have no idea where this might have happened?"

"NO." She propped herself up wearily and stared at him with an exhausted and hostile expression. "Or why. Do you?"

He had more of a clue than she did, but not much and he had not had a chance to follow up on the emails he'd received earlier. As he turned angrily away, he asked, "So where'd you get the pot?"

"What?" He could hear the alarm in her voice.

"Your clothes reek."

She didn't say anything for a moment, but he stayed there waiting for an answer, the tension between them building. He heard her fall back heavily onto the pillows before she responded. "I got high after the movies with some guys I met there."

"Really. Some random 'guys' asked a pregnant woman to smoke with them." He looked back at her in blatant disbelief.

"Yeah. It works like that sometimes, Tyler." Her accusatory sarcastic tone made it sound like he was the idiot in this situation. "Now I'd like to get some sleep, if you don't mind. If you recall, I've been gone for five hours so *you* could have some alone time with your new girlfriend." She rolled on her side to face the wall and pulled a blanket over her still fully-dressed body.

Resisting the urge to slam the bedroom door, he stormed back into the kitchen, furious at her, and at how his perfect evening had been ruined by whoever this vengeful graffiti artist was. Pouring the last of the pinot noir into his wine glass, he shot it back like a jigger of whiskey, adding a rush of heat to his already flushed face. Then he sat down in an armchair by the woodstove and closed his eyes.

In the morning he would deal with the car and the emails. But right now he was going to deal with his suspicions about Chloe. He quieted his breathing and sat very still, waiting and listening for sounds from her room. Eventually he heard her get up, fumble in a drawer, use the bathroom one more time and then turn out the light. He waited another fifteen minutes before creeping silently through her darkened doorway.

As his eyes adjusted to the dimness, he could just barely make out the rise and fall of her chest under the covers. Touching the nightstand next to the bed, his fingers almost immediately came in contact with her phone. There was a moment of resistance that sent a tremor of anxiety through him and then he realized there was a cord running from it; of course, she was charging it overnight. Carefully unplugging it, he carried it out into the living room with him.

What was he really looking for, he asked himself as he scrolled through the few calls she had made. There were no names attached, nothing in her contacts folder. Other than his own number, there seemed to be only one phone she had texted recently, with a Vermont area code. He quickly scanned the last message. *"Leaving now. First stopping for groceries. See you soon."*

Ho – that was interesting. She seemed to have been smart enough to cover her tracks, however, since this was the only visible message to this number. She was definitely up to something. Could it possibly have anything to do with Tucker? He realized now that was what he was hoping to find – info about his son's whereabouts.

He went back to her home screen – she had downloaded a Skype app, maybe that was how she was contacting him. Her wallpaper picture was of a big striped cat held on someone's lap. Photos – there might be something there. He clicked on her Gallery page.

There were only five photos, but then he remembered she'd only had the phone for a couple of weeks. Two were naked selfies of herself from the hips up, enormous belly and enlarged breasts. Worth documenting, fair enough. The other three were downloads; one was the full picture of the striped cat sitting on a lap that looked very male, worn jeans and a black wool sweater. The next was a photo of a middle-aged woman leaning against a very old building on a narrow street in what looked like a French village. Huh. The third was an artsy picture of two pairs of feet, one in beat-up brown leather hiking boots, the other strapped into dainty red leather high heeled shoes. Go figure.

He moved quickly on to Skype. The app opened to show her list of contacts which was very short – it included him, Tucker and someone named Annabel. He hastily clicked on Tucker's name – their last conversation via Skype had been back in October and had been little more than a cursory text exchange: *Are you coming home this weekend?...Yes, Be there Saturday afternoon.*

Annabel was a different story. Their most recent Skype call had been yesterday and had been 25 minutes long. He wondered who she was.

Frustrated, he went back to the photographs, zooming in on the details. There was a young man's hand holding the cat, the fingers still unwrinkled but definitely calloused from hard work. He wore a piece of braided rope around his wrist that had a couple of colored beads woven into it. Tyler remembered Tucker wearing something similar for a while. He looked at the photo of the older woman; she had a pleasant freckled face and unruly strawberry blonde hair that blew around her head in the wind. Maybe this was Annabel.

Finally he ended up staring at the footwear pic trying to figure out what struck him about it. The women's feet definitely looked like Chloe's, with nails painted black and a tiny silver ring on one toe. When he zoomed in, it looked like the shoes didn't really fit her but it was hard to tell the way her legs were in the air, the short spiky heels resting on the top of the rugged hikers. They almost looked like tango shoes...

"Holy shit." He froze when he realized he had spoken aloud but there was no sound from Chloe's room. He tiptoed stealthily back in and replaced the phone on the charger. Then, grabbing his own cell, he slipped on his boots and hurried outside to make a call.

"Kind of late for you to be up, isn't it, old boy?" Sarah's voice had a humorous edge.

"I knew you would still be working. It's Saturday night. Listen, what are you doing on Tuesday?"

"Let me check my calendar...looks like working at the West Jordan Inn. Why, what's up?"

"Can you come to Windfall with me for tango class?"

He heard her laugh. "Tyler, I'm no dancer."

"Better yet, let's go in your car. Nobody knows your car. Or you." The wheels were turning in his head so fast now he could barely keep up with the possibilities. "I'll leave the car for Chloe. Oh, yeah, oh yeah..."

He could hear her mirth suddenly disappear. "Does this have to do with Myles?"

"Yeah, I think it might. That's what we're going to find out."

CHAPTER TEN

FEBRUARY 2017

With a quick look in the rearview mirror, Chloe made a right-hand turn, skidding a little on the hard-packed snow of the narrow secondary road. She lightened the pressure on the gas pedal; there was no need to speed now that she had managed to lose Tyler and Sarah, and there was still probably thirty minutes of daylight left.

A half mile further, she went right again at a fork, driving on until she came to the circular turnaround where the roadway ended abruptly. Turning off the engine, she stepped out into the still chill of late afternoon, the sun already down behind the nearest mountain. Reaching beneath her sweater to unhook her overalls, she squatted down at the edge of the road to relieve the pressure on her overburdened bladder. It was hard to balance in this position now that she was so front heavy and even harder to get up afterwards. Using the nearest snow bank to push herself to standing, she kicked some snow over the yellow stain she had left by the side of road. Like a cat, she thought.

The phone in her pocket chimed, and she quickly checked the screen, assuming it was Myles telling her he was on his way. Instead she saw that it was an email from Annabel. Receiving a message from Annabel was like getting a package of home-baked cookies at sleep-over camp, and Chloe smiled as she opened it.

"Chloe, mon cheri! So wonderful to see those amazing photos of your belly. As always, I am so inspired to paint your pregnancy! Please send some pics I can use – you know the poses I like." (a smiley face and a heart icon inserted here) *"Sold another set of 'the series' last week. Miss you so much, my beauty. Dublin so dreary after the*

wonderful light and life of southern France. Thinking of you. Our time together will always be a highlight of my life experiences. Skype me when you can, love."

Chloe's eyes started to fill with tears and she quickly dashed them away. Annabel had been everything to her that she had needed at the time – friend, lover, mother – and the feelings still overwhelmed and confused her. She knew it was a chapter of her life that she should let go of now, but it was hard not fall back into the lush memories of those autumn weeks in Greece and France.

By early September she'd been so lonely on Skyros that she began to fall into a hazy depression, left to her own devices living in the dark little room under the family house off Niko, Tucker's boss. Tucker was gone for twelve days at a time, home from Saturday afternoon to Monday morning every other week, during which time he talked only boat talk when he wasn't showering or wanting to have sex in a rough and ravenous way. He didn't want to hear about what she was doing to keep herself from going out of her mind in a village where she couldn't speak or even read the language, where they had only a small room with barely more than a bed and a hot plate, and where she knew no one. The only thing he noticed different about her since she'd returned from her secret rendezvous with Myles on Ikaria was that she no longer had any tan lines. She'd been lucky enough to be able to say truthfully that she'd finally found a nude beach on the island.

Tucker would pay their rent and leave her a meager pile of Euros to get through until he returned again. Fortunately food and wine were cheap and if she wasn't extravagant, she would not go hungry. Her life fell into a repetitive pattern that might have seemed chill if she wasn't so sad. She would sit outside at a small café by the waterfront and drink wine past midnight. Then, if she closed the shutters on the one window of their mean little room, no light would come in and she could sleep later and later into the day, making time crawl by infinitesimally faster. In the afternoons, she would walk way down the coast to a private protected cove that had the small sandy beach where she could actually take off all her clothes and sunbathe until the sun disappeared into the water and she had to make her way back before dark. As the days got shorter and the air began to cool, the tourists started disappearing, and hotels and restaurants closed for the season.

The local people were kind and friendly to her, at least the men were. The women seemed a bit stand-offish and disapproving of her vagabond girl status and scanty clothing. Since there was no hostel nearby, few backpackers came through and most of the fall travelers were much older than her, primarily white-haired retirees that spoke other languages.

In the two cafes she frequented, the waiters were solicitous, always making her aware of the least expensive daily specials and, in exchange for her grateful smile, sometimes bringing her an extra glass of wine or a tasty dessert. She practiced her rudimentary Greek with them and they appreciated her uneven attempts at conversation. Occasionally she had to rebuff an aggressive local who wanted to walk her home, but she had no problem with this aspect of her life and a firm "no" was always respected here.

As the days began to shorten and the arc of the sun became lower, her time on the beach became more precious. She could not imagine what she was going to do with herself when it became too cold to soak up the rejuvenating rays of light or swim in the still warm sea. Overcome by this thought on one sunny afternoon, she laid out her faded linen spread on the small patch of sandy ground, slipped out of her bikini and escaped into a deep lazy sleep.

When the shadows of the inland hills finally cast the beach into shade, she awoke, shivering and disoriented. She scooped up the blanket and, wrapping it around her naked body, she looked up at the sky.

"No. Wait – please!"

A few feet away, a woman sat with a portable easel in front of her and a paintbrush in one hand. "You've been such a lovely and patient model all afternoon." She laughed apologetically. "I hope you don't mind – come take a peek, I think you'll like it."

Chloe froze in place, too astounded to speak, and quickly assessed the presumptive artist. Her first impression was of soft, freckled rosy skin and fair flyaway hair clipped back in a haphazard way beneath a crushed straw hat. She wore paint-stained khaki shorts and a long-sleeve blouse decorated with colorful but faded embroidery, her motherly figure displayed by the wide open neckline.The deep wrinkles of crows' feet accented her light eyes as she smiled warmly at Chloe, inviting her to look at the artwork. There was nothing threatening about her.

Chloe moved forward slowly, tightening the blanket around her body, still feeling dazed from the unusually lengthy nap. "Tell me what you think," the older woman said, moving aside so Chloe could take her place. "Have I captured the feeling?" Her accent sounded British but with some sort of brogue.

Chloe caught her breath as she observed the amazing intricacies and sensuous lines of the watercolor painting. Her golden nudity took focus in the foreground, the shape of her figure a curvaceous counterpoint to the bold landscape of the sea, sky and rocky shore.

"You made me look like...a goddess. Or a spirit... of the sun." Her wonderment made the artist laugh with delight.

"You are a goddess! And I am your worshipping devotee now." She opened a sketchbook. "See what you think of these. I hope I haven't overstepped my bounds here. If you are upset, I will throw them away – but I warn you, it would break my heart."

There were three pages of line drawings featuring parts of Chloe's body, up close and intimate, as could only have been done from a few feet away. Detailed sketches of her eyebrows, the darkness of her nipples, jeweled bellybutton, and the vee beneath her pubes where the curve of her thighs opened out to show just a little of the darkness between. There were some other views of her when she had rolled onto her side, the roundness of her breasts together, the arc of her hipbones, the creases behind her knees.

"You – you got really close, didn't you." Chloe finally raised her eyes to meet the artist's kindly and expectant gaze, their faces only a few inches apart.

"I did. I feel like I know you so well already." Warm fingers brushed a stray hair from the side of her face and lingered for a moment against her skin. Despite her bewilderment, Chloe could not help but close her eyes and savor the sensual touch. They stood that way for a few seconds, long enough for an electric tingle to run between them before the woman began efficiently packing up.

"Can I buy you a glass of wine? To thank you for being my model and to find out your name? And to maybe convince you to do it again for me another time?"

A sudden gust of wind whipped at the thin blanket, pulling it away from Chloe's long tanned legs, exposing the lower half of her torso. There was no point in being modest here. "Sure," she responded, dropping the blanket and striding naked over to her bag. "Let me just get dressed."

She had brought only her bathing suit and a long gauzy sweater with her. Abandoning the bikini top, she wrapped the sweater around her, secured it with a piece of twine at the waist and then strapped her sandals around her feet and ankles. "Ready."

"Wearing only a jumper tied with string and you look ready for the fashion runway." The blue eyes took in the way the neckline of the sweater fell open to Chloe's waist, exposing the unbroken brownness of her skin between the cleavage of her very visible breasts, before moving up to meet Chloe's still wary gaze. "I'm Annabel, by the way."

A carafe of wine later, the warmth between them was of friends who had known each other for years. After a shared meal and another carafe, Chloe was ready to do anything for this wonderful woman who had made her laugh, talk and confess feelings like she hadn't done in weeks. She wanted to believe it was just the fact she was actually having a real conversation in English with someone besides Tucker, but she could not deny how enchanted she was by Annabel's personality and talent. She could think of nothing she would rather do than be an artist's model for her, if it meant being able to share her company.

"Shall we leave here and go back to my place, love?" The question was casual but the fingers that caressed the inside of her bare thigh under the table were not.

Chloe caught Annabel's hand and their eyes met. "I'm not–"

"Not?"

I mean, I've never –"

"Or haven't yet." In the shadowy evening light of the nearly deserted outdoor café, Annabel leaned forward and put her lips on Chloe's and suddenly she was falling into a cloud, a soft comfortable pillow of positive emotion. With a gasp, she leaned back against the hard cast iron of her chair, unable to process what she was feeling. Her sweater slid askew, revealing one bare shoulder and most of her right breast.

"I can't – I don't know how…"

Annabel laughed merrily as she pulled Chloe to her feet. "Oh, I think you do. Now fix your cardigan or everybody will be following us home." She straightened Chloe's sweater, the fine fingertips lingering long enough to enjoy the hardening of a nipple beneath the loosely knit fabric. Then she slipped her arm through Chloe's and led her out onto the cobblestoned street. "I think you'll like the place I'm staying. It has a balcony overlooking the sea."

Chloe didn't return to her own room for three and a half days. There didn't seem to be anything to go back for; with Annabel she had more than she could ever imagine wanting or needing. But on Saturday morning, Annabel convinced her she needed to go home for the rest of the weekend and be with Tucker. "I'm not going to be here forever. And you have some history you need to work out with him. He's probably waiting for you by now. And besides, I need to finish this painting of you without any more distractions."

So wearing one of Annabel's long blouses like a mini dress, Chloe took a straw shopping bag and some Euros ("Your pay for modeling," Annabel had insisted. "Tell him you had a job this week.") and stopped at the market and bakery on her way back to Niko's, arriving at home to find Tucker laying on the bed, freshly showered with a towel around his waist, impatiently scrolling through their ipad.

"Where have you been?" he demanded. "I've been home nearly an hour."

She almost dropped the groceries and ran out, but she knew Annabel would be disappointed with her if she did so. "Buying food before the stores closed. I got a job for a few days so I could buy some things we've been wanting." She forced a smile as she held up a jar of peanut butter, a bag of peaches and a container of real cow's milk.

"You're working?" He propped himself up on his elbows, a smile playing on his lips. "Doing what?"

"Artist's model for an Irish woman who's vacationing here for a couple of weeks." She turned away from him as she opened the food cupboard.

"Nude?"

"Yeah. I don't have any problem with that. Do you?"

"No, in fact, the idea of it is turning me on. Come here."

Reluctantly she went to him, and sat on the edge of the mattress. You can do this, she told herself, as he slipped his hand beneath her clothing and between her legs.

"Oh, apparently it turns you on too," he laughed and she swallowed the lump that was forming in her throat. "Where'd you get this...whatever it is you have on?"

"She gave it to me one day to wear when I was cold. Told me to keep it."

And so it went. She realized that for weeks she had only been going through the motions of being married, but now she was allowing herself to feel the despair of the situation. Tucker was in a good mood, happy that she was happy he said, and then spent the rest of the time talking about his adventures on the Mediterranean. Chloe felt inordinately tired and dozed deeply a few times during his long monologues. After he left before dawn on Monday morning, she found herself in the bathroom, vomiting from a wave of sudden nausea. Climbing under the covers again, she sobbed herself back to sleep.

When she finally returned to Annabel's hotel at noon, she felt drained and sad, and it took another day before she reblossomed under the artist's nurturing comfort and experienced touch. She still seemed to be suffering from exhaustion and sometimes spent hours napping in the porch hammock after Annabel had arranged her limbs in an appealing way for sketching. They hiked out to remote cliffs and coves, where Chloe could shed her clothing to pose and where they could make love on a blanket afterwards. As the week progressed, they were both aware of the limited time they had left together.

"Can't you stay another week?" Chloe begged.

"The house in France is rented for two months starting Sunday. But I suppose I could stay a few more days." Playfully she ran the tip of her paintbrush delicately across the tips of Chloe's breasts, enjoying the tremor of desire it seemed to arouse in her. "Besides, all these good meals with me are putting some meat on those skinny bones of yours. You seem to be filling out in some of my favorite places."

The next morning Chloe was again seized with an episode of sudden vomiting that passed as quickly as it came on. She chalked it up to nerves and her worries about what would happen to her once she was alone in the village without Annabel.

"Will you do something for me if I stay for another half week?" Annabel asked her one night after they were more than a little drunk on wine and sex. "You can say no," she said, stroking her lightly in the way and the place she knew Chloe liked best.

But by then, Chloe was completely under Annabel's spell. She could never say no to her.

A familiar owl-like hoot from the woods sent heat through her body in a little rush of anticipation. From behind a large boulder that concealed the start of a trail, Myles emerged cautiously, peering down the length of the road before stepping into the clearing. Chloe moved quickly towards him, her lips finding his, her cheek scratching against the short bristly beard hairs that now covered the lower half of his face. Beneath the edge of his wool cap, his gray eyes looked heavy with weariness.

"You okay, babe?" She touched his nose with the thumb of her mitten.

"Yeah, just tired. Not sleeping that well. How about you?" He brought her face to his shoulder, leaning his head against the top of hers.

"Eh. Okay. It's hard to breathe sometimes. My lower back hurts. And I've had some little false contraction pains. But fine."

He pulled away and looked at her in alarm. "Contractions? Isn't it kind of early for that?"

"No, no, it's normal. We talked about it in birthing class last night. Braxton-Hicks, they call them. Don't you remember when I read you that part of the book?" she scolded him teasingly. "Come inside the car and I'll turn on the heater. Let's sit in the back where we can cuddle."

"And eat. I haven't had anything since breakfast." Myles pulled his gloves off and looked through the bags of groceries on the seat. "Mmmm, tortilla chips. Good call."

"There's some salsa too, but you might want to keep that sealed for the hike home. But this needs to be eaten." She pulled out a container of store-made guacamole and flipped the lid.

"Oh, my god, you are truly my guardian angel." Myles stopped speaking, his mouth now full of chips and spicy avocado.

"I am, aren't I." She touched his hand. "So here's the bad news."

He paused with one hand in the bag, waiting for her to continue.

"The reason I have the car today is that Tyler talked your mom into going to tango class with him."

"My mom? Sarah?" He resumed eating, but Chloe noticed his fingers trembling a bit. "That's crazy," he mumbled. "She doesn't dance."

"I don't think she came along to take a lesson. She's probably here to ask people about you. But I'm not exactly sure. It could have something to do with this." She hauled herself out of the car and motioned for him to follow her, then tapped her hand on a cluster of four "Bernie for President" bumper stickers that were plastered on the back door.

"It's a little late for that, don't you think?" Myles laughed curiously.

"It was the easiest way for him to cover up the graffiti painted on it. It happened some time on Saturday night when I had the car. It says "pervert" in caps."

"What?!" He stared at the Subaru suspiciously. "That's just weird and random, right?"

She shrugged. "I don't know. He's all wigged out about it. And he asked me a ton of questions about where I went and what I did. We need to be careful. I think they were trying to follow me today, but I managed to lose them when I stopped in Littleton to buy groceries."

"Shit." Myles slumped against the car, his posture dejected, his eyes downcast.

"You ought to call them. Your parents. Just to let them know you're okay. I think they're going crazy."

He snorted derisively. "They've got the girls now. They're getting their parental fix again, they're fine."

"Oh, come on. Maybe I've got some new motherly instincts, but I'm sure they're worried about you."

"When was the last time you called one of your parents? And I'm not talking about Tyler." His defensive response was met with silence and they sat there without speaking for a few moments. Outside the car, darkness settled into the forest around them.

"Let's get out of here," he said suddenly.

"What do you mean?"

"I mean, I haven't been out of the woods in a month. Let's go for a drive. I need to see something besides trees. Maybe even get out and walk around some place where nobody knows us." He climbed from the back of the car into the passenger seat and sat there expectantly.

Chloe got out of the car and stretched for a moment. She did not feel like doing any extra driving but she knew Myles was going more than a little stir crazy. "Okay, where should we go?"

With his directions, they drove out of town on several winding back roads that avoided Main Street and the more populated areas. She was surprised when they eventually emerged onto the highway just south of Littleton. She pulled into a parking lot where they had a view of the liquor store and a 24-hour gym. In the brightly lit interior, a handful of people were jogging on machines and lifting weights. Chloe and Myles watched them, transfixed by their rhythmic robotic movements.

"Its' like we're watching fitness center TV or something," she commented wryly. "And they must have a bathroom in there. I need to pee."

"They must have a shower in there too..." Myles gazed wistfully at the sweaty patrons conducting their normal daily routines.

Chloe was already getting out. "I'll let you know." She crossed the parking lot and reached for the door of the gym but it was securely locked. Putting her face up to the window and peering through, she could see a woman standing in a corner putting on her jacket and she knocked and motioned to her.

"Thanks. I hope nobody minds letting a very pregnant lady use the restroom." No reason not to play the maternity card.

As she made her way to the rear of the building, she was given the once over by the primarily male customers, enduring looks that ranged from amusement to disgust. Emerging from the bathroom, she stopped to get a drink of water from the wall fountain and when she straightened up, there was a stocky man blocking her path. Despite his iron-pumping and barbell reps, the strongest thing about him seemed to be his acrid body odor. His stringy pale hair was pulled back in a rubber band at the nape of his thick neck; his jaw was clenched beneath a scraggly beard that ended in a long thin man-braid and he glared at her with eyes as icy as the Bering Sea.

"You're his chick, aren't you?"

Chloe had no idea who he was and tried to step around him.

"I know you are; I saw you with him once at Martin's. And it looks like now you're having the murderer's baby." He nodded intimidatingly towards her stomach.

"Get away from me. I have no idea who you are or what you're talking about." She tried to step around him but he stepped in front of her again.

"I'm the real keyboard player for the Why Mo Boys. But you wouldn't know anything about real, hanging out with that poser." He moved in closer and she tried to back away, colliding with the metal frame of the water fountain. "So he must be hiding out with you, right?"

Chloe took a deep breath; she knew how to deal with male assholes, she was Chloe the vagabond world traveler, she could handle anything, right? When she finally spoke, it was in a low controlled tone. "If you don't move out of my way right now, I am going to scream rape and I won't stop until they haul your ass into jail, motherfucker. I don't know or care who the fuck you are, but I advise you to step aside. This minute."

She was shaking so hard even her eyelids were twitching, she was sure he could see it, but she stood her ground. In her peripheral vision she could see that a few of the other members had stepped off their machines and were standing in the background waiting to see how this played out.

"Gray!" one of them called. "You must be desperate to put the moves on a pregnant lady, even if she is a beautiful babe."

"Chill, man!" another chimed in. "Don't fuck up your probation."

With a last dark look, Gray stepped back and let Chloe pass. Without turning around, she headed for the exit, praying that Myles had not gotten out of the car for any reason. Then she saw him, standing by the front bumper, trying to watch the drama that had been happening inside the gym, craning his neck to get a better glimpse of the aggressor.

"Who was that guy?"

"Get in the car. Right away." The serious command of her voice spurred him into immediate action. "No, you drive."

She sat in the passenger's seat, holding onto her abdomen, trying to relax. Her fear and adrenalin had prompted another series of false contractions and she breathed deeply, waiting for them to stop.

"What happened in there? Where are we going?"

"Anywhere. Just go."

He drove the car across the highway and pulled into a parking lot behind a small Chinese restaurant. When she told him about the confrontation with Gray, he put his head down on the steering wheel and spoke in a low mumble.

"The guy is psycho. He freakin' hates my guts. I've never had enemies before. Chloe, what am I going to do? What am I going to do..."

She rubbed the back of his neck. "How about some egg rolls and shrimp lo mein?"

Slowly he pulled his body up and gave her a brave smile. "You do know what I like, baby."

By the time Annabel left for France, Chloe realized she was pregnant. She sat for hours on the balcony, staring out at the navy blue waters of the Adriatic Sea, unable to comprehend what her future entailed, taking whatever pose Annabel gently asked, as long as she could keep gazing at the endlessness of the Mediterranean. On their last night together, Annabel pulled Chloe into her lap and wrapped her arms around her, trying to discuss the options, but Chloe did not want to talk.

"Just hold me. Love me."

"Sweetie, you know I am here for you."

They had parted at dawn, with a promise to be in touch as often as possible, and Chloe had felt like her heart had been broken in half again. First Myles, now Annabel. She needed someone, something, to love. She could not get rid of this baby.

But that weekend, when she told Tucker, he looked at her with a blank, uncomprehending face and then said, "Well, you can take care of that, right? They must have abortion clinics here in Greece."

"Tucker, I want to have it."

"What do you mean? How can we have a baby? I hardly make enough money to take care of us. And I don't want to give up my job. I've just barely started." His already ruddy cheeks darkened and he glared at her. "Damn it, Chloe. How did you let this happen?"

"Fuck you, Tucker. Can't you just for once think about somebody or something besides yourself?"

And so it went. By the time he left, they were more sad than furious with each other, and both promised to try and see the other's perspective in the next twelve days. Tucker went out sailing again and Chloe stayed home, throwing up in the morning, sleeping in the afternoon, and going out in the evening to drink bottled water while yearning longingly for the oblivion of red wine. She desperately tried to track back to when she had become pregnant; it had been more than two months since she had been with Myles. She'd gotten her period as soon as she returned from Ikaria and it had been after that when she had gone into the funk and forgotten to take the birth controls pills for several days.

She knew this had made her more fertile during her next ovulation, which had been during the next weekend that Tucker had been home.

Which made her almost eight weeks into it; Annabel had told her the way pregnancy was counted should be from her last menstrual cycle.

There were fewer and fewer afternoons warm enough for the beach but on these rare occasions, Chloe would find a protected place in the sun and stare down at her body, watching for changes. She had been so nauseous and upset, she thought she had actually lost weight. Her stomach was still flat, only her breasts continued to grow bigger and now they felt sore. She hardly knew anything about pregnancy or giving birth. Sometimes she became so overwhelmed that she thought maybe Tucker was right and she should look into ending it.

But when she received the message that he had to work overtime and wouldn't be coming home for another two weeks, she could see the writing on the wall. She decided to fight it any way she could, telling her landlady, Niko's wife, Thea, that she and Tucker were expecting a child and finally receiving the enthusiastic response she felt she deserved. As anticipated, the news was all over the village by nightfall and quite suddenly she was accepted into the fold – a villager about to add to the dwindling local population. Every place she went, people hugged her and cared for her, adding treats to her market basket, and offering her a chair.

"Kalimera, kyria Mackenzie! Syncharitíria!" they called, congratulating her. She stopped feeling so sick all the time, the waistline of her skirt got a little tighter and she could see a slight curve to her belly now. It was happening.

Tucker went ballistic when he returned. "How could you make this decision without us discussing it further! You know I am so NOT down with this. You are so selfish. You don't care about my career at all. How can you do this to me..."

The only time they spoke all weekend was when they were fighting. In the middle of the night, when he reached for her in bed, she rolled away angrily. "You've got to be fucking kidding me."

In the morning when she turned from the sink after brushing her teeth, he was scowling at her nakedness, the new roundness of her abdomen evident beneath breasts that were already a cup size bigger, if she were to wear a bra. She let him look for a moment, taking in her newly acquired womanliness, and then she covered herself with the long sweater and turned her back to him.

"It's not your choice anymore. It's my body and I'll do what I want with it."

An hour after he was gone, she began packing.

It took three days of hard travel to get to the village in Provence via ferry, plane and train with long layovers between her last minute reservations. Chloe was more than exhausted by the time she fell into Annabel's arms; her eyes itched, her back ached and her feet hurt from being laced into boots for the first time in months. Still she was awed by the autumnal glory of the southern French countryside, the golden light, the ancient architecture, the classic landscapes.

She could have put the last year behind her if her rapidly expanding body wasn't a constant reminder. Annabel kept a roaring fire going on the hearth, trying to raise the temperature inside the old stone cottage so that Chloe would be warm enough to relax into natural poses for her. Their days and nights settled into a pleasant companionable routine into which Chloe found it easy to disappear. But the albatross that hung over them was that the house was only rented until mid-November, at which time Annabel would return to Dublin – and to the woman she lived with.

"Does she know about me?"

"She's seen the artwork."

"Would you leave her? For me?"

"You are the light in my heart...but she is my life partner."

Chloe tried not to be devastated by this news or overwhelmed by the uncertainty of her future. But she had no idea what was to become of her – she couldn't picture what she was going to do or where she was going to live with her baby or how she would get by without Annabel's comforting presence.

And then one day she discovered a message from Myles on her Skype account. It was more than a month old.

"Myles? Is he the one you spent the week with in Nas?" Annabel was massaging her shoulders, looking at the screen with her. "The one who went home to college?"

"Yes. Only it turns out he didn't."

Myles and Chloe ate Chinese food and then cuddled in the back seat, trying to find each other's skin beneath the heavy layers of winter clothing. "Oh, my god, I miss this. I need you so much. I'm going to find a way to get you up to the cabin. A sled. Or a snowmobile." He put his face against her sweater, his hands finally inside her overalls resting against her warmth.

"Babe – you know we're going to need a second cradle." She tried not to think about what was going to really happen after she gave birth. How would she ever get up to the sugar house pushing a double stroller?

CHAPTER ELEVEN

FEBRUARY 2017

"I still can't believe she lost us that quickly. She's a slippery one, that Chloe." Tyler slung his daypack over his shoulder as he got out of Sarah's car.

"I agree. From what you say, I think there's a whole lot she's not sharing with you." Sarah did a quick scan of the parking lot beside Martin's Mountainview. "Looks like they do a pretty brisk Happy Hour business here."

"You know how it is when it's the only game in town. Come on, I want to introduce you to a few people before it gets really busy." He led her into the darkened interior of the bar.

"Do I get to guess which one is your girlfriend?"

"Now you know that's not what you're here for. And look at them all looking at you coming in with me. We've started the small town gossip mill rolling already. And wait until they find out who you really are." Tyler was more than a little nervous about the various ways the evening might play out.

They approached the end of the bar, where all the seats were already taken. "Babs! I want you to meet someone." He waved at the bartender who held up a finger as she opened another beer for Butch; he slouched several seats away, surveying them from beneath the brim of a cap that bore the imprint of years of grimy fingerprints.

"This is my friend, Sarah," he said, watching the two women look at each other, their eyes experienced in the art of sizing up people in a matter of seconds. "She's Myles's mom."

Babs' expression registered a series of emotions and then settled into the softness of sympathy. "He was – is – a sweet boy. One of my favorites. Any word from him?"

Overcome with unspoken feelings, Sarah shook her head.

Tyler spoke up. “We were hoping Sarah could talk to a few people here who knew him. We think he had a girlfriend he might be staying with. Also can you get us a couple of Margaritas.”

“Well, strangely enough, Butch over there was pretty good friends with him.” Babs tilted her head towards the logger who had suddenly straightened up on his stool and was staring at them intently. Tyler signaled a hello to him but Butch did not seem to notice. Beneath the grease streaked across his cheeks, he seemed to be growing pale and then, suddenly he rose, put a grubby hand over his mouth and bolted for the back exit.

“Is he all right? He looked like he was going to be sick.”

Babs glanced at the empty space that Butch had been occupying seconds earlier. “Huh. That is unusual behavior for him.” Babs looked worried, showing the universal concern that all bartenders share for their regular customers. “I heard a rumor that he may have something wrong with him. Like something major.”

Tyler swallowed the remark he wanted to make about Butch having a lot of things wrong with him. “Like health-wise?”

She nodded as she pushed their drinks across the bar. “But don’t say anything. I heard it from a friend of mine who’s a nurse at the hospital.”

Sarah and Tyler made their way towards Butch’s empty seat, awaiting his return.

“Not the type of person I would expect Myles to be friends with,” Sarah commented, looking around at the other patrons.

“Hey, he had a good education in North Country relations, growing up at the West Jordan Inn. Oh, see those two guys playing pool? They’re in the band he used to play with. Let me introduce you to them.”

Aidan and Liam were warm and compassionate towards Sarah, and Tyler felt fine leaving her with them for a while. Curious about Butch's hasty departure, he peered out the window in the fire exit door, trying to see into the parking lot behind the building. A middle-aged man and a younger woman were sharing a cigarette on the wooden landing, but the paranoid way they acted when they saw Tyler looking at them, made him think maybe they were sharing a joint.

A refreshing blast of cold air hit his face as he stepped outside. "Hi. Did either of you see which way Butch went?"

"Butch? You mean the crazy logger guy?" Whatever it was they had been smoking, the woman was stubbing it out against the railing.

"He took off in his truck a few minutes ago. Running like he got toned out to a fire or somethin'," the man informed Tyler.

The woman giggled a little. "He's such a weirdo. Ever see his one hand? It totally creeps me out."

Tyler paused, one foot still wedged between the door and the frame to keep it from closing. "His hand?"

"Yeah, he's missing a couple of fingers. Or like the top half of them. Logging accident or something."

"Both hands actually." Her companion shook his head. "If you ever look carefully, you'll see he's missing part of his pinky finger on the other hand too. That's what happens when you drink and work at the same time."

It reminded him of something or someone but he couldn't think of what or who. Tyler shivered a little and went back inside.

By the time he figured out where he had left his drink and located Sarah, he saw that Fern had already arrived. She was sitting at a table in the corner, her hand on the arm of a robust bald man with a large mustache, and she was speaking intimately and animatedly in a manner that Tyler knew only too well. He was a little disappointed – Fern was a key person that he wanted Sarah to meet, and if she had brought a new hot date to tango class it might be a little harder. They probably ought to get right to it.

He was surprised to see that Sarah had actually relaxed enough to be enjoying a game of pool with the boys from the band. "She's really good," Liam muttered to Tyler. "Myles never mentioned he had a mother who was a pool shark."

Tyler laughed a little. "Did he ever mention that he grew up in a bar?"

"Actually he never talked much about anything. Except music sometimes." Liam stared thoughtfully at the colored glass light shade over the pool table.

"Did he ever talk about his girlfriend?"

He shook his head. "Nah. She only came here once and sat way on the other side of the room, away from the stage and the bar. I don't even remember what she looked like."

Fern and her date had their second martini glasses in front of them when Tyler managed to get Sarah over to their table. Despite his intimidating size and appearance, the man had a pleasant genuine smile and seemed to be enjoying Fern's sense of humor.

"Tyler!" she greeted him. "Heartsafire treating you right, I guess?" Her sharp eyes quickly assessed Sarah, from long silvery braid to angular body in black sweater and jeans, her gaze lingering on the sheepskin-lined boots, which were obviously not meant for tangoing.

"This is my old friend, Sarah, who also happens to be the mother of Myles." He flashed Fern a warning look that she blatantly ignored.

"So you're not one of his online conquests then." She held out her hand to Sarah.

Sarah grinned at Tyler. He had not seen her like this for some time; it was clearly good for her to get out of Dodge every once in a while. "Apparently not. We met long before the internet was invented."

Fern's companion also held out a meaty hand with fingers that looked a bit like small sausages. "Milt. Nice to meet you. Are you dancers too?"

"Tyler is, not me. I'm just here looking for information about my son. I hear he house-sat for you after Christmas."

Boldly Sarah sat down in the seat next to Fern and folded her arms across her chest, clearly not going anywhere until this topic had been addressed.

Almost imperceptibly, Fern moved to her left, putting a little more space between herself and Sarah. Milt misread her intention and leaned towards her so that their shoulders and arms were touching.

Caught between a rock and a hard place, Tyler thought to himself and had to turn away momentarily to keep from laughing aloud at his private joke. When he looked back, Fern was draining her second martini. She placed the glass down a little too loudly before speaking.

"He did. He and his girlfriend."

Sarah and Tyler exchanged glances. "I never met his girlfriend – what is she like?"

Fern shrugged. "She didn't come to the house with him when I showed him around. I only met her once at the library a couple of months ago. You know, she was like him, dreadlocks, outdoorsy looking."

Sarah frowned, a few deep creases showing between her eyebrows. "The last time we saw him was Christmas. So you actually saw him after we did."

Fern blinked a few times. "No, I don't think so. I never saw him – them – when they came to stay at my house, I was already gone, and then I left him some cash in an envelope here at the bar. So I'd say I haven't seen him since…I don't know…the third week of December?"

There was something cagey about her answer, but Tyler didn't think Sarah was aware of it. "So he never came to the library in that week before – Sloane died?" He worded the question carefully.

"I don't think so. I could check the sign-in book if you want. Or the security camera." She giggled. "But I hate that thing – it makes my butt look bigger than it already is!"

Security camera. Tyler instinctively looked up at the corner of the restaurant's ceiling where a small electric lens was recording everything that took place. "Could we?" he asked suddenly. "How far do the videos go back?"

"Well, I think the computer at the library has copies of the last three months. But what do you think you are going to see?" She turned to Milt and patted his arm. "Honey, would you get us a couple more drinks and a menu? I am suddenly starving."

"I'd love to, babe." He squeezed his sturdy body out from behind the table, which seemed dwarfed by his bulk.

"Looks like you might have reeled in a good one this time," Tyler teased her.

"Oh, I've caught some good fish before – they just got away from me." The reference did not escape Sarah's notice and she kicked Tyler under the table as she rolled her eyes.

"Okay, seriously. If you still have the tapes, or the files, whatever they are now, from December, I'd like to take a look at them, see if we can maybe get a picture of the girlfriend, even identify her. Sarah's pretty desperate to find her son."

Fern hesitated. "I'm really not supposed to share that with anybody who isn't authorized." Sarah and Tyler waited expectantly, their disappointment hanging over their heads like a heavy banner. "But I'll tell you what. I'll go through the files and see if I can find a picture of her for you." She touched Sarah's arm with much the same gesture she used a moment earlier on Milt. "But I can't promise how good the quality will be or if there is even a shot of her face."

Tyler saw Eva pushing the outside door open, struggling to carry her portable speakers inside and he leaped quickly up to help her. "Thanks, Fern!" he called over his shoulder.

Gratefully accepting his assistance, Eva gave him a quick kiss on the cheek. "That's all I get?" he laughed.

"You know I need to be professional here!" she shot back. But he also knew now how protective she was about her private life.

He looked over his shoulder at Sarah and Fern who both sat watching him intently for different reasons. One of them he knew and trusted as much as anyone in the world;

the other he knew enough about to know there was a whole lot he probably didn't know about her.

But somehow he knew that he needed to see those security videos as soon as possible.

Sarah eventually drank enough that Tyler was able to coax her out on to the dance floor to learn a basic tango walk. By then she had spoken to at least half the people in the bar. "You see that guy down there on the end? Kind of stocky with the scary eyes and the braid in his beard? They told me to stay away from him."

As they circled the pool table, Tyler glanced over at the person she was indicating. Gray was glaring at them, his whole body rigid with animosity. "Oh, that's the not-very-talented keyboard player I told you about. The one who hates Myles's guts."

"Don't say that kind of thing to a boy's mother. I'll go punch his lights out in a heartbeat." Sarah's grip on Tyler's shoulder tightened instinctively.

As if on cue, Gray was suddenly on his feet and heading towards them. "He's a loose cannon. Try not to react to anything he says to you." Tyler spun Sarah around so he was between her and Gray – unfortunately this also had the effect of putting her face to face with him.

"So you're the one that gave birth to that son of a bitch. Which makes you the bitch, doesn't it."

Sarah stopped moving which forced Tyler to stand still also and then the next couple bumped into them, causing all of the dancing to come to a slow awkward halt.

"Don't rise to it, Sarah." Tyler spoke in a low voice, not turning around.

"I've heard he's the one who started the whole 'Gray-hole' thing." A purplish red flush was creeping up his face from his chin to his forehead. "That fucking dickhead comes in here, doesn't know anything about me, or this town, or the band and he's like a goddam celebrity, taking advantage of the fact that I'm down in county doing my ninety days–"

The entire bar had gone silent now; the only noise was the tinny sound of the tango music coming from the portable speakers. Tyler could see a couple of well-muscled customers moving into defensive positions, ready if needed. From the other side of the room someone quietly taunted, "Gray-hole," and a few others snickered.

Gray snapped his head around to look in their direction and then back at Sarah, so angry now that his eyes bulged and spit flew out of his mouth as he ranted on. "And on top of being a dickhead, he's a mother fucking cowardly murderer as well. Ran away rather than face the heat. I hope your rock star son rots in hell, you old cunt–"

Despite Tyler's hold on her, Sarah slipped through his grasp and, with a sound like a war cry, literally leaped through the air at Gray. At the same time, Milt stepped into the space between them, breaking Sarah's attack as he knocked Gray's drink out of his hand and twisted his arm behind his back. Then the rest of the home guard moved in and held Gray away while moving him swiftly towards the door.

"So much for your probation, buddy," someone called after him and the noise of the bar resumed, closing in over the gap left by Gray's angry presence, as though nothing unusual had occurred. Except it had.

Sarah had actually fallen to her hands and knees, and was panting hard, trying to calm herself down, her salt-and-pepper braid grazing the floor. Tyler moved swiftly but Milt was already helping her up. "Thank you," she gasped out between breaths. "I'm sorry I pulled the crazy Ninja lady act. I didn't even realize I had done it."

"Well done," Tyler murmured to Milt.

"Ex-cop. Moonlighted as concert security." He returned to Fern's side, and she hugged him adoringly, flashing Tyler a strangely triumphant look over Milt's shoulder.

"So maybe this wasn't such a good idea," Tyler admitted. "We should probably go home."

"No, no. Finish your class. I'll be fine. Let me just sit down. Go on. Dance." Sarah gave him a little push in Eva's direction and then returned to her chair at their table, leaning her head back against the wall.

This was not the way he had hoped the evening would go. As he started up with Eva again, he could see a single tear running down Sarah's cheek. "Sorry," he apologized to Eva for the interruption they had caused.

"Everything okay?"

"Not really." He ran his hand down the curve of her spine and quickly moved it to the correct position at her reproving look. "Would rather be stuck in a snowstorm with you any night."

Chloe was already asleep by the time he returned home. Before removing his boots, he slipped quietly outside to the car to check the mileage. Nearly ninety miles – where had she gone – that was even more than his round trip to Windfall. In the dim illumination of the overhead light, he looked around the seats for any clues. In the back seat there was a scattering of crumbs and a narrow strip of paper wedged beneath the middle seat belt.

Holding it up to the light he read, *"You will inherit a large sum of money."* He chuckled to himself. Too bad fortune cookies were hardly ever right.

There was certainly nothing suspicious about a very pregnant lady with a craving for Chinese food. Except that she had driven forty-five miles for it.

He had hoped to get back over to the Windfall library the next day but then luckily he remembered it was Wednesday and the library would be closed. He had a commitment on Thursday to cover a story on the local high school play and then Chloe needed the car on Friday for her weekly doctor's appointment and by then it was the weekend and he realized he might as well wait until Tuesday when he would be in Windfall again. On Monday, temperatures rose into the fifties for the first time in weeks and there was a huge thaw, followed by freezing rain and ice the next day and to his great disappointment, tango class was canceled. So it was nearly ten days by the time he was able to actually get to the library. Already the beginning of March.

Meanwhile Fern had sent him a fuzzy black and white picture of the back of a girl wearing a hat and sweater and sitting at a computer. "All I've got right now. No time to look for more," she had texted.

Her expression registered something more than surprise when he walked in the door, but he wasn't quite sure what. "Hi, Tyler. What's up?" As she talked, she continued alphabetizing books on a rolling cart, getting them ready to return to the shelves.

"Just wondering if I could look at that security video myself, see if I could get any other clues from it." He gave her his widest and most charming smile, knowing they were past the point where he could flirt his way into any opportunity here.

"Ummm…" she glanced around the library at the two older women browsing the "New Books" area. "Okay. You'll have to sit here at my desk. Wait a second."

She swept some folders off to the side and rearranged the old-fashioned ink blotter calendar that covered the scarred wooden surface. Sitting down at the computer, she closed out of several programs and then reopened another. "I can't remember which day it was…" She picked up a loose-leaf notebook and flipped back through several pages until she found the day she was looking for.

"All right, here it is. It's probably about an hour in. But be as quick as you can. Remember, this is against the rules." She gave a nervous giggle and stepped aside so he could occupy her chair.

"Thanks. I owe you one." He began fast forwarding through the grainy video marked December 15, looking for an image that matched the one she had sent him. His vision started to glaze over as he watch the pixilated silent movie of a quiet afternoon at the library go by at sixteen times the usual speed. Finally he could see two shadowy images come in through the front door and move to the computer carrels.

He slowed down the film and enlarged the image. The tall one was definitely Myles, the other must be his girlfriend. She was looking down at something in her hand and he could not see the features of her face at all.

"Damn." He watched the slow motion action of the two figures take off their daypacks and each sit down in front of a computer. He could almost make out the girl's profile as she leaned in towards Myles, appearing to whisper something in his ear. It looked like they shared a quick kiss and then settled down at their respective screens.

Something brushed against his back and then he felt Fern's breath hot against the side of his face. "Any luck?" she asked, peering over his shoulder.

"Well, I'm there. Haven't been able to get a good look at her yet though."

The girl pointed at her screen and Myles lean towards her to get a better look and put her hand on the back of his neck. There was something unnervingly familiar about the way she moved, like he'd met her somewhere. Maybe she was a girlfriend of Myles from high school, but he couldn't recall who that might have been. She had dark polish on her nails and a couple of rings on her middle finger. He wished she would take off her hat.

"Yeah, there isn't much more. Call me if you need help." Fern moved a few feet away and opened a drawer.

Tyler sensed she was definitely hovering for some reason. He continued watching the two people on the screen until eventually they stood up and turned to go, Myles helping the girl put her backpack on over a large shapeless sweater that made it hard to identify her body type and then wrapping a long scarf protectively around her neck a few times.

He caught his breath and felt suddenly dizzy. Was it possible? He tried to recall some key dates from a few months earlier but was too dazed to think clearly. He stopped the video. "Do you have a calendar?" he asked Fern.

"Right there, under everything." She indicated the large pad that covered the desk.

"No, I mean like from the last six months."

She handed him the computer sign-in book, opening it to the inside cover. At the same moment, a half dozen toddlers were ushered in the front door by a very harried young woman. "Oh, hell. Story hour already. You're on your own." Fern moved around the desk to great the children. "Hi, kids!"

On his own – she could not have said sweeter words to him. Tyler swiftly leafed through the pages, looking for Myles's name. It seemed to appear fairly regularly for a few months on Tuesdays and Thursdays and then on Friday, December 22, there was the addition of the words *and guest* next to his signature. But that was the last time his name appeared in the book for December. On the off chance that he'd brought his "guest" earlier and had maybe forgotten to sign her in, he changed the date on the security video search to the previous day. Keeping an eye on Fern, who was now completely wrapped up with the preschoolers, he began quickly scanning the new date.

He was disappointed to see Myles entering the library alone but he continued to fast forward through, hoping the girlfriend might appear. Instead he saw Fern approaching Myles and then watched as she got so close to him that his body language became rigid and defensive. He slowed down the footage, trying to figure out what was going on. Was she actually coming on to him? Hadn't Tyler himself still been involved with her in mid-December or had he already ended their affair by then?

"What are you looking at now?" He had been so deep in thought that he hadn't seen or heard Fern returning until she was next to him speaking.

"Nothing. I mean, I was just checking a few other dates that Myles was here, just to see if she might have come along but not signed in." He fumbled with the back button trying to return to the previous video he had been perusing.

"I think it's time for you to leave now." There was a hard edge to her voice that he had never heard before and he realized he had been caught overstepping the parameters she had set up, limits designed to protect her own reputation.

"Let me just ask you a question," he backpedaled, returning to the place where he had paused the video on Myles wrapping the scarf around the girl's neck. "Do you remember what color that scarf was?"

"Funny you should ask that. I do remember because around the same time I lost one in the same shade but of a different style. A little silk scarf that I was very fond of."

She was acting so odd and cold, he was not sure how to respond. Before he could speak, she had reached across him and clicked the program shut on the computer.

"Wait - " but he could tell that there was no changing her mind now. He stood to go. "Sorry to hear about your scarf. I hope you find it. So what color was that again?"

"A lovely shade of heathered plum."

What the hell kind of color was that, he thought. "So that's like…frosty purple?"

"Frosty. That's a good word for it." It was also a good description of the strange smile frozen onto her lips. "Does that help you?"

"Yes. Yes. It does. Thanks." Under her watchful eye, he hastily collected his belongings, still trying to shake the sense of disbelief that had overcome him.

"Why? Do you know her?" Fern's own curiosity seemed to have gotten the better of her now and she dropped the ice queen act for a few seconds as she asked the question.

"Actually, yeah. I think I do."

With zombie-like movements, he walked away, ignoring her as she called after him,
"Who is it? Where does she live?"

CHAPTER TWELVE

MARCH 2017

Myles shaded his eyes as he stepped outside into the warmth of the midday sun. The glare of the melting snow was almost blinding but the temperature felt amazing. Sitting on the edge of the porch, he stripped off his thermal long-sleeve shirt and let the healing rays infuse some Vitamin D into his winter white skin. He couldn't remember the last time it had been as far above freezing as this. For a few seconds he almost felt free-spirited and happy and normal. Diva wandered out the open doorway and rubbed up against his bare back before jumping daintily off the step onto an exposed patch of frozen ground.

If only this was really spring, not just the false promise of warm days still in the distant future. The cabin, which had seemed so cozy when he and Chloe had occupied it together, now seemed like a deep dark hole that threatened to swallow him up along with his sanity.

In the distance he could hear the sound of a hammer striking metal. But after a few minutes there was, once again, only the familiar silence of the woods around him, punctuated by the now constant drip-drip-dripping of the snow as it melted off the overhang of the roof.

He needed to get out, take a walk, maybe hike up to the top of the mountain and look at the view. It might help him figure out what he was going to do with his life when the winter was over. Somehow he had to get out of Windfall, start over somewhere again. What had been a really good new beginning last summer had now deteriorated into the greatest clusterfuck in modern history.

At this moment he hated even going back into his cave of a cabin to put his boots on. He grabbed a light jacket, remembered to put his cell phone in his pocket in case

Chloe called, and then stopped at the cooler on the porch to pick up a hunk of sharp cheddar and an apple. Food was becoming an issue, especially now that Chloe was approaching her due date and eventually would not be able to shop for him. Even his supply of rice and dry beans was getting low. Dangerous as it was, he was going to have to venture down the mountain soon and visit a few of his favorite kitchens.

Hell, he didn't even know what day of the week it was. In the last two months he had slowly lost track of time, first the date, then the weekday, then the hour. None of it had any meaning for him in his current lifestyle, where time was determined by the space between visits from Chloe and satisfaction was only measured by the amount of weed he had left. Luckily she had been able to cop some for him before their last rendezvous or he would surely have gone insane by now.

As he headed off between the trees, he heard the hammering start up again; it seemed closer now. He proceeded cautiously, using a path that ran parallel to the old logging road from Sloane's. He kept trying to keep his eyes open for anything out of the ordinary in his peripheral vision, but after taking a few hits of the pot, which had turned out to be some really good shit, he was having trouble doing anything except being dazzled by the color of the bluebird sky and the sensation of the mild breeze in his hair.

So when he came over a small steep ridge and found himself face-to-face with Butch holding a hammer in one hand and a sap bucket in the other, it took a few seconds for him to realize what had just happened. Myles froze in his tracks, suddenly as alert and cautious as a bobcat, unsure of whether his best option was flight or fight.

Butch got over his surprise first, an amused leer spreading across a jaw that appeared not to have been shaven for several days. Myles was aware of an unhealthy yellow hue that seemed to pervade his complexion; even the whites of his eyes looked a bit like watery beaten eggs.

"Well, well, looky what the sun drove out of hibe-uh-nation. How you doin', boy?" Butch coughed and then spat a wad of phlegm onto the ground before hanging the bucket on the trunk of a large maple tree he had just drilled a tap into.

Myles blinked a few times, still feeling really stoned, trying to decide if Butch was friend or foe. All F words ...flight, fight, friend, foe... "Fucking A," he said aloud and then laughed. "I guess I'm okay, Butch."

"Here." Butch handed him a stack of stainless steel buckets nested inside each other. "Carry these for me, would ya?" His movement down the path was stiff-legged and jerky.

Myles picked up the sap buckets and followed him, as if it was the most natural thing in the world to be working in the woods tapping trees, as though he had not been a fugitive in hiding for the last two months. "How about you? You all right, Butch?"

"Doesn't mattuh. When the sap's running, you got to get to work." A few yards down the path they stopped at another maple and Butch pulled a hand drill out of his pocket. "How's that girlfriend of yours? Still preggers?"

"Uh, yeah, she is." Had he really told Butch that Chloe was having a baby? He couldn't remember; he knew he used to tell him all kinds of shit he shouldn't have.

As Butch held the drill against the tree trunk, Myles noticed that a couple of Butch's fingers were partially missing below their joints; on the other hand most of his pinky finger was gone. "Logging accident?" he asked.

"Huh? Oh, sumpin' like that. Portable saw mill took these two. The othuh one..." his gaze narrowed and he suddenly seemed to be scrutinizing Myles's face. "You don't want to know about that one."

His answer, of course, made Myles want to know everything about how Butch might have lost his little finger.

"How 'bout you? You got enough to eat?"

"What? Why would you ask that?" He handed Butch a tap.

"Cause it's that time of year. When all the animals who live in the woods start to get hungry."

Myles said nothing for a moment, the truth of Butch's words rattling around in his head. "I'm getting by." He wanted to change the topic so he said the first thing that popped into his brain. "How're things at the bar?"

"Don't know. Ain't been in a while." Butch began hammering a nail into the bark for the sap bucket.

"You what? You haven't gone to Martin's?"

"Sumpin' wrong with yuh hearin'? Now hand me that bucket. You only got one frickin' job hee-yuh and you can't even do it."

"So...like you got thrown out for something? Like drinking while intoxicated?" Myles laughed at the joke he had inadvertently made. He was so high he almost didn't know what was coming out of his mouth.

"Very funny. No, just not goin'." Butch stopped working and began studying Myles's features again until Myles felt like he had to run his fingertips across his cheeks to see if there was dirt or snot or something on them.

"What?" he finally demanded.

"Nuthin'." Butch turned away. "Just wonderin' if someday you might end up lookin' like me."

It was a scary thought and Myles instinctively reached to touch his own face again.

"Can't really see whatcha look like with that bee-yud."

He had forgotten that Butch hadn't seen him since he started growing his beard. "That's kind of the point, you know."

"Heh heh. Right." They worked in silence for a while, except for the labored wheeze of Butch's breathing, which sounded kind of ragged. Almost syncopated, Myles reflected, and started playing an accompaniment to it in his head.

"So you stopped going to the bar when?"

"You still thinkin' about that?"

"Yeah, I guess so. Just can't picture it, that's all."

"Coupla weeks, I guess. Cheaper drinkin' at home anyway. Speakin' of beer – go get us a coupla cold ones outa the cooler in the truck." Butch nodded down the hill in the direction of the path that Myles no longer used. When Myles hesitated, he said, "It's off the road, in the turn-around by the skidduh." It took a second before he understood that Butch mean the log "skidder."

It felt odd to walk down the trail he had been studiously avoiding for the last several weeks, but as he watched his footprints blend into the slush with Butch's, he realized there wasn't much danger in going partway.

The black pick-up was parked by a few logging machines which hadn't been there in January, the last time he'd taken this route. Both doors to the cab were wide open as was the tailgate. Stupid and/or lazy, Myles thought. Any wild animal could get in.

He looked on the floor and behind the seat but there was no cooler, just a bunch of trash, candy wrappers and empty bottles. He finally found it in the back beneath a black tarp and retrieved a couple of Budweisers. A few months ago he would have turned up his nose at cheap domestic beer; now his mouth was actually watering at the idea.

Thinking that maybe he should close the doors, he checked inside again, just to see if there was a valid reason that Butch might have left them open. Like maybe it stunk really bad or he had a pet dog that liked to rest on the seat. Myles picked up a stick from the ground and poked around in the garbage in the well behind the passenger's seat. It looked like the dump or the house of some hoarder and he found himself vowing that no matter how bad things got for him, he would not get like this.

As he slammed the door, a receipt fluttered out in the wake of its closing and fell onto the ground. In a well-trained automatic gesture, he picked it up, feeling resentful that he had to clean up Butch's trash. Before he crumpled it into his pocket, he looked at it, just curious what Butch might have spent his money on besides beer.

It was from a local gift shop on December 24; had Butch actually been Christmas shopping? Myles looked at what he had purchased. Just one item. A cheese and sausage gift basket.

He leaned against the truck and gulped down one of the Budweisers in under two minutes, tossing the empty over his shoulder to join the growing pile already there. Fucking Butch. It had been him; somehow he had known all along that Myles was living in the sugar house. Of course he did – he worked this sugar bush, logged this mountain, knew the terrain like the back of his own deformed hand, would have noticed anything new or out of the ordinary.

Jesus Christ, he had even brought him a fucking piano. The man was his goddam guardian angel. But the question was – why?

Myles belched as he started back up the trail, carrying the six-pack minus one. Shit, he even sounded like Butch now, burping Budweiser up. If he stayed out here in the woods, would he turn into him? He remembered Butch's creepy remark about whether Myles would resemble him when he got older and he shuddered. It could happen; stranger things had occurred.

Angry and confused, he strode towards the figure in the trees, watching as the older man suddenly began coughing violently, finally leaning over as if he was going to puke. When he saw Myles approaching, he straightened up and passed the back of his hand across a forehead now shiny with perspiration.

"What the fuck – how come there's only five beers?" he grunted.

"Why the fuck do you think." Myles threw the six-pack on the ground at Butch's feet and turned away, feeling emotional and disoriented. He wanted to confront him, yell at him, ask him why he'd done all those things, but what did it matter. The man was old and sick. He had known for months where Myles lived and what his game was and he had never told a soul. He had, in fact, even one-upped him on it, stealing and moving a half ton of unused piano from one of Windfall's entitled wealthy families. There was nothing to talk about.

He reached down for one of the Buds, twisted the cap off and then he handed it to Butch.

Without ever speaking about it, they fell into a daily work pattern. It was just for a few hours in the afternoons, but Myles was grateful for the break in the monotony of his lifestyle and really he couldn't take Butch for much longer than that at one time. Myles carried and emptied sap buckets, moved some wood that had been cut into stove lengths and needed to be stacked. Each day, when Myles got ready to leave, Butch would slip him a couple of twenty dollar bills, which Myles gratefully accepted. The was the beginning of his "Get Out of Windfall" fund – for the first time he let himself dream about a future that was not a black hole of unknown horrors.

Butch apparently did his boiling down in a shed behind his house, wherever that was, and eventually Myles was rewarded with a pint jar of Grade A first run syrup. "You know many gallons it took to get that, boy?"

Myles actually did know the equations associated with sap to syrup. "Well, if it's forty to one, then I am going to say five gallons."

"Huh. Yeah, I'd say that's 'bout right."

"Seems like a lot of work for a little sweetness, doesn't it?"

Butch shrugged. "Don't mattuh. It's what we do. Every yee-uh."

Myles wanted to save it to savor on a pancake breakfast with Chloe someday, but could not even begin to picture when that might ever occur again. Except vicariously through a text message photo. He sent her a selfie of himself licking the sticky pure maple off his fingers with the warning – *"Love it and then let it go. Just wanted to share this sweetness with you. Please delete after viewing!"*

But then, with the full moon, the temperatures dropped below zero again and a heavy snowfall changed more than just the landscape. The first sap run was over and the final ravaging of winter took hold. High winds rattled the cabin walls and caused snow to drift across the porch; it obliterated paths and broke branches and even blew down some large trees. Myles huddled indoors, eating rice and beans, working out an intricate blues melody on the piano. Gusty backdrafts blew in down the stove pipe and sometimes filled the sugar house with gray smoke that made his eyes water and his throat ache. Myles could feel himself sinking once again into a cloudy miasma that more than once threatened to choke him off with its darkness.

On stormy days like this, his solar chargers were worthless and he had to carefully monitor his usage of all his electric and electronic devices. As the chill of the evening took hold, he wanted nothing more than to get under the comforter and call Chloe, but he knew he needed to save the little charge he had left in his cell for emergencies rather than "phone sex" as they laughingly called it. Although his mental state was beginning to feel like an emergency when the only person he'd had contact with in days was a whacko half-human woodsman.

Sometimes he had long one-sided monologues with Diva, who was always supportive and responsive, but couldn't really offer much in the way of conversation. He was starting to have long bouts of homesickness, where he missed his family more than he would have believed possible, wanting to share thoughts and feelings with Sarah and Hunter in the open way they always had until last summer, wishing he knew what his older sister and younger brother were up to these days.

Diva was nearly out of cat food. Myles weighed his options...he could try to talk Butch into buying some for him next time he saw him. He could ask Chloe if she might be able to get the car and come over. Or he could venture down the mountain and see if he could obtain it himself. It was dangerous, but he knew some rich cats that could spare a few pounds of the best.

When the sun finally came out and he was able to put his phone on the solar charger, a text message was waiting for him from Chloe. She said Tyler had been acting strangely towards her.

"He knows something he's not saying. He's waiting for me to fuck up somehow."

"Be careful. I'm fine right now," he lied. *"I love you."*

Then he put on his outerwear, grabbed his backpack, kissed Diva on one striped ear, and headed down the mountain. Unless he ran into Butch, somebody's privileged lap cats were just going to have to share.

He didn't see Butch again until a day later; by then Diva had enjoyed a dinner of Fancy Feast Chicken Divan and had enough dry food to last another week. He himself had enjoyed thawing a frozen steak and grilling it with some potatoes that had just needed their sprouted eyes cut out, washing it all down with a few glasses of some expensive French red wine. He was feeling so well-fed that he actually slept halfway into the morning and it was nearly noon before he ventured down the trail in search of Butch.

The buzz of a chainsaw up on a ridge led him to the old logger hidden behind a stand of pines. He looked worse than usual, dark bags forming half circles beneath his bloodshot eyes, his jowls drooping beneath several days' growth of unshaven beard. Without a word of greeting, he handed the running saw to Myles and sat down heavily on a fallen log nearby. Myles finished cutting up the large white ash tree, an apparent windfall victim of the last storm. He recognized the tree by its distinctive bark; it was one of the hardest woods in the forest, it made a good hot fire that lasted. He wouldn't mind having a few pieces for really cold nights.

When he finally turned the saw off, he heard Butch gagging behind him and looked around just in time to see him spew up a bunch of vile-looking bile with red spots.

"You all right?" Despite his revulsion, Myles moved a little closer.

"What do you think." His voice sounded hoarse. Pulling a Budweiser out of his jacket pocket, he rinsed his mouth out and spit into the snow.

"Sounds like you're fucking dying." Myles regretted the words as soon as he said them. "I mean, sounds like you ought to see a doctor."

"And you oughta see a lawyuh. But hee-yuh we ahh – bucking up fi-yuh-wood."

"Yeah, here we are, bucking up instead." Myles laughed ruefully.

Butch didn't respond, just sat there with his eyes half closed, squinting at the other side of the clearing.

"Uh, so what else do you want me to do here today?" He felt a bit lost with Butch not running the show.

"Haul that wood down on the sledge and stack it in the back of the pick-up. Should be near to a half cord."

Myles was glad to have a mindless job to lose himself into. Butch's behavior was making him nervous and he had no idea what to do about it. The man wasn't his responsibility but he did feel like he owed him something in a really skewed way. He threw himself into the work and was soon sweating enough to strip off his jacket and cap.

"Yo, boy! When'd you do that?" Butch was staring at him.

"What?" Myles didn't want to stop working because if he quit moving, his sweat would dry and he would start to get chilled.

"Your hair."

Instinctively he touched his head and then realized Butch had never seen him without his dreads. He had kept his head covered in the weeks following the haircut before he went into hiding, and then had not removed his hat on the previous days he had worked with Butch.

"Months ago. Where you been?"

"Shit, you look almost normal." Butch wheezed a little.

"Don't worry, I'm not."

By mid-afternoon Myles had filled the truck and Butch was looking a little better. He hadn't vomited again since that first time and had managed to keep a few beers down. "You think you'll be out this way again tomorrow?" They didn't usually make a plan, but for some reason today, Myles felt the need to ask.

Butch shrugged. "Probably." He thrust a hand deep into the pocket of his grease-stained pants and pulled out a handful of cash. "Here."

"Woah –this is way too much…" Myles began to protest as he realized how many twenties Butch had transferred into his palm.

"Who the fuck cares. Ya might as well have it now. Can't take it with me." Butch began limping away down the path.

Myles had this weird scared feeling that Butch was talking about dying. "Hey! Wait!"

"What." Butch stopped but didn't turn around.

"You got a cell phone number? Why don't you give it to me?"

"Why - you gonna call me so we can chat?" Butch's shoulders heaved a little with the effort of snorting.

Myles reached into his jacket for his phone and then realized he had left it on the solar charger. "Just give it to me, you jerk." He could memorize the seven digits after the 603 area code.

"Don't be callin' me a jerk. I'm your employuh." He tossed an ancient flip phone to Myles. "You look it up. I don't remem-buh it – I nevuh call myself."

Myles could barely recall how to use a cell like this one, but he found the number and committed it to memory. And then, just in case he forgot it, he placed a call to his own phone before Butch shoved it back in his pocket as he lumbered down the trail and out of sight.

Myles counted the wad of bills he was still clutching. Nearly two hundred dollars. What the fuck, he thought, and then quickly amended that to, who cares. With more money he could get out of Dodge all the sooner.

As he neared the cabin he noticed that there was a steady stream of gray smoke coming out of the chimney and he began to move faster. He was sure the stove had been damped down and nearly out when he left home earlier.

He stopped short when he saw a set of fresh footprints coming into the yard from the opposite direction. Someone was in his house. In fact, they had not even shut the door behind them. Unconsciously he pulled the splitting maul out of his wood-chopping block and held it in front of him defensively as he moved silently up the outside steps. He paused, listening for movement inside, noticing a yellow stain in the snow where whoever it was had taken a long whiz off the porch.

After a moment he heard a long low moan on the other side of the door. Without making a sound, he peered curiously around the edge.

Then a dry hoarse voice whispered loudly, "Myles? Is that you? Oh, my god, where have you been?"

CHAPTER THIRTEEN

MARCH 2017

For the third time in ten minutes, Chloe leaned against a tree trunk to rest. She was breaking all the rules – going against the doctor's specific orders, defying the safe parameters she and Myles had defined, violating Tyler's trust in her – but she had to do it. There would be no other chances in the months to come and it hurt her heart so much sometimes she could hardly bear the prospect of it.

Breathing heavily, she put her hand beneath her swollen abdomen and tried to support the extra weight. A sudden tightness made her gasp a little; it felt as if an elastic band was tightening around her waist. The false contractions were happening more often these days; sometimes they even woke her in the night out of her increasingly restless and mostly uncomfortable sleep.

She looked at the steep snow-covered trail that lay ahead. She was only about a third of the way there. The new path that Myles used was longer than the one down to Sloane's house that had been too dangerous for him to travel on since January. Chloe had only gone this way once with him, but it was pretty clearly marked by his travel, even though his most recent tracks had been covered by snow. With a deep breath, she started off again, slowly putting one foot in front of the other, up the side of the mountain.

For the last week Tyler had been acting very strangely towards her and it had begun to make her nervous. She couldn't put her finger on exactly what the change in his attitude was, but he seemed quieter, more thoughtful maybe, sometimes angry but not saying why. Occasionally she found him studying her from across the room, with a serious, almost mean look on his face. "*He knows something he's not saying,*" she had texted Myles. "*He's waiting for me to fuck up somehow.*"

She had been excrutiatingly careful for the past few days, covering her tracks, never leaving her phone unattended, even keeping it in under the covers with her when she was in bed. The only places she had gone were to birthing class and to her doctor's visit, and Tyler had accompanied her to both of those. Her prenatal appointments had been increased to twice a week, along with the warning that twins often came early and to try not to do anything that might increase her blood pressure, which was apparently on the rise now, as were her sugar levels.

But she was going crazy in the house, watching the snow melt outside and the mud start to surface, only to have the snow cover it again. A couple of warm days had started "the sap running," which she learned meant that maple sugaring season had begun. This major Northeast Kingdom seasonal event was more important to some residents than any national holiday and also signified that spring might actually occur one day soon. When Tyler went off one morning to cover a story on tapping trees and boiling sap, Chloe was overwhelmed with memories of Myles and the sugar house and couldn't stand it any longer. Since her last visit with him, she had been obsessing over the bleakness of their future and how and when they would ever get to be together again.

Filling her daypack with food, she dressed warmly and comfortably and then set off to hitchhike to Windfall. If all went well, she should be there before noon and then be able to get back before dark. It would be fun to surprise Myles – she could only imagine the look on his face.

It had not been hard to get rides – most people wouldn't pass by a pregnant woman on the side of the highway in the winter – but she hadn't factored in the half mile hike down the dead-end side road that led to the foot of the trail. By the time she headed up the mountain, she was more tired than she had expected to be. Hauling around an extra forty-five pounds was hard on all her systems and she had not done this level of physical exercise for a while. Also squatting to pee in the woods wasn't as easy as it had been a few months earlier when she had been living up here.

Another contraction came on suddenly, stronger and surprisingly painful, enough to make her stop in her tracks and double over for a minute.

Go slow, take it easy, she calmed herself. As she stood still, she could hear the distant sound of a hammer ringing through the forest. She wondered if it was Myles and what he might be doing. She didn't know how he filled his days now. Maybe she should have let him know she was coming. But she knew he would have tried to stop her.

She reassured herself that it was only a few hundred more feet before the path leveled off and then the terrain was pretty much flat the rest of the way. All she had to do was make it to the top of the hill and everything would be fine.

When she finally caught sight of the cabin fifteen minutes later, she felt a powerful sense of relief. The hike had been way more stressful than she had expected, and all she could think about was lying down on the couch with her head in Myles's lap and resting. She could see a wisp of white smoke curling up from the chimney, indicating the temperature might even be cozy inside.

As she came around the final bend where the path opened into the dooryard, her belly tightened up into a hard ball and a sharp pain ran up the front of her body, bringing her to her knees.

"Oh, my god, no," she whispered, instinctively panting as she rested on all fours. "Make it stop."

Amazingly, several long seconds later, the pain seemed to drift away and she was no longer some primal creature but just Chloe again, kneeling in the snow, with wet circles growing on the lower legs of her pants. Relieved she staggered clumsily to her feet and called, "Hello? Myles?"

At the same time she felt a trickle of something wet down the inside of one thigh. Had she peed herself during that bad contraction – she hoped not. These were the only clothes she had to wear today. Distressed, she looked down at the leg of her overalls where a pale red stain told a different story.

"Myles? Are you here?" She did not like the panicky way she was speaking and breathing; it made her even more anxious when she heard herself. Pushing open the door, she peered inside; compared to the mid-day sunlight, the cabin seemed gloomy. And very unoccupied. From somewhere out in the woods behind her, Diva came running and darted between her legs, greeting her with a squeaky meow.

With a groan, she lowered her body onto the sofa and examined the brownish-red trail on her pants leg. The words "mucous plug" and "bloody show" floated through her brain – did this mean what she thought it did?

Whatever she was thinking went out of her head as the next sharp pain took hold, this one going up her back with a dull throbbing ache. Hell, this could not be happening. Not here. Not now. Where was Myles?

When the cramp subsided, she dug out her phone and called his number. The sound of his ringtone came to her from outside on the porch before she heard his voice mail response in her ear. Shit, he was charging his cell outside and did not have it with him. Wherever he was. But where the hell could have gone to?

A tear trickled down her cheek as she tried to calm herself down. He must be out on the mountain somewhere. He would be back soon. Everything would be fine. It had to be. She was just going to take a little nap and then either Myles would show up or she would head back down the trail.

Two hours later the contractions were coming regularly ten minutes apart and she was starting to freak out. She knew this stage could last for a really long time, that labor pains with such long intervals between them could go on for hours or days. But already sometimes the cramping was so intense that she felt she might split in half and she was afraid to try walking back down the trail. She drank some water and put some more wood in the stove so that she could keep the door open for fresh air and still feel warm enough. Diva had snuggled against her side and gone to sleep, her midwifery skills limited to purring.

Between contractions Chloe alternated between dozing, crying and berating herself. What was she going to do? If she called Tyler, or worse, dialed 911, Myles's hideout would be totally blown and he would end up in jail because of her stupid idea of a surprise. She felt vulnerable and idiotic. Could she and Myles deliver these babies here? It was too early; they were going to be premies, small and underweight. Unless she had been more pregnant all along than anybody thought.

She thought about the little outfits she had been collecting from thrift stores over the last few months and the tiny sweaters she had been knitting, the soft flannel sheets and cozy fleece blankets folded in the bottom drawer of her bedroom. The pile of infant equipment that had begun to stack up in the corner. The car seat/baby carriers that would be needed to transport them home. There were so many things that hadn't been dealt with yet – like where were the babies actually going to sleep? They hadn't even bought a crib. Or two cribs.

Her thoughts flew away as the next contraction started, building like a heavy rainstorm. She breathed through it like she had been taught in class, trying to concentrate on nothing but the breath until it subsided.

Afterwards she was damp with sweat from the effort and could think only of getting her overalls off of her hot and heaving body. They were gross now anyway. Unhooking the straps she struggled to her feet and let them drop around her ankles. But after the initial cooling effect was over, she felt unnaturally chilled. Would it matter if the fancy-ass blanket draped over the back of the couch got stained with her body fluids?

No, there were no fluids coming out her body now, she reasoned. And who cared anyway...wherever the rest of her thoughts were going, they disappeared into the next waves of pain that shot up her back and around her sides before settling into a basic contraction. Back labor...that was a thing, right?

Afterwards she needed to pee and had to get herself up from the couch again. Stepping outside bare-legged and barefooted, she found she couldn't face going as far as the outhouse. Holding onto one of the porch posts for balance, she peed in the snow beside the stairs and then lumbered back into the cabin. While she was up, she put another piece of wood in the stove.

Please, Myles, please come home, she prayed. Time moved so slowly when you counted it in ten minute increments that ended in blinding pain.

She had lost track of the hours by the time she opened her eyes and registered his horrified face hovering inches above hers. Bursting into tears, she threw her arms around his neck and squeezed until the sobs subsided.

"Oh, my god, what are you doing here, how did you get here, how long have you been here..." His questions crashed over her like surf breaking on a reef as she held onto him, so happy just to have his chest to lean on and his shoulder to cry into.

"I came to visit, I thought you would be happy. But the babies–" she couldn't even say the words aloud.

"The babies are what? Really getting big, right?" He pulled the soft knitted blanket down to look at the amazing hump of her belly just as her whole body stiffened into another labor spasm. "Chloe – what – that's just one of those fake contractions, right?" Myles's voice rose with panic as she gripped his arms so hard he could feel her nails through all the layers of his clothing and then expelled the air from her lungs like a stove bellows. "RIGHT?"

When she could finally speak, the terrified look in his eyes told her that he understood what was happening and didn't have a clue what do. "They're coming," she whispered as he mopped the perspiration from her brow with the sleeve of his jacket.

"What are we going to do? We're not ready for – a home birth. Two home births. Oh, my god. Shit." He stood up and paced back and forth twice and then stopped as suddenly as he had started. "Okay. Okay. Just tell me what to do."

An unexpected bubble of laughter rose from her throat as, for a brief moment, everything seemed normal. They were Myles and Chloe, superheroes who could conquer the world and manage anything that came their way. But then she saw her blood-stained overalls crumpled on the rug and the reality of the situation set in.

"You have to get me out of here." The words came out hoarse and harsh, but she couldn't manage any better. She squeezed his hand and closed her eyes, waiting for his response.

"Okay. Okay. Um, can you walk at all? I mean, can you lean on me so we can get down the mountain to the car?"

"I can walk. Except when the labor comes. But I don't think I can walk that far." She felt tearful again, this time with the basic feeling of not wanting to disappoint him.

"Okay. Let's see..." He looked around the room as though there might be an answer waiting there somehow, then snapped his fingers. "I can get you down on the toboggan most of the way, probably. How does that sound?"

She didn't like the thought of bouncing over roots and rocks above the snow but at least it was a solution. She kissed his cheek. "Thank you. But – Myles. There's just one thing."

He had already leaped up and was heading for the door. "What's that?"

"I didn't come in the car."

"What?"

"I hitchhiked here."

He stared at her blankly, clearly unable to wrap his mind around this new obstacle. Before either of them could speak again, another contraction took hold and she couldn't keep herself from shouting this time, as the pain seemed to rip through her abdomen in a trail of fire. When it finally settled she realized he was holding her just the way he was supposed to, his legs around her, supporting her back with his chest, mostly just being there for her.

"Myles?"

"Yes, I'm here."

"You can just leave me at the side of the road. Someone will pick me up. I'm in labor, for Christ's sake."

"Don't be ridiculous. I'm not going to leave you."

"But–"

"Shush. I know what to do. Where's my phone?" He disappeared outside and a moment later she heard him speaking.

"Hey. Are you still on the mountain?...Shut the fuck up, this is an emergency. My girlfriend needs to get to the hospital...yeah, she's here at the cabin and it's time...No, she can't walk, it's already happening. I'm going to bring her down on the sled...Okay, we'll meet you halfway."

She could not imagine who he was talking to and then he was back at her side, a ghost of a grin on his face. "Come on, let's get you dressed. I got you a ride."

The cold air felt good on her skin as he bundled her onto the toboggan, dressed in a pair of his sweatpants, wrapped in the expensive sofa blanket, and cushioned at her back with a few bed pillows. "Wait, wait. Let's not go until the next contraction passes – that will give us a good...seven minutes of travel before we have to stop again." She hated admitting that the pains were coming closer together now.

Myles nodded, although she could see he was anxious to be on their way.

"So this guy – he knows where you live?" she asked curiously as she braced herself for the next round.

He nodded again. "He does. He has. He's a total weirdo but in his own warped way, for some reason he's got my back."

"Keep talking," she said, falling into her breathing pattern as she felt the labor beginning.

Myles fell to his knees and held her shoulders. "I don't get it. I only figured it out today. He's the one who brought the piano and left food. I've been working with him in the woods for the last week or so. He pays me. He's obnoxious, and anti-social, he smells bad, he's a drunk and I think he might be dying so he doesn't give a shit about anything. Sometimes I hate his guts. But we have this strange connection." He stopped his chatter, realizing she was no longer listening but concentrating on getting through the pain.

A moment later, they started out in the direction of the old trail to Sloane's house. Myles pulled the sled as fast as he felt was safe but it was difficult to maneuver over the foot trail. As they moved, the distant sputtering of an uneven motor engine grew louder and louder until suddenly an ungainly yellow apparition appeared before them, like a giant insect crawling up the hill.

Myles let go of the sled's cord and waited for the machine to stop on the trail. "You brought the log skidder?" he shouted over the noise.

"Backhoe, dumbwad. This ain't the skidduh. Let me turn it around first before you load her on." Expertly Butch maneuvered the equipment until it was facing downhill.

"Load her on? She's a person, not a log, Butch."

"Well, whatevuh you want to call her, she's gonna have to ride in the bucket. Let me tip it up so she don't fall out."

"Myles, this is no time for jokes." Chloe's utter disbelief was evident as he helped her get up from the toboggan.

"This is no joke, honey. It's our only option." He swept up the blanket and pillows. "It's not that far. His pick-up is down at the bottom." He gave her a quick hug. "Come on, I'll go with you. It'll be fun. Like a ride at the Caledonia County fair."

She watched dubiously as he padded the scratched cold metal surface of the back hoe's front bucket with the pillows and then climbed in, holding out his arms. "Here, you sit on me and I'll put the blanket over you..." His voice trailed off as he saw her squat and then kneel as another contraction took hold.

Jumping quickly to his feet, he shouted to Butch, "Hold on a second. She's in labor!" and then got down beside her.

"Holy fuckin' Christ. I shoulda brought a few beers." Butch spat a mouthful of phlegm onto the ground and revved the motor.

"Yeah, I know, he's an asshole, but he did come when I called." He pulled his glove off with his teeth and stroked the side of her face as she panted and grunted. Through her daze of pain, she distantly noted how rough and chapped his fingers had become over the hard winter.

"It's okay. I'll be all right – in – a minute." She wasn't going to complain. She just had to get to the hospital. One foot in front of the other. One step at a time.

"Ready?" he asked when he sensed her tension had subsided. "Let's go." He tossed himself into the curved metal scoop and reached out to her. She lowered her body slowly onto his, trying to get comfortable as he pulled the blanket around both of them.

"Okay, Butch. Let's roll!" Myles banged hard a couple of times on the engine housing and with a jolt they moved forward, down the trail. Chloe closed her eyes and buried her face into Myles's arms that were wrapped tightly around her, trying not to picture the precariousness of the situation.

Contractions were her measurement of time now, although if she used them as the sole indicator, time was speeding up, which meant the world must be turning faster. She knew roughly how long it took them to get down the mountain because she had one contraction in the bucket that left her nearly unconscious and then another just as they got to the bottom of the hill. She barely registered the fact that somehow she had ended up in the cab of the pickup with Myles squeezed in beside her, trying to shield her from the hair-raising view of the road in front of them as Butch sped down through Windfall and then onto the interstate, pushing the truck to nearly ninety miles an hour as they approached the exit to the hospital.

She didn't know if she had fallen asleep or passed out, but the next thing she was aware of was standing in the emergency room propped up between Myles and Butch who had somehow, together, managed to maneuver her in there. She could not think straight, but even in her "state of emergency," which she told herself she must be in if this was the emergency room, right?, she knew that Myles should not have ventured this far.

"Go," she whispered. "You don't have to stay."

"I'm not leaving you." Gently he lowered her into the wheelchair that an orderly had rushed over. "I'll be right here."

"Are you the husband?" A man with a clipboard had appeared at her side as well.

"Uh – yes. Yes, I am." Myles had started to turn away, but straightened up and faced the emergency room nurse.

"Then you can come along. But only immediate family. What about him?" The distaste in the man's voice was obvious as he tilted his head towards Butch, who was slumped into a waiting room chair already and looking rather green.

"I'm his uncle," Butch called and then put his head between his legs and vomited on the tile floor.

"He's not – well." Myles turned to the nurse. "Sorry about that. He's actually quite ill. Maybe someone can have a look at him."

"Only immediate family can be in the birthing room. We'll get someone here to clean that up. What's wrong with him?" The orderly began to push Chloe's wheelchair down the hall with the nurse walking alongside.

"I don't know. Something bad. But Chloe and the twins are more important." As she rode along, Chloe realized she was clutching his hand so hard that she might be hurting him.

"Twins? Oh. That's exciting," said the man flatly without showing any emotion, while his face displayed how many new calculations he was making as to their needs. "Chloe? That's your name, hon? I'm going to have to take you on your own for a few minutes while your husband goes back to the office and gets the admission process started. Mr....?"

"Mackenzie."

Even as she felt the next contraction starting to overtake her, Chloe looked up at him in surprise.

"Tucker Mackenzie," Myles said, extricating his hand from her grasp and holding it out to the male nurse.

She could not help but admire his quick thinking. It would at least work for a little while.

"Tucker..." she whispered, unable to keep a little smile from playing on her lips, even as she breathed through the pain. "Don't leave me."

"I'll be back soon. Don't worry. I've got this covered."

For now, was her last thought, as she watched him loping away down the hall.

By the time he found his way to her room, she had been hooked up to more machines and monitors than she believed possible and had been attended to by an equal number of maternity nurses, doctors and hospital officials. She had caught bits of conversation about how they were not equipped for any seriously premature neonatal situations and that it was too dangerous for her to be ambulanced to Dartmouth Hitchcock but that the helicopter crew should be on call. Mostly she cared about none of it; the contractions were now only two minutes apart and all she could think about was getting these babies out of her birth canal.

"Would you like to take over?" A nurse with a blonde ponytail and bright blue plastic eyeglasses stepped aside so Myles could sit in the chair beside Chloe.

"Thanks, I like your outfit." As he took her place, he nodded towards her tie-dyed scrubs and orange rubber clogs.

"Thank you..." she checked the chart at the end of the bed. "...Tucker. I'll be right outside if you need me. Or just push this button and someone will be with you in a jiffy. Oh, and keep feeding her ice chips. She needs to stay hydrated."

"Hi." He seemed shy suddenly as he looked at Chloe propped up against stark white pillows and sheets, an IV in her arm, and with cords running from various parts of her body.

"Everything okay?" she asked him, her wary expression letting him know exactly what she was referring to.

"Fine. No problems. They found your info in their shared medical database somehow."

"That's good, I guess?"

"Yeah, all clear. And they admitted Butch as well." He tried not to frown as he said this.

"And?"

"Nothing. Turned out they had his records too." She felt his leg move up and down nervously. "I'll tell you about it later."

"Tell me now. I need some distraction. You've got about thirty seconds."

"I don't want to tell you now. You've got other stuff to worry about. All I will tell you is that he apparently also listed me as his next-of-kin. But they don't know that's me."

"What? That's crazy." She could feel the next one starting and sensed it was going to be a whopper.

"Yeah, he's as loony as they come. Okay, here we go again...breathe...breathe..."

CHAPTER FOURTEEN

MARCH 2017

"Tyler. We have to get ready to go. I don't want to be late." Eva's fingers were like delicate bird wings tracing his closed eyelids, running down his cheekbones and across the softness of his lower lip.

"Can't you just call and say class is canceled? It must be bad weather somewhere. In fact, a storm is coming. It's growing in strength, right here." He pulled her warm body even closer to his. "Feel it?"

She laughed and tried to slide out of his grasp. "I'm serious. You have totally derailed me this afternoon."

Really? Because I thought we rode the rails pretty well, especially through the last tunnel – oh, no, runaway train just jumped the tracks. Call 911." He reached after her as she slipped out from under the comforter and streaked, lithe and naked, across the room to the bathroom.

"And now I have to shower all over again!"

"No, you don't. You smell fantastic." He closed his eyes, savoring the scent of her that seemed to cover him everywhere.

"I can't dance close with people like this – everyone will know!" she called over the sound of running water.

"I want everyone to know," he murmured, grinning broadly at the ceiling, feeling more content than he had in months, or maybe years.

When he had let himself into her living room an hour earlier, she had just come out of the bathroom, her hair clipped up on top of her head, a fluffy white towel wrapped around her middle and tucked neatly under her arms. "Oh, you're early," she said, but he was not listening, fixated on the beautiful lines and olive brown color of her bare shoulders and the graceful sweep of her arms around the towel.

"Good thing," he had replied, moving toward her, overcome by attraction, unable to stop the trajectory of what he was about to initiate.

"Tyler. Not now," she had started to protest before he began kissing her.

"Yes, now." For the first time he could feel her really responding to him in a way she had not previously allowed herself to and there was no way he was going to let this moment slip away from him.

Now, feeling contented and relaxed as he listened to the sound of the shower running in the next room, he could only think about how many hours it would be until tango lessons were over and they could be here again. He was so enjoying this pleasant, dreamy state of being that he did not realize that someone had been banging insistently on the front door until he heard a shrill voice come grating through his fantasy.

"Hello? Eva?"

How could Fern's timing be so bad? He considered pulling the sheet over his head and pretending that he wasn't here but he realized his Subaru in the yard probably already gave him away. Might as well just let Fern be the first to know the truth. Then everyone in town would know sooner than later.

"She's in the shower," he called back and was rewarded with the sight of a startled face framed in the bedroom door. "Yes, I'm here." He stifled a smile and sat up, making sure Fern could see his naked chest.

The range of emotions and colors that crossed her face was as breathtaking as the view from the top of Mt. Washington. "Oh, sorry... I didn't know you guys...She said I could borrow a pair...I didn't realize that was your car...Thought she might need a ride..." Her features finally settled into the usual smirk of one of her smart-assed replies. "Not bad, Tyler. Didn't take you too long to get to where you've wanted to be all along."

Something in her green-eyed gaze unnerved him and he found he could not come up with a sassy zinger in response. He slid back down into the coziness of the tangled sheets and averted his eyes, staring at the ceiling as he said, "Yeah, well, she doesn't need a ride. Now what is it you wanted to borrow?"

He could feel her spite charging the air between them before she spat out the words, "Shoes. She said she had a pair I could try tonight The gold ones aren't working out." And then suddenly, she was in a hurry to leave. "Just tell her I stopped by. I've got to go. I forgot something at home."

"Milt coming tonight?" he called after her.

"...history..." was the only word he could make out over the sound of the outside door slamming.

"Was that Fern?" Eva reappeared looking almost the exact same way she had when he'd first arrived, making him feel a little déjà vu for a minute, as though he had just imagined everything in between. "Damn. We might as well walk into the bar carrying a sign. Everyone will know before we even get there."

For the next few hours, Tyler didn't notice much beyond the circle of light cast by his own glow, but he did think that Fern was actually acting somewhat more subdued than usual. She'd sat out a number of rounds, sitting straight-backed on a padded bench by the wall, guarding their table of drinks and pizza from early collection by the over-eager young waitress who worked on Tuesday nights, graciously handing Eva and him their margaritas when they returned to their seats, and then begging off the rest of the evening with the excuse that she was coming down with a cold.

"Give her a break. She's jealous and has every right to be. She's the one who brought you to this class to begin with and now you've run off with the teacher." Ben's joke made Eva blush and Tyler felt a little bad – but only a little. The group awareness of the jump that their relationship had taken made all the students respectfully pack up quickly at the end of the lesson and give them the space they were clearly craving.

"Finish your drink," he whispered to her. "I feel feverish too."

She laughed and downed the rest of it in one large mouthful; Tyler was glad to see her finally loosening up. "Here, drink the rest of mine too. I'm the one driving home. And I like seeing you get really relaxed, lady."

Unfortunately the extra alcohol did not have the effect on Eva that Tyler had been hoping for. By the time they had turned into her driveway, she was unusually quiet and when the car stopped, she was looking pale with a pained expression on her face.

"I feel like I'm getting a really bad stomachache. In fact, I think I'm about to throw up right now." And as she heaved over and over again into a snow bank, Tyler knew the romance of the evening was over.

Two hours later he was ready to take her to the emergency room but she begged him not to. "I hate hospitals. I just need to drink more water, that's all. Please get me some more water." She was curled up on her side on a bathmat on the floor a few feet from the toilet, which was as far away from it as she had been since staggering into the house.

"And I hate seeing my girlfriends die of dehydration. If you can't keep this water down for the next thirty minutes, I am carrying you out to the car." He helped her to a sitting position and held a large glass to her lips. "Don't drink it so fast this time." He brushed some stray locks of hair behind her ears as he had already done countless times since the ordeal began. The pallor of her complexion was not improving and he made the silent decision that if she did not stop vomiting soon, or would not come willingly out to the car, that he was going to call 911 for an ambulance.

He would have guessed food poisoning if they had not literally both consumed the identical meal, right down to sharing the same pieces of pizza. He did feel slightly nauseous himself but nothing that rivaled Eva's upset stomach.

As he held her upright, waiting for her to finish sipping the water, he tried to remember what his personal commitments were and what he was supposed to be doing the next morning. He could barely recall the responsibilities in his own life and then realized he had not checked in with Chloe since he'd left West Jordan mid-morning. Well, if he had not received any frantic phone calls or text messages then everything was probably fine at home.

"I think I'm okay." Eva gave him a feeble smile over the half-empty glass.

"Drink it all and get up off the bathroom floor and I'll believe you."

"You're a hard-hearted nurse, Tyler Mackenzie."

"And you're a terrible patient. We're a perfect pair."

By the time a pale gray light could be seen in the eastern sky, Eva was finally too weak to protest any longer. She was limp and shivering in his arms as he carried her out to the car, wrapped her in blankets, and then skidded swiftly along the back roads that led to the highway and the hospital.

After being up all night, Tyler's eyeballs felt as though he'd rolled them in gravel and inserted them back in their sockets and he was squinting painfully as he pulled up to the emergency room entrance. He was grateful for the efficiency with which Eva was taken from his care, put directly onto a gurney and rolled into an examining room. He took off his glasses and rubbed his eyelids with the back of a less than clean hand as he sank into the seat across from the admissions clerk and tried to answer her questions. She looked as tired as he felt and had clearly been at her shift for several hours, her fingers punching listlessly at her keyboard.

"Mackenzie – is that Mac or just Mc... and what'd you say your first name was...huh...this is such a weird coincidence..." She suddenly seemed much more awake as she stared at the screen. “Your name is Tyler, not Tucker, right?”

“Tucker’s my son.” He sat up straighter also, his exhausted brain unable to process the reasoning behind her question. “Why would you ask me that? I mean, he’s not in your system, is he? We don’t use this hospital.”

Her cheeks seemed to get a little pink and he was surprised to see her suppressing a smile as she rose stiffly from her desk chair. “Excuse me for just a minute, Mr. Mackenzie.”

He rested his head against the wall next to his seat and was unaware that he had actually fallen asleep until he felt himself being shaken awake and heard his name repeated over and over.

“You’re here with Eva Melendez, right?” The admissions woman was hovering over him, a nurse with a clipboard at her shoulder.

He nodded slowly, unsure of how long he had been sitting there or if maybe it wasn’t even the same day.

“But can I confirm that you are the Emergency Contact person for Chloe Mackenzie?”

Tyler stared at her uncomprehendingly. “Yes, but...how…”

“And she hasn’t called you since last night?”

He was on his feet now, wary as a cougar. “What’s this about? Is Chloe okay?”

Both of the women were smiling at him now and then the clerk stepped aside and left him with the nurse, who said in a pleasantly brisk voice, “Please follow me, Mr. Mackenzie.”

“What?” He trailed after her, trying to keep up as she moved rapidly down the hallway, away from the emergency wing and then stopped suddenly in front of an elevator. “Where are we going? Where’s Eva? Why did you ask me about Chloe?”

He had never felt more confused.

“Well, I’d say congratulations are in order, but I think your son and daughter-in-law would probably like to tell you themselves." She stepped into the elevator and put her hand on the door, waiting for him.

"Congratulations?"

She laughed aloud now, clearly enjoying his bewilderment. "You have no idea, do you? Tucker and Chloe are the proud parents of two tiny baby girls. You are a grandfather."

By the time they had reached the maternity ward, Tyler had recovered from his initial shock and was now trying to clear up the gray clouds of confusion that obscured his understanding of this situation. "But – I don't get it. I was the birthing coach. When did she get here? Why wasn't I called?"

"You? But your son brought her in. She was nearly six centimeters dilated by the time they arrived and she needed immediate attention. And just so you know, he did a great job. You raised a very nice young man." She stopped outside a long window and pointed. "There they are."

But he had ceased walking and was standing in the middle of the tiled hallway, staring at her in dumbfounded amazement. "You're saying my son is here? In this hospital?"

"Shhh. Please don't shout. Look at how sweet they are. We thought initially we might have to airlift them to Hanover but they are both a good solid four-and-a-half pounds and we think they'll be fine if they stay here a few extra days."

Despite his growing anger and anxiety, he followed her gaze and finally saw them – two tiny pink bundles, swathed tightly in blankets with knitted caps pulled low over their miniature heads, their soft little faces each a perfect balance of the crescents and curves that defined their features. And then, with that innate, centuries-old fascination with newborn life, he found he could not look away, mesmerized by just watching them breathe and sleep.

After a few moments, the nurse touched his arm and nodded down the hall. "They're resting in Room 205, but if they're still sleeping, I wouldn't disturb them. It was quite an ordeal."

His desire to continue looking at his beautiful granddaughters was not as great as his need to see how his son had suddenly materialized for the birth of his children. In a few long strides he was outside the door she had indicated, peering into the darkened room beyond.

As his eyes adjusted to the dim light he could see the outline of Chloe's body in the bed, her short disheveled hair framed by the pillows behind her head, her belly still a surprisingly large bump beneath the covers. And stretched out in a reclining lounge chair next to the bed, a slim long-legged male figure snored unevenly, his face wedged against the padded armrest, one slender-fingered hand stretched out to rest on the sheets next to Chloe, where her own fingers had apparently slipped from his grasp.

His initial jolt of disappointment was replaced by a wave of wry disbelief as the answers to all the mysterious questions of Chloe's behavior over the last few months now fell into place.

He backed quietly out of the room, put a finger to his lips at the nurse's inquiring look and then pulled his cell phone out of his pocket as he moved swiftly down the hall towards the elevator.

"Sarah? It's me. What? Oh, sorry, I have no idea what time it is. I'm at the Littleton Hospital...Yes, everything's fine...it's not even why I came here, I came here because of Eva..." He'd all but forgotten Eva. He had to go check on her. "But yes, we have babies. Both girls...Yes, yes, thanks, but...actually that's not why I'm calling. I mean it is, but..." He ducked into the stairwell and lowered his voice. "You need to get over here right away. And I mean now."

Eva was hooked up to an IV and appeared pale but stable. He was informed that they had taken some of her blood to the lab for testing but did not have the results yet.

She smiled wanly at him and squeezed his hand when he whispered the news into her ear.

"I'm good. Go do what you need to do. You don't have to stay here with me."

At the moment all he really wanted was a giant mug of coffee. Satisfied with an extra-large cup of dark roast from the cafeteria, he wandered back to the emergency waiting room and anxiously watched the entrance for Sarah's arrival.

"Sorry to bother you again, Mr. Mackenzie." He was surprised to see the emergency room nurse with the clipboard one more time. "But we were wondering if you could clarify something for us."

Tyler held his breath, bracing himself for whatever unexpected question could possibly come up now, hoping it would not interfere with his own surprise plan of attack.

"Are you related to the uncle who drove them here?"

"The uncle?" He nearly spat a mouthful of coffee out on the floor. "Oh, really? My 'son' has an 'uncle'? What's his name?" It was hard to keep the sarcasm out of his voice.

With the tip of her pen, she pointed to the top line on a printed form. "Well, Butch Evans. But I doubt that's his real given name. We couldn't get much more out of him. He's in Room 113."

"Butch?" Now Tyler was choking on the coffee he had managed to keep in his mouth. "He brought them here?" He shook his head, unable to conceive of what curve ball might be thrown his way next. "Yeah, he's not a real relation. Sorry. One of those euphemistic neighborhood uncles, if you know what I mean."

"Oh, that's too bad. Before he collapsed, he told us your boy was next-of-kin, but there seems to be a different name here." She was frowning at the page on her clipboard. "We don't have any other information for him, not even an address."

"Collapsed?"

She looked at him primly before she turned on her heels to go. "Mr. Evans is a very sick man."

Could the morning get any stranger, he wondered. Life had seemed so simple when he'd arrived at Eva's yesterday afternoon.

He hoped Sarah would get here soon – more than anything he wanted to go see those babies again. He realized he wasn't totally comprehending that his life was never really going to be the same as it used to be.

"Where is he?"

Tyler opened his eyes to see Sarah standing over him, pale and grimly determined. Despite all the caffeine he had ingested, somehow he had fallen asleep again sitting up in an uncomfortable waiting room chair. He leaped to his feet, careening dizzily in his drowsiness, and she put out a hand to steady him.

"Wow, you're a mess. Maybe you ought to get out of here for a while. But first, point me in the right direction."

"Thanks for your vote of confidence. You look stunning too," he remarked, noting that her braid was still askew and unbrushed from a night's sleep and that her sweater was actually on inside out. "Let's go."

They did not speak as he led her up the stairwell to the second floor and proceeded towards 205. But as they passed the nursery window, he stopped moving and touched her arm. "Oh, Tyler," she gasped and her face seemed to display every emotion ever associated with motherhood and parenting.

"I know. Can you believe it…"

They stood silently admiring the twins until finally Sarah said, "I need to see him."

They walked the last few yards and peeked around the doorway. Chloe was still sleeping in the bed, but the reclining chair next to her was now empty.

"Shit." Tyler swore loudly and Chloe's eyes fluttered open. She stared at him blankly before she registered her surroundings as well as her visitors and her hand flew to her mouth and her head whipped sideways to see the vacant lounger.

Falling back on the pillows, she sighed deeply and said, "Hi. I was going to call you... Did you see them?"

Sarah's restraining hold on his arm was all that kept him from shouting.

"They're gorgeous, sweetheart. Congratulations," Sarah said softly.

Chloe looked at Sarah, the meaning of her presence finally sinking in and her eyes filled with tears. "Thank you. Will you call the nurse for me? I need to pee."

"Sure, we'll just be outside." Before Tyler could respond explosively, Sarah pulled him into the hall. "What is wrong with you?

"Only about a million things." He took a few steps away, blew out a long breath and then turned back to her. "Room 113."

"What?"

"Just go. Quickly. I think that is where you'll find *your* son." Then, swallowing all the emotions he felt, he headed for the nurse's station.

CHAPTER FIFTEEN

Myles sat on the edge of the chair, surreptitiously feeding himself forkfuls of rubbery scrambled eggs from the breakfast tray next to Butch's bed.

"I ain't got no interest. You might as well eat 'em," Butch had muttered in a scratchy, barely audible voice. "But I wouldn't mind a can of Bud with a straw if you could go out and get me one."

"I'll need the keys to the truck for that." Myles eyed the pale excuse for wheat toast and the cardboard containers of butter substitute, trying to determine if he was really that hungry and decided he was.

"Must be in my jacket pocket. You ought to take 'em. You know, in case they never let me out of here." Butch coughed a little, then more, and then uncontrollably, and just when Myles was beginning to get alarmed, he stopped abruptly. A moment later, he was snoring loudly.

Holding the limp toast in one hand and a plastic container of orange juice in the other, Myles used his foot to move his chair over so he could read the patient chart attached to the metal footboard. The words blurred in front of his eyes; the adrenalin rush he'd had from helping to birth two babies was wearing off and he knew that soon his tiredness was going to catch up with him.

"What the hell, Butch?" He spoke aloud, knowing there would be no answer. "Advanced stage four cirrhosis of the liver? Even I know that means you're nearly dead. Fuck." He looked up warily, suddenly thinking that the old logger might stop breathing at any second, but Butch's chest continued moving up and down. Licking the fake butter off his fingers, Myles carefully lifted the first page of the chart to read the next.

There it was on the line for Next-of-Kin, 'Myles Scupper-Adams.' "You asshole, you have such a warped sense of humor." Then in a flash, he actually felt sad; maybe Butch had no relatives. He certainly didn't have any friends. But what did it mean – was Myles going to have to be responsible for him in some way? Shit, what if someone at the hospital recognized his name from all the bad press about Sloane's death and reported it to the police?

He moved over to the window and stared sightlessly at the view of the parking lot. The sun was now up which meant it was really morning, although he had no idea what time it was. Chloe's labor had lasted way longer than he thought it was going to; he had expected that the babies would be born a few minutes after they arrived at the hospital, but instead it had gone on several more hours. Near the end even he was crying from seeing her deal with the pain and then crying again from the miracle of the twins coming into the world. They'd let him cut the cord, because they thought he was Tucker, and he knew that right now he felt more like a father to those girls than Tucker ever would be.

A warm wave of relief swept over him and he leaned his forehead against the coolness of the glass pane. Nobody here knew his real name; as far as the hospital staff knew he was Tucker Mackenzie, Chloe's husband. He was safe – for a little while longer at least.

"Myles?"

He turned at the sound of the familiar voice. And as swiftly as it had come, his sense of security disappeared.

"Mom." The sight of Sarah standing in the doorway filled him with such a strong cocktail of emotions, that he felt dizzy and almost drunk. "How – how did you – what are you doing here?"

'I should be asking you that question." A few seconds later she was by his side, her fingers gripping his upper arms as her eyes hungrily roamed his face, searching its familiar landscape. "Oh, Myles." She wrapped herself around him and despite the alarm bells that went off in his head every time she said his name, he found himself giving into the faint aromas of home that emanated from her hair and clothing, smells he was accustomed to but had forgotten all about, a mixture of almond soap, restaurant kitchen and antique pine. "We miss you so much," she whispered. "Where have you been?"

Myles glanced nervously at the door; at any moment one of the hospital staff could appear. "I'm fine. Fine. I miss you too. But you get it, right? Why I can't call or come home." He felt so weak-kneed that if she hadn't been holding on to him, he might have slid to the floor.

"But–" she nodded and then shook her head. "But you're innocent, aren't you? Hiding out makes you seem guilty. We don't understand. I mean, you didn't do it..."

"Why would you say that? There's so much you don't know. About me and about what has happened." Something about being held by his mother made him feel and act like he was a small boy and he found himself wishing desperately that she could just wipe his tears away and make everything right, the way she used to.

"Because I know you. You're a good person, you are kind, loving, loyal, you do the right thing."

"Wait – what are we even talking about?" Myles felt like he was falling down the rabbit hole, unsure whether Sarah was referring to Chloe or Tucker or Sloane or any of the other people or crimes in his life. "How did you know I was at this hospital? They don't know who I am." A new sense of paranoia began settling over him. "Look, Mom, we can't talk here."

"Tyler called me." Her anger and hurt hissed at him like hot steam.

"Tyler."

"He's upstairs with Chloe. And yes, I guess he already had that part figured out." Now Sarah looked at him wild-eyed and waved an arm at Butch. "Here. What is here – what are you even doing in this man's room? Who is he?"

She peered suspiciously at the jaundiced and grizzled face in the bed.

But Myles was barely listening to her ranting now. The walls of his world were collapsing in on him, like a house being swept into a cyclone. Tyler had somehow found Chloe at the hospital, in New Hampshire, and now he, Myles, was losing Chloe all over again already...

He had to get out of here. He needed the keys to that truck, the ones that were in Butch's pocket. Across the room he could see the filthy work jacket hanging in the narrow closet, taunting him with the prospect of escape. Myles began edging his way along the wall when a raspy command rattled out.

"I wouldn't come any closer if I was you, Sarah. You're makin' me violate the terms of my restrainin' order."

Myles froze, the only part of his body moving was his eyes as they whipped rapidly back and forth from Butch's heavy-lidded smirking gaze to Sarah's expression of stunned terror. He watched his mother's features settle into a look he had never seen on her face before, one he could only describe as hardened hatred.

He remembered then, the conversation he'd had with Butch at the bar, it seemed like eons ago, when he said he'd known Sarah in West Jordan.

"I – I forgot you two were already acquainted," he stammered, but his words seemed lost in the dynamics now charging the air of the small room.

"I never thought I'd have to see you again, Lyle." She turned to Myles. "What is your relation to this – this person?"

Butch wheezed out a sound that resembled laughter but quickly dissolved into a coughing fit that prevented him from speaking.

"His name is Butch," Myles said loudly over the noise. "He's just a – my..." He did not know what to call Butch. "He brought us here. But he's sick."

"You know very well what our relationship is, Sarah," Butch managed to gasp out. "And there's ain't no order against him."

"Mom?" Myles sounded as young and clueless as he felt.

"Well, I see you haven't really met. Let me introduce you to your Uncle Lyle, my half-brother." Sarah spoke with undisguised revulsion. "My *father*, your grandfather, was also his father."

Sarah caught up with Myles just as he was starting the engine of the pick-up.

"Myles, wait!" She banged on the window of the passenger side and then wrenched open the door, hurling herself into the seat.

"You owe me a big fucking explanation." He gunned the motor and the truck shot out across a row of empty parking spots towards the hospital exit.

Sarah pulled the seat belt across her chest and looked desperately through the accumulated trash in the console as she tried to locate the buckle end. "Okay, okay, but don't kill us both until I tell you the story."

Her usual biting sarcasm calmed him down a little and he slowed to twenty miles an hour as he ran the stop sign, careening left towards the highway.

"And then you owe ME a big fucking explanation." With a satisfying click of the buckle, she sat back, her death grip on the door handle the only indication of the tension she was feeling. "Deal?"

"Yeah, well, you start." The heaviness of his foot on the gas pedal kept both of them intent on watching the road rather than looking at each other.

Sarah was silent for a moment and Myles stole a sideways glance at her. There were lines in her face he had never seen before; furrows in her forehead that had deepened since he had disappeared and he guessed he was probably at the root of the distress that had recently aged her. At another time he would have felt bad for her; right now he only felt sorry for himself.

She cleared her throat. "Your grandfather, Travis Monroe, was a …well, let's just say he was not a nice man," she began. "He abused my mother, gambled away her family's savings and had sex with her housekeeper. After my mother died when I was an infant, he moved to Havana. I only met him once, when he was old and ruined and living in Atlantic City."

Myles could barely comprehend the wealth of information she had just revealed in a few sentences. "How is it I never knew any of this?"

"Because I hate talking about him." The venom in her words was something he had also never heard before. "There is nothing positive to say about my father and I did not want my children growing up with his cloud of depravity hanging over their heads."

"But didn't you think we had the right to know about our family?"

"Yes, you probably did. I'm sorry. But you had Hunter's parents and relatives in California and they provided all the love and attention that my side never could. Even if you didn't see them very often. You were happy – and when you got old enough to understand, you never asked."

It was true – he had barely spent any of his childhood wondering what his mother's parents must have been like. Sarah had been given the inn by an old man named Woody, who had been a family friend and as much of a grandfather figure to him as he ever needed.

Feeling distracted by all the questions and answers in his head, Myles slowed the truck down and looked for some place safe to pull over. He had been driving aimlessly and had no idea where they even were, but a turnaround by the edge of the river offered what he needed. He put his head down on the steering wheel, trying to sort through the confusion he was feeling.

"You look exhausted." Sarah's hand gently touched a bare spot on the back of his neck and for a second he almost allowed his vulnerability to get the better of him.

"I am, but go on. I need to know how Butch fits into this picture." He sat up and stared ahead, grim and determined.

"He shouldn't. But unfortunately he does." She sighed. "I truly haven't thought about him in years. And rightfully so. After he tried to kill me, he wasn't allowed to come within 300 feet of wherever I was."

Despite his resolve to be unfeeling, Myles turned towards her in disbelief. "You're kidding, right?"

"If only I was. None of this would have happened if Tyler hadn't showed up in West Jordan to do a story on my mother and started poking around in the past."

"Okay, so she's the one who did the stained glass window in our bar, right?" At least this was a family legend he had grown up on, a story that had been shared with patrons and visitors time after time. His grandmother, Winnie Scupper, had been a famous glass artist whose work embellished several local buildings around West Jordan as well as a few in New York City, as far as he knew.

"That's right. So up until Tyler showed up and started asking questions, nobody in the village had realized who I was, because I was going by the name of Monroe. But once it became known and Lyle figured out his relationship to me, he felt like I owed him something."

"We're talking about Butch."

"I guess that's what he calls himself now. His mother worked as my live-in nanny when I was a baby. She was from a poor family who lived down in the hollow. No surprises here. A beautiful young girl, Travis promised her whatever, got her pregnant, abandoned her, etc. It's a story as old as time."

"And?"

"When she tried to extort money from him, he did some unsavory things to blackmail her into keeping quiet. Tyler actually never told me the details." There was an uncomfortable pause as the two of them imagined the worst and then refused to believe it. "Needless to say, Lyle – Butch – grew up somewhat mentally…uh…damaged."

It was hard for Myles to absorb this new reality where both of his worlds collided. He swallowed and asked the burning question. "So why did he try to kill you?"

"He thought I was rich." Sarah gave a sardonic chuckle. "Thought I had grown up privileged with lots of money, with everything he had never had. Little did he know, my father – his father – had burned through that before I was even born and not only left us penniless but left my maternal grandmother footing the bill for his gambling debts. Travis Monroe was so suave and selfish, he pretty much ruined everything and everyone he came in contact with."

Myles had never heard his mother speak so bitterly about anything or anyone. He did feel bad for her now, but he felt bad for Butch too, and he still needed to know more. "So what did Butch do to you?"

"He came at me after the bar was closed one night, told me the truth." Sarah shut her eyes, obviously picturing the circumstances. "It doesn't matter – in the end, I took him down. Literally. We broke the Night Heron window. And they put him away. For a long time. In the state mental institute. And when he got out, he wasn't allowed to come within 300 feet of me ever again. And I've never seen him since. Until today."

They sat there for a long time, not talking, just watching the icy waters of the Connecticut River race by them. Finally Sarah said, "It's a lot to process, I know."

"None of his other Evans relatives are still alive? Am I really his next-of-kin? I mean, not counting you."

She looked startled. "I – I have no idea. Yes, I think they're all dead now." Her surprise turned to puzzlement. "How did he find you, anyhow?"

Myles shrugged. "It was just coincidence. Two people in a bar. He was a weirdo that nobody liked and I guess I felt sorry for him. And then, after a while, I guess he felt sorry for me." He paused. "But he KNEW. And he never said anything. He's dying, you know. He's dying and we're sitting in his goddam truck."

Then suddenly he was pounding the steering wheel and the walls and the ceiling and sobbing loudly. "What if I end up like him? I mean I AM just like him. We even have the same friggin' DNA!"

"So what, so do I!" she yelled back at him. He couldn't even remember a time when they'd ever shouted at each other like this. "And we're all directly related to fucking Travis Monroe. But that doesn't mean we're like him! It's about how you were raised and how you live your life, Myles. You know that."

"I know! And I've been doing a really bad job of it lately."

For a while there was no sound except for a few deep sniffles as he tried to suck all the fear and sadness back inside him. He knew she was waiting for him to tell her about his life. But instead she asked, "What's he dying of? Alcoholism?"

"Of course. What else?"

"That should have killed him years ago. Or some accident caused by it. Even back then, he was one of the worse drunks I ever knew."

They slipped into silence again, but now Sarah sat sideways taking in Myles's appearance. "New sweater?" she asked. "And where'd you get this?" She touched the soft, brick-hued scarf wrapped around his neck. "Feels like cashmere."

The sound of Sarah's cell phone ringing brought them back to the present situation. "It's Tyler," she said looking at the incoming number. "Hi, yes, I'm with him. We're..." she looked around, "...somewhere. In Ly- Butch's truck. How are the babies?"

Myles suddenly realized that Chloe was probably wondering why he had not come back. He felt around for his phone and then swore. It was in his jacket, which he had left in her room. When he'd run out of the hospital he'd been so worked up he hadn't even felt the cold. Now he realized he was chilled to the bone. He didn't need the coat – he had others back at the cabin, but he needed to see Chloe.

"Tyler, tell me the truth," Sarah was saying. "Do you really not know who Butch is?" Her eyes met Myles's and she shook her head. "You're slipping up, Tyler Mackenzie. Must be getting old...See if you can figure it out. We'll be back in a bit...Yeah, I'll tell him."

"Tell me what?"

"Chloe's asking for you. And Tyler wants to talk to you."

"No doubt." Myles laughed morosely. "He must be pissed that I impersonated his irresponsible son."

"You mean your best friend?"

"You mean my former best friend." He turned the ignition key and then turned it off again. "I don't know if I can go back in there. Has he told them who I really am?"

"Myles. He's on your side. He's been searching for you for months."

"Mom. That's because of you. He's on *your* side, not mine. I'm a murderer and a thief."

"Myles, you're not a murderer..."

"Listen to me!"

She settled back into her seat, leaning against the passenger door, arms crossed over her chest. "Okay," she said. "Talk."

He told her everything, starting with Istanbul and ending with the birth. He told her about how he'd started to "take" things from the wealthy of Windfall who had more than their share of good fortune and how then he couldn't stop. More than once, he had to turn the truck heater on to keep from shivering. And finally, sobbing, he told her about the night he had accidentally backed the truck over Sloane's body and how, with the help of Chloe and more recently Butch, he'd been in hiding ever since.

Sarah squeezed his hand, which she had been holding through most of his story. "Myles, listen to me now. You didn't do it."

"How can you say that, Mom? I just told you what happened!"

"Because she was already dead when you hit her. That wasn't what killed her."

"How can you possibly know that? Fern saw what happened. She told me–" He stopped, thinking harder over the sequence of events.

"Fern? The librarian? What does she have to do with this?"

"Nothing." Myles pulled his hand away from her and started the engine. "We need to go. I have to get back to Chloe."

Sarah opened her mouth to protest and then seemed to think better of it. They drove in silence for a few minutes, with the heat blowing at full blast, before she spoke again.

"He really brought you a piano?"

"He didn't just bring me a piano, Mom. He STOLE me a piano. Don't you get it? Fuck." But he knew she didn't get it, because she didn't want to.

After a while she said, "We'll talk about Sloane later. But there is one more thing I need to ask you before we get back to the hospital."

When he didn't respond, she went on.

"The twins. Are they yours?"

His grip tightened on the steering wheel. "You mean biologically? Because you, more than anybody, should know that isn't what's important." Shit, he could be as sarcastic as her, he thought when he saw her flinch at his reply.

"Okay, but yes, that's what I mean."

"She says she didn't get pregnant until late August. So no, I'd say not."

And although they didn't say anything else on the rest of the ride back, he knew she was doing the math in her head just like he had. Over and over again.

Myles and Sarah met Tyler just as he was leaving Chloe's room. He put his finger to his lips and, despite protests from Myles, led them a short distance down the hall. "She's just fallen asleep again after feeding both of them. And they're both in there with her for right now." The trepidation in his eyes spoke to the foreseeable and unforeseeable hours of baby care in his future. He looked directly at Myles. "What are their names again?"

"Athena and Artemis. Can't I just take a peak? Besides, I need to get my jacket. Believe me, I am an expert at getting in and out of places without making a sound." Not waiting for anyone's approval, he slipped silently into the room.

"My poor boy. He's so troubled. And he thinks you're mad at him," Sarah remarked.

"It's not him I'm angry at, but I don't dare say anything to her right now." Tyler tried not to let his irritation out, but he was too tired to make a good show of it. "She's been lying to me for weeks. I don't know if she's ever told me one true thing. I don't know if those babies are even really my granddaughters."

"Shh." Sarah looked around, afraid someone at the nurses' station might hear him. "You need to believe they are."

"But who was the first person she went to when she came back to the United States? She didn't come to me until she had nowhere left to go. I don't know much, but I've figured that much out." He started striding quickly towards the stairwell.

"Where are we going? I have stuff to tell you."

"They're ready for Eva to check out. I've got to take her home." He stopped and leaned heavily against the white-washed brick wall. "I feel like I'm losing it. I don't know how I'm going to do all of this, take care of all these...females... in the next few days."

"Don't worry," she reassured him, clearly suppressing a smile. "We'll help you. We're old hands at this. And that boy in there–" she nodded back the way they had come – "He's really good with kids, just like his father."

Tyler looked at her wearily. "But is he coming above ground now?" He gave her a small grin. "Much as I hate to say it, his impersonation of Tucker was a brilliant move. And I haven't told anyone otherwise yet."

"Yeah, somehow I don't think that would work very well back in West Jordan where he grew up. And then there's the matter of...Butch." She pushed open the heavy fire door that led to the stairs and motioned for him to follow.

"Holy fucking shit." Tyler's voice resounded up and down four flights of metal steps. "I can't believe I never recognized him! And damn him, I remember that first time I met him at the bar in Windfall - he knew exactly who I was. And Myles has been hanging out with him and Butch never told him either?"

"That's only part of the story. Let me tell you the rest."

By the time they reached Eva, who was pale but patiently waiting for them in a wheelchair outside the emergency room cubicles, Tyler had heard more than he could absorb or process. "I've got to get Eva home and then I've got to get some sleep," he told Sarah. "Help me out – do whatever you have to and keep Myles where we can reach him. Tell him to stay here and continue being Tucker if he wants to do that. But I need time to figure this out. And I need him to help me do it."

CHAPTER SIXTEEN

April 2017

Butch's truck almost didn't make it all the way to the cabin, but in the end it did. Myles had waited for a night when the temperatures dropped into the twenties again for several hours. He could not believe he was praying for cold weather to return after the spectacular warmth of the early April thaw, but he knew there was no way the pick-up could navigate the mountain without getting mired in the mud unless the road froze up again. Lucky for him the weather forecast predicted three sub-zero nights in a row. That gave him time to drive to the sugar house before sunrise, pack the truck and get down the next morning, and then maybe even do it again.

He'd left West Jordan just as the eastern sky began to grow pink along the horizon. By the time he'd reached Windfall, the low rays of the morning sun were already glistening off the heavy coating of frost on the flattened hillocks of grass along the roadsides. He drove slowly, making sure there was no traffic in either direction before he turned into Sloane's driveway, shifted into four-wheel-drive, and then headed up the logging trail.

It had been almost a week since the last time he'd been here to check on things and to make sure Diva had enough food and water. Fortunately she was a self-sufficient woods creature, happy to slink in and out of her cat door to hunt and play, and then return to curl up in the down comforter, evidenced by the thick layer of cat hair that was accumulating on it. Random mouse tails and guts on the floor indicated that she was also still performing her household duties as caretaker and exterminator.

He didn't know what was going to happen to her. Thinking about the uncertainty of Diva's future brought on another wave of anxiety in the turbulent ocean of apprehension that threatened to drown him these days. He had to put her out of his mind and focus on the monumental task at hand. Once he took care of this part of his life, he and Tyler could focus on the next part.

Opening up a kitchen cabinet, he stared bleakly at its contents. Then slowly he began to transfer items to an empty box from the pile he'd brought in from the truck. After a moment he stopped and retrieved a few more cardboard cartons. He might as well start sorting things out now.

He knew his mother must have had a hand in convincing Tyler that it would be a good choice to have Myles around when Chloe and the twins came home from the hospital. There was no question that it was an all-around awkward situation, but given how clueless Tyler seemed to be about childrearing, he was grateful for the help, not just with the babies but also with Chloe's postpartum personality. Myles was less than comfortable with being an outlaw in his own village, unable to go anywhere beyond the small bungalow and its backyard without fear of being recognized. More than once he had to disappear into a bedroom when visitors stopped by. The only perk of the circumstances was that his parents were able to pay regular clandestine visits and offer their support.

Tucker's childhood bedroom was as crowded as a tenement with a single bed, two cribs and a futon mattress on which Myles slept in the remaining floor space. Sometimes he dragged it out into the living room when the claustrophobia of the close quarters became too much for him. It would probably be years before he and Chloe were ever going to be able to have sex again, and there was no way he was ever going to do that in Tyler's house anyway. There were limits to this weird arrangement.

But he loved being close to those sweet twins. Some days and nights it seemed like all Chloe did was either breastfeed or express milk and Myles found himself folding laundry or washing dishes with either Athena or Artemis strapped to his chest. It wasn't easy, but he'd even figured out how to play his fiddle with an infant in a front carrier. If he kept the music soft, it seemed to soothe them, and it certainly eased his own stress. After a week or so, he even took over the midnight feedings, and before long he was an expert at how to thaw breast milk and heat it to just the right temperature, while juggling one or sometimes both crying babies.

Relieved to have Myles there to rely on, Tyler spent much of his time closed up in his office working and a lot of hours not even at home. He cradled the girls gingerly, as if he might break them and seemed afraid to get too close to them. Myles found himself looking for ways to trick Tyler into having to watch the babies for a while. Sometimes, when he thought no one was looking, Tyler would stroke their cheeks and study their little faces intently. They never discussed it, but Myles knew what he was doing – searching for definitive clues that would tell him if he really was the grandfather of these beautiful children.

But while they didn't talk about the twins' DNA, they did talk at length about Myles's dilemma. As they marveled at the wonders of birth, they struggled with the disparities of death. Tyler walked him through the events and timeline of Sloane's murder, trying to get him to remember all the details he had repressed, trying to piece together what had actually occurred and how they were going to prove it while keeping Myles out of jail.

Tyler had not known that Fern had been present that night. "Funny that in all the discussion of Sloane's death, she never mentioned that." His voice was heavy with cynicism. "No wonder she knew so much about it."

But when Myles described the parts of the conversation he had overheard that night, Tyler had paled a little and Myles knew exactly why. "It was you they were arguing about, wasn't it, dude? You threw Fern over and she didn't like that very much." He scrolled through his phone until he found a photo he had taken when they had been housesitting at Fern's. "Do these names mean anything to you?"

Tyler squinted at the picture of neat printing on yellow-lined paper and then the color in his face faded away. "Damn that jealous bitch." He started to slam the phone down on the table but Myles neatly grabbed his wrist in the nick of time.

"Don't wreck my phone! So you know these women? Caroline, Wendy, Magda, Eileen?"

"I know those names. It turns out that those women don't actually exist." Tyler stood up abruptly and opened the refrigerator, staring inside. "Shit, it's times like this that I wish I kept alcohol in the house. I could really use a beer right now."

Myles hesitated before pulling his pipe out and offering it up. "You want some of this?"

Tyler shook his head. "No thanks. That won't do it for me. I want something that will dull the pain but still let me think clearly. For a while. Until it doesn't." He paced back and forth a few times and then sat down. "Okay, I'm over it." He pulled out his notebook and turned it to an empty page. "Myles, let's nail this bitch."

"So did I miss something? How do you know these people who aren't even real?" Myles had hoped Tyler would want to smoke with him; he left his stash on the table just in case it might help him change his mind.

"You know how Fern and I met, don't you?" When Myles gave him a blank look, Tyler told him about his online dating experiences. "It became a little bit of an ego-booster for me and after a while I couldn't stop. Especially when I wasn't getting anywhere with Eva. Then I seemed to hit a string of bad luck where this series of women were standing me up and dissing me online. I realized my account had been hacked and I shut it down. Which was a good thing for me. Because I really didn't need it anymore."

"Fuckin' Fern, man. What a piece of work." For a second Myles didn't feel so bad about his own transgressions against her.

"Hell, then this means…" Tyler started making a list as he spoke. "If she hacked my account, then she's the one who spray-painted my car. She's most likely the one who slashed Eva's tires. And chances are I bet she's the reason Eva ended up in the hospital as well." He stood up and then sat down again. "Shit. We left her at the table that night during tango class - she was probably trying to poison both of us. But I didn't finish my drink, Eva did."

There was so much about this that Myles hadn't known about.

"So the night Sloane died…" Tyler turned to a fresh page, and then, pen poised, looked up questioningly. "She and Fern actually got violent over…me?"

"Not exactly. They were talking about me too." Myles frowned trying to recall. "I remember being shocked that anyone could get so upset about a cookbook. Sloane was defending me. I saw Sloane fall down but I wasn't sure why. That was when I ran up there. When she didn't get up, I got in the truck because I was going to take her to the hospital."

Tyler's eyes became small slits for a second and then he got up again, this time returning with a large book that he dropped on the table in front of Myles. "Was this the book perhaps?"

Myles felt his cheeks go crimson and he turned his face away.

"I'm not going to ask why."

"Chloe really liked it." It was a lame excuse and he knew it. He did not want to start trying to explain his thievery to Tyler when he could no longer justify it to himself. Without further explanation, he stood up, grabbed his coat and went outside to smoke a bowl.

A few nights later, Tyler handed Myles a beer and they resumed the conversation, at which time Tyler revealed a fact that Myles hadn't known. For a small fee, Sarah and

Hunter, as Myles's parents, had been able to acquire a copy of the police report of the alleged crime. The findings had revealed that although Sloane's legs had been crushed when the truck tires had backed over her, it was not what had killed her. Autopsy toxicology showed that the actual cause of death was poisoning; the details of which could not be revealed by order of the victim's lawyer.

Myles couldn't believe what he was hearing. "So I'm not guilty? But Fern..."

"What about Fern?" Tyler pressed him. "Notice there is no mention of her at the scene. And she's never said anything about it. You're the only person who knows she was there."

Myles squeezed his eyes shut as though that physical act might actually make him recall the sequence of events better. He remembered Fern yelling at him through the open window of the truck, saying she was going to go to the police and him yelling back to her that he knew all her perverted secrets. How she had threatened him and he had threatened her and how he had slammed the gears into reverse and put his foot on the gas and then the sickening thud. How he had leaped out of the truck and tried to pick Sloane up and how Fern had stopped him and told him to run. That she wouldn't tell anybody how it happened if he disappeared and didn't talk about it. When he refused and wanted to take Sloane to the hospital, Fern had said she'd have him arrested not only as a murderer but as a thief, she said she knew all about him.

They had essentially blackmailed each other. The difference was that he had disappeared in a cloud of guilt and she had returned to her daily life as though nothing had happened. He had acted as though he were at fault; she had been the innocent gossip of local news.

"Myles?"

He opened his eyes. Tyler was looking at him with questioning concern. Myles realized that he had not said anything for several minutes as he went over the happenings in his mind. He had been clutching the bottle in one hand, gripping the printed report with his other. He upended the now-warm beer, finishing it in one long fraternity-party-worthy guzzle and then brought his fist down on the wooden surface of the table.

"That fucking bitch."

"I'll drink to that." Tyler finished his own beer in a similar fashion. "Because, let's face it. It's not just you who she's been trying to bring down. And if I'm hearing you correctly, I'm the reason she went to Sloane's that night – she thought I was back together with Sloane. Because I had wanted her to think that so she would leave me alone." He gave a rueful laugh. "That plan backfired – unfortunately on you." Then he became somber again. "And now that I think about..."

"So what do we have to do to clear my name? How can we prove that Fern is responsible?" One of Myles's legs began to twitch nervously as a sense of frantic urgency overtook him.

"Very carefully. The woman is lethal. And I mean literally. Promise me you won't do anything crazy until we've thought this through."

The laugh that Myles gave was almost manic. "Crazy?" He waved his arm at the living room cluttered with baby paraphernalia. "What could be crazier than me being here in your house in the middle of all this? After just finding out about that? How could my life get any more insane?"

Tyler was clearly becoming alarmed that Myles was verging on hysteria but covered it up with a warning finger to his lips. "Shhh. You'll wake the babies. And maybe Chloe. Not sure which would be worse." At times Chloe's lack of sleep made her the scariest force in the household. He opened the outside door and motioned for Myles to follow him onto the porch.

The cold air brought Myles around like a smack across the face. Despite the sense of his life having suddenly fallen into a new incomprehensible vortex, he felt suddenly clearheaded and alert as he turned towards Tyler.

"I'm ready for anything that will make this right."

Tyler clapped him on the shoulder in an unusually masculine gesture. "So we need to do this very carefully. But in the meantime, there's something you should probably do first..."

And that was how Myles had ended up at the cabin on a cool spring afternoon, folding merino wool blankets and linen sheets. He was almost finished with the small stuff; tomorrow he would work on getting the larger pieces of furniture into the truck. It was going to be difficult alone, but somehow he had managed to get it all up here in the fall.

The elephant in the room was, of course, the piano.

He was not even sure who it belonged to. It was going to be awkward, but he would have to give Butch a call. He had not spoken to him since he'd run out of the hospital that day, although he had called a few times to see if he was still there. Myles had driven Butch's truck back to Tyler's and parked it behind the house. He had only used it on his irregular trips to the cabin to feed Diva, check on things, and then padlock the door behind him.

He knew he was overdue for a real conversation with Butch, but he hadn't been sure what to say or whose side he was on now. With all the hoopla surrounding the twins and getting everybody settled at home, it had been easy to put Butch on the back burner.

He sat down on the porch steps while he waited for the call to go through, looking around at the sky through the treetops. It wouldn't be dark for another hour but the sun had already disappeared behind the mountains and a chill was settling into the shadows.

"This is Myles Scupper-Adams? I'm so glad you called. We've been trying to reach you."

"You have?" He did not like the sound of this.

"Mr. Evans has taken a turn for the worse, he probably won't make it through the night. It might be good if you come in as soon as possible."

"What? Um, I don't think..."

"When he's conscious, he's been asking for you. We think it might give him some closure. And you are listed as next-of-kin, so there will be some paperwork to sign."

Myles leaned his head back against the nearest porch post and closed his eyes. "Is he still in the same room?"

"Yes, you can just come on up and stop at the nurse's station. We'll be waiting for you."

Tyler would shit bricks if he knew. His mother would shit a whole chimney. But Butch wasn't the only one who needed closure. Myles shut the door to the cabin and flipped up the tailgate of the truck. Maybe he could get something to eat at the hospital too.

He hated to admit it, but Butch already looked dead. His skin was a translucent grayish-yellow hue and hung loosely from all visible parts of his body. Tubes ran from his nose and his arms and with every breath, his chest rattled like a loose window shutter.

Myles got as close as he dared and gazed down at the ghoulish specter of Butch's face. He was amazed when suddenly the familiar wild eyes opened and stared at him with recognition.

"Where the fuck you been, asshole..." It was barely a whisper but the words managed to convey all the usual sentiment.

"Been busy, you jerk. With the babies. How you doing?" Myles dragged a chair as near as he could to the bed and straddled it backwards, leaning his chin on the frame.

"How's it look like I'm doing." The strain of even these few sentences seemed almost too much for him and he closed his eyes again. Myles thought he had fallen asleep but then he realized that Butch was speaking.

"...inside my jacket..."

"What is? There's something in your jacket you need?"

"Brilliance...runs in the family..." Butch could apparently not resist wasting his last breaths on sarcasm.

Myles went to the closet where the same greasy jacket still hung in the same place it had weeks before when he had retrieved the keys to the truck. Cautiously he pulled the filthy fabric back to look for inner pockets. With one finger he explored first the right one and then the left, but they seemed empty.

"I don't feel anything, Butch," he called over his shoulder. "Are you sure?"

"...folded small...in they-uh..."

"I don't know about that." Myles checked again, feeling deeper and then he saw there was another compartment, a smaller one, with a flap up by the chest area. "Oh, here we go." He retrieved what appeared to be a piece of graph paper that had been folded several times into a tiny square. Is this what you're looking for?"

"Open...it."

Myles sat on the edge of the chair and carefully unfolded the well-worn sheet of paper and peered at the crude pencil marks on it.

"It looks like a map." He rotated it a few times, trying to understand what he was seeing.

"Duh...Now don't go losin' it."

"Me? Why? What's it for?" There was a square drawn in the middle and then some X's and numbers around it.

"...for you...no one else knows about it..." His lips seemed to draw back into a ghost of a smile. "Go now...before they take..." Butch's facial muscles slackened and then he choked a little.

"Okay, okay. But Butch. You have to tell me where it is. And what I am looking for." Myles started to feel a little desperate, as Butch seemed to be slipping away again. "Butch!"

"Yeah...yeah...don't fuckin' yell...it's my house....and my money..."

"Your house? I don't even know where you live!" he whispered loudly. "Never mind, I'll figure that out. But what do you mean – your money?"

"...Shhh..."

Myles moved closer so that his ear was nearly next to Butch's mouth. His breath smelled foul, like the gaseous odor rising off a manure pile. "Okay, tell me now. No one else will hear," he said softly.

"...cans...buried in the yard...you go get it..."

Myles sat up and began to protest but the pleading look in Butch's dark eyes stopped him.

"...you...closest...I got...enough...should be..." Butch's head fell slackly to one side and his eyelids slowly shut. He was clearly exhausted by the longest conversation he had conducted in days.

Holy shit, had this really just happened? He looked at the tattered hand-drawn map hanging from his fingers. "Okay, Butch. You got it, buddy. No problem." That was what you were supposed to say to dying people, right?

He sat there for a few more moments, watching the ragged rise and fall of Butch's chest, and then he remembered why he had wanted to contact Butch in the first place.

"Butch? What about the piano?"

At the mention of "piano" Butch's fingers moved a little but his face remained immobile.

"Where'd you get it? I need to give it back."

There was no response but Myles thought he saw the corners of Butch's chapped lips twitch a little. He couldn't tell if the old man was sleeping or just comatose.

"Damn you."

He began to delicately refold the paper and then stopped. Pulling out his phone, he took a picture of it, before gently finishing the process and stashing the one-of-a-kind document in his own jacket pocket.

He was surprised that he actually felt teary-eyed as he left the room.

"I bet he was glad you came to visit," the nurse assured him as he walked blindly by. "We'll call you."

"Hey, isn't that the guy..." a second shrill voice seemed to pierce the back of his skull. "It is, isn't it?"

Myles walked faster and did not look back. There would be no returning to the hospital now. Good thing it was dark out.

His first stop was the Emersons. He stood in their yard under the dim light of the waning moon and realized that he was never going to be able to put things back to how he had found them. Anywhere. There was no replacing camping gear in its original packaging or making boots unworn or pots unused. And there was certainly no giving back food he had eaten. If he hadn't promised Tyler he would do this, he probably wouldn't be bothering with this craziness.

He might as well just be up front about it. He put three large boxes on their screened porch with a scrawled note that read simply, "Thanks and sorry," and then got back into the truck and headed for the Carters. It had been months since he'd made the last trip out to their mansion on the hill; he could see the blinking red light of a new alarm system that must have been recently installed. There wasn't much to leave here; most of it had been consumables from the refrigerator and cabinets but there had been a few really nice things from Madison's closet he had lifted for Chloe. He'd brought those with him from Tyler's house, with Chloe's blessing.

"It was fun while it lasted," she had whispered, digging in her drawers. "I can't wear pearls and cashmere now anyway – no point with babies around. But I'm glad we got to eat all that Spanish cheese and tapenade." Reluctantly she had even relinquished her favorite piece of clothing, the extra-long purple scarf.

He put a large carton under the table on the Carter's back deck with the same message and continued on. But by the time he left the Franchettis he was starving – he remembered he had been hungry when he'd headed to the hospital and he'd never gotten anything to eat. He wondered whether he could get into the convenience store unrecognized. It was going to be tricky. It would be so much easier to lift one last meal from a refrigerator somewhere.

Maybe he could just dash into the little food mart at the gas station and be on his way. Unless old Mattie was working the night shift. She would know him in a heartbeat. He pulled into the parking lot and drove slowly past the pumps, trying to peer through the windows to see who was working behind the counter. Damn, he couldn't tell. He was going to have to get out and look.

But just as he opened the door, he saw Aidan and Liam come out of the store toting a six-pack and a bag of chips. Myles froze and they passed by without looking in his direction. But the image of his two former band mates seemed to seer itself into his brain, taunting him with its normality. Just a couple of friends having a regular night together, probably playing some tunes, watching some TV, drinking beers and smoking weed. Myles resented how much they probably took their freedom for granted, not appreciating the privilege of it. He felt like he would give anything right now to have his old status quo back.

Putting the truck into gear, he headed south on the highway. He'd have to drive through the notch down to Lincoln and get some food there, in a town where nobody knew who he was. He hoped.

CHAPTER SEVENTEEN

The call came in at 6am the next morning. Butch had died two hours earlier, but they had waited respectfully until dawn to notify Myles. When they asked him about "arrangements," he had been too dumbfounded to respond and told them he would call back later. Then he rolled over and put the pillow on top of his face. But there was no chance he would be falling back to sleep now. He might as well get this day over with. He folded up the bedding and shoved it into a pillowcase and tossed it out of the loft. He'd been trying to remember whose house it had come from. If he couldn't remember by the end of the day, he would leave it at the town church. Maybe some other deserving poor person would get a chance to sleep in 500 thread count sheets under a European down comforter.

The registration to the truck was actually exactly where it should be, in the glove compartment. Butch's address was listed as 720 Harley's Pond Road; Myles had a sense of where this was because Fern's house was on the same road but closer to town. That was cool; as long as he waited until Fern left for the library in the morning, he could save himself a trip and stop at her place to drop off her possessions on the way back. He had no idea what he was going to find at Butch's. He'd already returned the garden spade to the Franchetti's so he hoped Butch had some tools at his house.

Temperatures had dropped again in the night and with an overcast sky and a light wind, it felt more like winter than spring. His phone told him snow flurries were possible and depressing as this news was, at least it meant that the road would probably not get too soft today. He had to get the piano out of the cabin and down the mountain, even if it meant taking it back to Tyler's place until he figured out where it belonged. He hoped whatever awaited him in Butch's yard would not take too long to find or he would have to come back another time. Which he seriously did not want to do.

Unsurprisingly, Butch's residence was not much to behold. Small and square, the one story building was sided with dirty yellow shingles, had a gray metal roof and windows that did not appear to have been washed for several decades. The idea of going inside freaked Myles out more than he could express, even to himself. He did not want to see or smell the decaying possessions of the old logger's life. He pulled the pick-up around to the back of the house and was relieved to see a few open outbuildings and sheds. Any kind of shovel would probably be there.

As he climbed out of the cab with the map clutched tightly in one hand, the wind whipped his fleece jacket away from his body. Zipping it up to his chin, he pulled his hat down over his forehead, wishing he'd brought some gloves. It had been so warm just a few days ago. He stepped inside one of the three-sided garages to get out of the wind and peered at the map, trying to orient himself.

There were numbers next to the X's and he assumed that maybe these were feet or paces. In the light he could see faint dotted lines running from the corners of the square that represented the house. Would Butch have used a tape measure? He tried to picture Butch's stride in his mind, but all he could see was an uneven and loping gait around the clearing on the mountain.

Well, only one way to find out. Armed with a short wooden-handled spade, he crossed to the nearest corner, pointed himself in the direction indicated and started counting his steps. They ended at the base of a gnarled trunk that he assumed was an apple tree from the rotting remnants of fruit littering the ground beneath it. Was he going to have to dig up the frozen earth all the way around it? How deep were these freakin' cans?

Eight minutes later a small metallic clang told Myles he had literally hit pay dirt. A moment later he held a rusting yellow "Chockful-of-Nuts" can in his cold trembling hand. Lifting the plastic lid, he saw it was stuffed with baggies full of cash. He dumped the contents out into the dirt and began counting. Ten thousand dollars in fifties and hundreds. Stunned, he shoved the bills back into the can and then stared speechlessly at the map. There were ten X's.

It took him half a day to recover eight more coffee cans. Their contents varied in amount from seven to eleven thousand. The last one he could not find and finally gave up on, under the assumption that Butch himself may have dug it up at some point. When he eventually got back behind the steering wheel of the truck, he was sweating as much from fear as from the effort. Nearly ninety thousand dollars in cash sat on the floor in front of the passenger seat. More money than he'd ever seen in one place at one time.

Had this been Butch's own form of a retirement savings plan? Was it money he'd earned legally as a logger or was it ill-gotten gains? He would probably never know the answer to any of these questions. All he knew was that the man he had never known was his uncle had just given him a lifeline to change his future.

Myles felt so blown away by this turn of events that he couldn't think clearly at all. It was already past noon. He needed to get back to the cabin and figure out how he was going to get the piano onto the bed of the truck – he'd had a plan for that when he'd left at dawn but couldn't recall the logistics he'd worked out. He hoped his tires wouldn't sink into the mud too much at this time of day; the sky had been spitting snow for the last few hours so with luck this cold weather might prove good for something. The trail just had to hold out for his final trip down. If the ruts got too deep the way would become impassable.

As he drove down Harley's Pond Road he remembered at the last second that he needed to swing by Fern's and drop off her stuff. The gravel driveway spun out beneath his tires as he veered around the corner. Not exactly a subtle approach but it didn't matter. Fern would be at the library this time of day.

Only after he had pulled up to the front of the house, climbed out and opened the tailgate, did he realize that not only was Fern's car still parked along the far side of the cottage, but another vehicle was as well. He froze with his hands still gripping the sides of the box. Shit, he was fucked. What was she doing here and who was she with?

He felt as though he was slogging through a swamp – he could not make his body move as fast as his mind wanted it to. Heaving the carton up, he hurled it onto the porch and began what felt like a slow motion run back to the open driver's side door just as someone stepped outside into view.

"Myles?" He heard her gasp, but a moment later it was not Fern who flung herself in front of the truck but someone else, someone male, wearing only a pair of jeans and some hefty looking biceps.

"You fuckwad. Don't try to drive away!" The voice was familiar but Myles couldn't place it and he didn't care. He put the truck in reverse and gunned the engine. The body on the hood slid to the ground, still waving a fist at him, a fist that was holding a phone. "I'm callin' the cops on you!"

"Gray, no!" For the split second it took to shift gears into first, Myles saw Fern run forward and grab the man's arm. Despite the adrenalin rush coursing through him, Myles had a flash of recognition. It was Gray, the piano player he had replaced in the Why Mo Boys.

It took all his concentration for the next few minutes to maintain the high speed at which he drove back into town, glancing continually at the rearview mirror to see if he was being followed. Occasionally he caught a glimpse of a small red car that seemed intent on catching up with him and he pressed on, knowing that if he could only get to the turn-off for Sloane's and then into the woods, there would be no way a regular vehicle could follow him up the logging road.

He sped through the center of the village at twice the legal limit, praying that the local cop would still be having lunch inside Martin's Mountainview and not be sitting with his radar trained on the road. By the time he was bouncing over the rocks and mud of the trail, sweat was pouring down his face as though it were the middle of August and not a winter throwback day in April.

Forcing himself to slow down so he would not break an axle or blow a tire, he finally allowed himself to think about what had just happened. Head in the clouds, he had nonchalantly waltzed into Fern's yard and caught her at home in the middle of the day with that shithead who was less than half her age. What were the chances…he realized suddenly that it was Wednesday; he had totally forgotten that the library was closed on Wednesdays.

Still – what was wrong with that woman. Gray was a jerk. Okay, maybe a very buff jerk. Really the question was, what was Gray doing fucking around with her… The rattle of the coffee cans on the truck floor brought his current reality into focus. He hadn't even thought about all the money he was driving around with – shit. He forced himself to slow down; the last half a mile up to the cabin was going to take all his attention. There were a couple of places where spring streams had washed across the roadbed making for an exceptionally rugged ride that required careful navigation.

When he finally reached the dooryard of the sugar house and was able to turn off the engine, he just sat there, breathing as hard as if he had just run the whole way up the hill. Then he sprang into action, putting plastic bags of cash into his backpack, tossing the empty coffee cans through the open truck window onto the ground. He would deal with them later. Now at least he could take the money and run.

He grimaced at his own dark humor and then put the pickup into gear again, backing it up until he heard it make contact with the edge of the porch. He leapt out and flung the tailgate open. It was almost flush with the decking; if he put down a couple of planks, the piano might just roll right onto the truck bed. Please, please, let this be a piece of cake, he prayed. If only he had someone else to help him it would be so much easier.

Something brushed against him and he flinched, feeling another surge of nervous energy. A loud and insistent meow at his feet enlightened him; Diva had returned. She was thin and scraggly in appearance, but as he pressed her furry body to his face, her familiar warmth threatened to undermine all his determination to get this job over with. If he could just crawl under the covers with her curled up next to him and make everything go away…

"What do you say, girl? Can you help me push the piano out of the house?" He let her leap down and she ran off to look for her food bowl. He'd forgotten about the cat dishes - hell, that was some Tiffany silver the Carters were never going to see again.

Myles moved the couch over as far as it would go, and put the kitchen table and chairs on top of it. He released the stops on the piano's wheels and then leaned against one end of it, rocking gently. With a little groan, it began to roll, almost as smoothly as it had the day he moved it inside. Slowly he began to maneuver it towards the open doorway, stopping every now and then to listen for any unusual sounds outside. The only thing he could hear was the crunching of Diva's dry food between her sharp little teeth and the branches of the trees scraping against each other in the wind.

As he shouldered the piano through the entranceway and onto the porch, his phone rang. It was Tyler – he thought about not answering and then decided that was stupid. "Yeah?" He knew he sounded rude, but he didn't want to fuck around with trite conversation

"Everything okay?"

"Hardly. I'm singlehandedly trying to put a piano on a truck." The sulkiness of his own voice brought a threatening flood of tears to his eyes. He staunched them with his fingertips; he couldn't cry now. "Do you, by any chance, know who this monster belongs to?"

There was a silence on the other end of the line and he thought Tyler had hung up. But then he said, "Hold on a minute," and Myles heard him moving around, opening drawers and searching for something.

"I don't have a minute," he muttered, putting the phone on speaker and continuing to slowly edge the piano over the door jamb. He peered cautiously around it to the other side; somehow he had managed to get the wheels to line up perfectly with the planks. He turned around and put his whole back into the next push and with some serious straining, he felt the first two wheels move over the lip of the wood.

"Myles, are you there?" Tyler sounded small and tinny through the phone speaker.

"Hang on a sec, I'm on a roll, I've gotta finish this," he called and then with a superhuman shove and a sumo wrestler's grunt, he forced the entire piano up onto the planks, where, with a satisfying metallic thud, it continued on into the back of the truck. "Oh, sweet Jesus." He sat down heavily on the floorboards of the porch and leaned back against the cabin, closing his eyes.

"Did you do it?" The phone was still on top of the piano, but between the pounding beats of his heart, Myles could hear Tyler perfectly.

"Yes, it's done. Now where am I taking it?"

"The Clarks is what I have in my notes. Do you know who they are?"

"Fuck no. Never heard of them." Myles felt tired and cranky. "Maybe I'll just bring it back to Vermont with me and we can figure it out later."

"Let me call Eva and I'll call you back."

"Thanks." He was grateful that Tyler had accepted his bad-temperedness without busting him for it.

Myles felt exhausted, both mentally and physically, but he knew he was almost finished with his task. The planks clattered as he kicked them aside. He needed to pull the truck forward a few feet so he could use the steps again. He jumped off the edge of the porch and climbed into the cab. Behind him he heard Diva's plaintive cry; she thought he was leaving her behind one more time.

"Don't worry, I'm not going yet!" he called to her. Tyler would be pissed, but now that he had the opportunity, he was going to bring Diva to live there. At least Chloe would be delighted to see her.

When he got out again he discovered that just a few feet of bouncing across the forest floor had moved the piano dangerously close to the back edge of the truck bed. He probably ought to tie it down with something. After a vain search for some rope, he finally remembered the clothesline he had strung from a porch post to a nearby tree. As he cut it down, he saw Diva pounce at something in the leaves and start to move towards the underbrush. He realized he better catch her now while he could.

Luckily she was a responsive cat and it did not take long to coax her into his arms. He shut her into the truck with an open can of cat food and her favorite alpaca wool blanket. Yet another thing that he would not be returning.

Then, with the clothesline in hand, he climbed up onto the roof of the cab and stood there in the wind, contemplating how to secure the piano for the ride down the mountain.

The sharp crackling of dry twigs on the path should have been enough warning, but Tyler's call coming in at the same instant distracted him. Instead of looking over his shoulder, he reached for the phone which was still where he had left it, on top of the piano.

Later he would remember how slow his reaction time had been and would blame it on his tiredness, even though he probably wouldn't have done anything differently.

"Hey," he said into the phone.

"Hey. So Eva says there are two Clark families in Windfall. They both–"

Behind him something heavy hit the hood of the truck and Myles jumped, instincts finally kicking in, the phone flying out of his hand. He whipped around in time to see Gray heaving another huge rock in his direction. It glanced off the side-view mirror, sending shards of reflective glass to the ground.

"So this is where you've been hiding out, fucktard." Gray's sullen face was red from the climb and he was breathing noisily.

"What the fuck is your problem, asshole?" From his vantage point on top of the cab, Myles looked down at his adversary and tried radiate the fearless confidence that he did not feel. "Because whatever stick you have up your butt has nothing to do with me." He wished he had something more substantial or sharp in his hands instead of a long length of clothesline.

"Actually I came to deliver your mail." Gray tossed something at him that floated to his feet. Myles stepped on it to keep it from blowing away – it appeared to be a postcard. He reached down to pick it up and put it in his pocket without taking his eyes away from Gray. "You, motherfucker, are a murderer, a thief and a liar, and you are going down." Gray came closer and began to circle the truck and Myles moved in a circle with him. He had never had a confrontation like this before in his life, he was not sure what to do, but he thought he should keep talking.

"First of all, you've got the murderer part wrong." His voice rang out clearly, as though he were a public speaking professional.

"Oh, really. Well, I certainly don't have the thief part wrong. Because it looks like you are about to take off with the Clarks' historic piano, the one that you stole six months ago. You are some piece of work, Mya…" Gray had been running his hand along the surface of the polished wood as he spoke. Now he flipped up the keyboard cover and, with his crazy gaze still on Myles, played a dramatic chord for emphasis. "Needs a little tuning, I'd say."

Myles couldn't keep himself from laughing. "Well, you've got that part wrong too. I actually didn't steal this piano. But just so you know, the man who did is dead."

He could see that Gray was a bit shaken by this last statement, but tried to hide behind his ongoing bluster. "So whoever that was, you killed him too. Was that before or after Sloane?" His fingers banged out a few vaudevillian-style musical bars as accompaniment to his words.

Myles used the muddy toe of his boot to kick the keyboard lid closed, forcing Gray to swear loudly as he quickly pulled his hands away. "Don't touch the merchandise, jerk. And if I were you, I'd watch your back. You're the one sleeping with the enemy."

"You know what?" Gray moved towards him now, putting one foot on the front bumper. "You're loony tunes and I am bringing you down and turning you in." In one swift motion, his powerful thigh muscles had him up on the engine hood, inches away from Myles.

If it came to a battle of physical strength, Myles knew he would lose. As he reflexively tightened his fists, he realized he was still gripping the clothesline in one hand. Without much thought, he lashed it out in front of him, striking the metal roof he was standing on with a threatening sound.

"Gray! Gray!" Neither of them had to look up to identify the female voice that was calling loudly. Through the woods, something bright and red was approaching and both of them stared dumbfounded as Fern staggered breathlessly into the clearing wearing a crimson leather jacket and matching cowboy boots that were caked with mud from the trail. Her inappropriate clothing underscored just how out-of-place she was in this setting.

"Fern – what the fuck – you followed me up here?" Gray shouted with angry disbelief. "Leave now. Do you hear me? Go back down the mountain."

"Don't – do..." She was panting too hard to speak clearly but as she leaned over, trying to catch her breath, she shot Myles a look that could only be described as pleading. "Myles...we...had...a deal..." She coughed the words out.

Gray's pale eyes widened as they moved from Fern to Myles and back again. Myles shivered and then recovered himself, forcing a derisive laugh. "I'd say the deal is off, Fern."

She straightened up and for the first time caught sight of the piano. "Oh my god, you were the one who stole it from the Clarks. You are so over-the-top, Myles. You do need to be locked up." Adjusting her skirt, she stepped forward and began to walk around the truck to get a better look at it. "And whose vehicle is this, anyway?"

"I didn't take it. It was given to me." His defensiveness seemed absurd at this point, but he couldn't help it. "And if the two of you would get out of the way, I can continue with process of returning this piano to its rightful owners."

"Oh, sure you can, Dudley Doo-right." Myles did not like turning his back on Fern, who was by the truck's open tailgate now, but he felt it was more important to keep his gaze on Gray's sneering face. "Fern, I am telling you to stay out of this. As soon as I bring this guy to his knees, I am calling the cops." Gray put his arms out and began moving back and forth in front of Myles like a boxer.

"Don't be ridiculous. This is not going to shorten your parole." Then Fern's tone suddenly changed from demeaning to demure. "Sweetie, this is really just between me and Myles. You don't need to defend me."

"I'm not defending you, you stupid cunt. I'm trying to give this impostor what he deserves."

Myles needed a plan to get out of here. It was possible that if he could get into the truck... Out of the corner of his eye he caught sight of his cell phone in the mud a few feet away, where it had fallen when Gray had startled him. He had been talking to Tyler... if Tyler was still on the call and listening to what was going on, Myles needed to use this ill-timed encounter to his advantage.

"Fern, why don't you tell Gray here what actually happened the night that Sloane died?" Myles began speaking loudly and clearly, hoping Fern would do the same. "What was it you used again to poison her? I can't remember what you told me."

Fern stared at him aghast as Gray stared at her the same way.

"Sorry, Fern," Myles went on, enunciating his words carefully. "I know I promised, but the gloves are off now. So let's tell your boyfriend what happened. Yes, I ran over Sloane," his voice trembled a bit and he steadied himself. "But that isn't what killed her, is it?"

Much as he didn't want to lose sight of Gray, he needed to look at Fern while he spoke to her. They faced off, he with his feet planted in a wide stance on top of the cab, she hands on her hips at the edge of the tailgate, the piano between them.

"You don't know what you're talking about." Her eyes flashed fire. "You're just trying to sleaze out of one more thing you've done wrong."

He felt his cheeks burning but he pressed on. "There's a toxicology report on Sloane. Tell me you didn't think of that, Ms. Librarian. Apparently not, because you tried the same trick again on Eva."

"What the fuck is he talking about, Fern?" Gray demanded.

But Fern just glared at them and said nothing and Myles glanced nervously towards the phone on the ground. He had to get her to say something.

"Tyler!" He shouted the name, not as much to unsettle Fern but to ensure that he had Tyler's attention. "It was all about Tyler, wasn't it? You were always jealous. You couldn't stand that he wasn't interested in you and your perverted sex games. Not like this one here, apparently." He inclined his head in Gray's direction and was rewarded with an unnervingly animal-like growl.

"Oh, please. That man doesn't warrant all this discussion." Fern gave an agitated laugh and dismissed the idea of Tyler with a wave of her hand. "Let's not waste any more breath on that piss-ant."

"Really. Because you certainly put a lot of energy into creating all those bogus e-dating profiles just to fuck with his mind. And the graffiti on his car? Nice touch."

"Ridiculous. You can't possibly have any proof of THAT." Fern sneered nervously.

"But I don't understand why you would go after Eva. You know the thing with her tires..." Myles couldn't remember the details of that incident but he could see she was really rattled now. "That wasn't fair to her, just because you were pissed off at TYLER." His throat was getting hoarse from yelling but he knew if he raised his voice, the others would too.

"It doesn't matter what I did, YOU CAN'T PROVE ANYTHING!" Fern screeched back at him and then seemed to regain her composure. "You know most of what you did was petty thievery, but this–" She rapped her knuckles against the side of the piano. "This is a valuable antique. This is grand larceny."

"Don't change the subject, Fern. We were talking about you, not me. Although a lot of this is about 'you and me,' isn't it? That day you invited me to your house to 'talk' about housesitting." He sensed Gray leaning towards him, Myles could feel the heat of his breath on the back of his neck.

"Because unlike you, Gray-hole, I rejected her. And she's been making me pay ever since." Myles knew he shouldn't have used Gray's unfortunate nickname, but he couldn't help himself. With a roar, Gray was suddenly up on the cab's roof beside him and Fern screamed.

"Gray, why don't you just go back to your car before you do something stupid that you'll regret?" she suggested anxiously.

"Because stupid is his middle name. What does he have to lose, he's already the biggest loser around."

Gray lunged at him and Myles lashed out with the only defense he had – the clothesline. As Gray's fist got caught in the tangle of dirty nylon rope, Myles twisted his body and tugged with all his strength, hoping to make Gray lose his footing.

The line grew taut as Gray struggled to keep his balance. One knee connected with the small of Myles's back, knocking him sideways in a graceless tumble to the ground. Still clinging to the end of the rope, Myles turned his head just in time to see the catastrophic effect of his defense strategy.

As Myles fell, the snarled clothesline tightened around Gray's lower arm and pulled him off his feet. For a brief second he seemed suspended in the air and then he flew backwards off the roof of the cab, his heavy muscular body slamming into the piano.

There was a rumble, a shriek and then a monumental crash that shook the earth beneath him. A resounding discordancy filled his ears, the musical travesty of too many keys being played at the same time, and then it faded into a deafening silence. From somewhere nearby he heard his name being called in a faint voice that sounded strangely like Chloe's, but that sound was drowned out by Gray's shouting.

"Fern! Oh, my god, Fern! Say something! I didn't mean to do it! It was an accident, I fell. I'm com – ow, ow, OW!"

Through Gray's bellowing, Myles heard the tiny voice again and turned his head to see his cell phone just a few feet away from where he had fallen.

"Myles! Myles! Are you okay? What happened? Myles!"

In one flying motion he leapt to his feet and swept up the phone, as Gray continued to howl. "My arm! My shoulder! You fucking idiot! It's broken or dislocated! Aaah, oh my god, do something!"

But Myles didn't care about Gray's pain. He stared stupefied at the wreckage of the piano and what was crushed beneath its ruined framework. All that protruded was a red cowboy boot on the end of a leg, which was twisted at a very odd angle.

He didn't remember much about the next few minutes. He knew he himself had screamed as loudly and incoherently as Gray had during the time it took to wrap the clothesline around Gray's ankles and drag him out of the truck bed and onto the ground. Then, while Gray had shrieked in agony, Myles had actually searched through his pockets, looking for Gray's car keys and phone.

"They'll be in your car. I need a head start."

"Ow, ow, ow. You fuckin' ass-wipe!"

"You'll figure it out," Myles said. Then he sobbed as he drove his truck too fast all the way down the mountain, not stopping until he came to the red car.

"Stay there!" he yelled at Diva through his tears. Traumatized by all the noise and Myles's unusual behavior, the cat cowered beneath the seat as he hastily got out to toss the keys and cell phone into the other vehicle.

Where was he going to go now? He was an outlaw with a truck, a cat and a backpack full of cash. And a postcard. As he started down the mountain, he fumbled in his jacket pocket to look at it.

On one side was a picture of cactuses against a backdrop of red mountains and blue sky. On the other was a message addressed to "Cute Blond Fiddler of Why Mo Boys, C/o Martin's Mountainview Bar, Windfall, New Hampshire." It was postmarked Mulege, Baja Sur, Mexico. His eyes scanned the unfamiliar handwriting of the message.

"Hola from beautiful Baja!The weather on the Sea of Cortez is perfect, the food is cheap and all that's missing is a good-looking musician. Love from Randy and Sitka."

CHAPTER EIGHTEEN

July 2017

The midafternoon sun shone mercilessly on the back deck and the air felt hot and heavy. Just how she liked it best. Chloe checked one more time to make sure the double stroller was situated well into the shade of the maple tree. Inside, beneath the tightly secured mosquito netting, Artemis and Athena slept soundly, wearing only their diapers, their little bare chests moving up and down in a nearly matching pattern of breaths.

Confident that they would be fine for at least the next hour, Chloe looked around, confirmed that she could not be seen by the neighbors or from the street, and then pulled her dress over her head and undid her bra. Free at last, she thought, as she stretched out on the lawn chair and exposed her pale skin to the burning rays. Hello, Vitamin D.

She took one fleeting look at the current shape of her body – after four months of nonstop baby-feeding, her breasts were the only part of her that remained large, the rest of her was thinner than she'd ever been in her life. Her figure was probably really sexy now, not that she ever thought in those terms any more. If there was one thing she didn't feel these days, it was sexy. With a last glance at the baby stroller, she closed her eyes.

Almost instantly, she could feel herself slipping away into the welcome embrace of sleep, lulled by the intense heat and her continual state of exhaustion. She had been alone with the twins for nearly a week now. She'd told Tyler she would be fine by herself, that he should just go to Greece, but despite her independent bravado she was insanely grateful for the daily assistance of Sarah and Hunter and their children, and had even been happy to see

Lucy, Tucker's manic mother, when she came to visit on Sunday afternoon.

Hunter had tried to persuade her to stay at the inn until Tyler returned. "It would be much better for your mental health, and the babies can get used to being around other people. You can have Dylan's room – we'll make him sleep on the couch."

But Chloe wasn't ready to deal with the Scupper-Adams family scene on an ongoing basis. It was hard enough trying to let go of having Myles in her life, without having to endure constant reminders of him everywhere she turned. His parents were still as traumatized by his departure as she was and she didn't need anybody else's stress when she could barely deal with her own. Even though she needed help with the girls, she was learning to manage, and she didn't want to feel like she'd have to pick her clothes up off the floor or wash yesterday's dishes that were still in the sink to meet somebody else's standards of housekeeping.

And now that they smiled and responded, Athena and Artemis were good company. Most of the time. Except when they were unhappy babies whose mother couldn't cope alone. And who sometimes lost precious sleep worrying about what would happen if Tyler actually managed to find Tucker and convince him to come back to Vermont. Or wondering if she would ever get to see Myles again.

Sometimes she woke up sweating with the memory of that day in April when he'd suddenly burst into Tyler's living room as though a big wind was pushing him from behind. Artemis had stopped nursing and burst into tears at the noise of the door slamming open and Chloe'd had to bounce and soothe her while Myles ranted wildly through the house, describing what had happened in broken and breathless phrases. The back of his jacket was covered with mud and one sleeve had ripped at the shoulder, the insulation spilling out like dirty snow, but as she followed him from room to room, she could not get him to stop and take it off.

"I need my passport, where is my passport?" He was rooting through boxes and dumping things out of drawers.

"Did you see Tyler? He left for Windfall to help you as soon as we heard what was happening. You didn't pass him on your way? We heard it all, you know. It was like a radio show. We recorded it on my phone from his."

Myles had only stopped for a second to stare at her blankly. "He doesn't know where the cabin is. He's never been there."

"I told him how to find it. Your mother picked him up in the truck."

"My mother?!" His reaction was so extreme it was only then that she realized how truly crazed he had become. "She went with him? Why did they go there? I'm not even there. She'll see her. She'll see Fern..." He shook himself. "Did I tell you Butch is dead?" He waved the passport triumphantly in the air before stuffing it into the back pocket of his pants.

"Butch is dead? Myles, it's okay. They'll straighten things out. You'll see." She didn't believe her own words but he needed to hear her say them. "You're okay, that's all that matters."

"It's not. Fern is dead too and now it's all totally on me. All of it. I threw the clothesline at Gray that made him fall on the piano. It's all my fault. I've got to go. I'm leaving." He was shoving random things into a cloth grocery bag now. "Where did I put my fiddle?"

"You can't leave! What about me? Us?"

"It's the only way to keep you out of it. Just pretend you never met me. That none of this happened. Tyler will take care of you. My family will..." he swallowed and blinked. "I've got to eat something." He was in the kitchen now, flinging open the cabinets, ripping open a bag of tortilla chips, stuffing them into his mouth.

"But where are you going? You don't have any money! And you can't go by yourself!" Her shouting had startled Artemis again who was sobbing loudly once more.

His eyes had grown large then and he had started to laugh, choking on the dry chips he was chewing, coughing so hard that tears ran down his face, but Chloe thought he was probably crying for real now.

"Remember the fortune in the cookie I got that night at the Chinese restaurant? *'You will inherit a large sum of money.'* Well, guess what. It came true. I do have money," he whispered hoarsely. "Fucking tons of it. And I'm not alone. Diva is in the truck."

"You have Diva with you? Bring her inside. You can't take her...wherever it is you're going. Shhh, shhh." She tried to get Artemis to calm down but now a wailing had started in the bedroom. "Shit, we've woken Athena up too. Will you go get her?"

"I have to go..." But then she saw it, the fierce walls of self-protection crumbling to reveal the sensitive, vulnerable Myles she knew so well, the one who dropped everything and dashed to the crib and picked up the baby. For a brief moment she thought everything was actually going to be fine and then he kissed Athena on her little forehead and kissed the back of Artemis's neck and then folded all three of them into a giant hug. "Take her. Please." He pressed the other baby into Chloe's free arm and stepped back. "I'll call you or message you in a few days. I love you. I promise we'll be together again."

"Wait! Wait!" Holding both babies she ran after him, catching the outside door with her elbow to keep it from closing. "Where are you going?"

"Mexico," he shouted. And then he was gone.

While she spent the next several hours in grief and disbelief, Tyler and Sarah had, both literally and figuratively, cleaned up the mess Myles had left in Windfall. They had managed to get Hunter's ancient and rusty pickup most of the way up the mountain trail, passing both Gray's and Fern's cars parked in the first clearing, stopping only when they reached some very deep and impassable ruts that Myles had left in his haste to get away. Along the way they had tried numerous times to reach him by phone but he didn't answer and the fact that his vehicle, Butch's truck, was missing made it clear that he had fled the scene.

Gray was still in the dirt where Myles had left him with his ankles loosely tied together with a piece of clothesline. Although it had been less than an hour since his abandonment, he was blubbering and incoherent and had done nothing towards attempting to free himself. But when they realized the full extent of what had occurred, and that Fern actually lay dead beneath the wreckage of the historic piano, they were baffled by how to proceed. Ignoring his pleas for help, they had sized up the entirety of this horrific situation.

"Are you sure she's...not ...alive?" Sarah had been paralyzed by the insurmountable awfulness of the accident and had watched as Tyler slowly circled the site, finally kneeling down to look beneath the ruined remains.

"It broke her neck. It was probably instantaneous. She's not breathing." He stayed on his knees for a moment, eyes closed, trying to find some place inside of him where the insanity of this scene made sense.

Using calm reasoning and classic scare tactics, the two of them managed to convince Gray that they would take him to the hospital if he never spoke about this incident to anyone ever again. Playing the phone recording of Tyler's interrupted call with Myles helped convince him that they had recorded evidence of him, Gray, admitting that he was the one who had pushed the piano.

"If you just keep quiet, you won't be implicated and your parole will not be affected." Whether it was a threat or intimidation, Tyler hoped his on-the-spot deal would be effective.

"Yeah, but what am I going to say about how this happened? And what's going to happen to Fern? And I've got to get my car out of here, man, they'll find my car, they'll know I was here…"

Sarah looked pleadingly at Tyler. "Lying is not my area of expertise," she murmured under her breath. "You help him come up with the story – I am going inside to see how it looks in there. And then we need to figure out who we are going to contact about… this… disaster. And how."

By the time she had closed the door to the sugar house, carrying only a cardboard box and a pillowcase of bedding, Tyler had Gray on his feet. Miserable and muddy, he cradled his bad arm and mumbled about possibly never being able to play a keyboard again.

"You'll be fine," Sarah assured him, while behind his back she threw a questioning look at Tyler. "They can do amazing things with surgery and therapy these days."

They let Gray set the pace and lead the way down the mountain to the truck, their collective tension growing.

"Won't they be able to trace the 911 call back to one of our cell phones?" Sarah asked Tyler quietly. "How are we going to call this in?"

Tyler pulled his hand out of his pocket to display an unfamiliar phone in a leopard print case which he held out gingerly in a loose glove. "Fern's," he explained. "I fished it out of her purse."

She shook her head incredulously but said nothing about Tyler's capacity for sneakiness. "I wish we would hear something from Myles. I need to know he's alright."

They had reached the truck and after opening the passenger door for a now very sullen Gray, Tyler climbed into the back and held on as Sarah navigated the rough road in reverse. When they reached Gray's car, Tyler hopped out. Sure enough the keys were on the seat as Myles had apparently promised him.

"It's an automatic," he announced as he started the engine and hid Gray's phone beneath the floor mat. Let him find it at a less emotional time, he thought. "You ought to be able to drive yourself to the hospital if I back it out of here and point it in the right direction." He held the door open while a very dazed Gray eased himself inside. "We'll follow you down."

"Do you trust him?" Sarah asked as they proceeded slowly out to the main road, a few feet behind the red sports car.

"Not at all. But we did the best we could." Then he carefully brought out Fern's phone and called 911, after which he wiped the phone clean of his fingerprints and tossed it out the window onto the side of the logging trail just as they came out of the woods into Sloane's driveway.

They both jumped when almost simultaneously another ringtone signaled a call coming in. "That's mine." Sarah's voice trembled. "They couldn't possibly... could they?" She fished it out of her own coat pocket. "It's Chloe. Answer it, will you?" She handed it to Tyler.

Even though Tyler had the phone to his ear, Sarah was able to hear Chloe's hysteria.

"Slow down, slow down," Tyler said. And then, "What did you say? Mexico?"

For the next month every day had felt like an extended nightmare to Chloe as they listened and waited for news. Word of Fern's unusual demise spread quickly; it was the headline story of the local and state television stations and even found its way to national reporting, particularly in light of the historic stolen piano which showed up as the "instrument of death." The proximity of the event to the location of Sloane's unsolved murder put Myles's name into the spotlight a few times, and although there was no evidence to connect him to this most recent accident, he was still reported to be "at large."

In Windfall, Fern quickly became a local legend of heroic proportions, with over five hundred people showing up for her memorial. A collection was taken up to dedicate a park next to the library in her name. In the village, the big news about Fern and the Clarks' missing piano overshadowed the smaller story that a number of residents had discovered their stolen possessions had been returned, some of them only realizing in the recovery of the lost goods that the items had ever been missing at all.

On the obituary page of the Littleton newspaper, opposite Fern's three-column tribute, ran a smaller one about the passing of Lyle "Butch" Evans. Across the river in Vermont, there was slightly more fanfare, when, much to Sarah's mortification, the St. Johnsbury daily paper ran a human interest story about the little known connection of Butch Evans to the miscreant husband of Winnie Scupper, the famous stained-glass artist.

When the dust had settled behind Myles's hasty departure, it fell to Tyler to keep up the spirits of those around him who were feeling bereaved, despite the fact that he was experiencing a great loss of his own. Eva had not been able to accept even the small amount of the story Tyler tried to share with her and they'd decided to put their relationship on hold for a while. In light of local events, tango class had been canceled indefinitely and Tyler no longer made the weekly trip to Windfall.

Chloe could sense that Tyler's forced cheerfulness was as much for his own benefit as for hers and Sarah's, and when he wasn't working on the paper, he threw himself into the care and full-on adoration of his granddaughters. But without Myles taking on the role of stand-in father, Tucker's conspicuous absence from the family began to nag at Tyler more and more, often obsessively, until one day he announced that he had booked a flight to Athens in mid-July.

"Maybe you don't ever want to see him again, but I do." On his laptop screen was a map of the Greek Islands, zoomed in on Skyros. "Now I need you to give me names and directions."

So Chloe had been left home with all the responsibilities – the newspaper, the babies, the house and garden. "Cinder-Chloe, Cinder-Chloe," she had complained teasingly, knowing that nothing would change Tyler's mind at this point and that she had been offered plenty of help from the greater "family."

Which, of course, made these few minutes of lazing in the sun even more precious. As she felt the rivulets of sweat running between her breasts and down the sides of her rib cage, she tried to think of something other than whether she could get Artemis to start eating a little rice cereal like Athena did now or whether Athena's diaper rash might be from the recent introduction of solid food into her diet. Her beautiful babies – what she felt for them was such a different kind of love than anything she had ever experienced. It was overflowing, all-consuming. Sometimes she couldn't even remember what it had been like to just be a young adult woman who defined herself by her sexuality in relation to other adults rather than by her infinite love and capacity to care for her children.

And, as always, whenever she tried to picture something other than the fresh faces of her infant twins, she found herself wondering about Myles.

He'd managed to get a message through to her once. Eight weeks after he'd left, she'd found a new Facebook friend request on her phone from Diva Gatotita. She cried and laughed at the same time when she saw the profile picture – it was a striped cat wearing a tiny sequined sombrero.

Diva's profile info said she lived in Bahia Concepcion, Baja Sur, Mexico and that she worked at "permanently camping on the beach."

Quickly accepting the request, Chloe typed in a message, *"We are fine and hope you are too. Love from C, A & A."*

She watched obsessively for a reply but none ever arrived. She researched Bahia Concepcion and found it to be 876 kilometers south of the border along the Sea of Cortez. It looked beautiful and unpopulated and as different from Vermont as any place on earth.

And then one day she realized that Diva Gatotita no longer existed, her profile was gone. Sometimes, when

Chloe was feeling depressed, she worried that the whole thing might have been a figment of her desperate imagination. But most of the time she knew that Myles was safe, an outlaw with a new life and probably a new identity.

From somewhere beyond her daydreams, a tiny sob became an ongoing wail. She felt the reaction in her breasts before her brain; it was post-nap feeding time and Artemis wanted to nurse. Now. As if on cue, Athena joined the chorus, her cries echoing loudly across the yard.

"Okay, babies, okay!" Chloe called. "I'm coming!" There was no point in bothering with the bra. She pulled her sundress over her head, using the hem to wipe the sweat from her brow. It was a tricky process, but at least she'd figured out how to nurse both of them at once.

As she carried Artemis and Athena into the cool interior of the house, she wondered how long it would be until Tyler came back.

ABOUT THE AUTHOR

A lifelong lover of travel, mysteries and creative expression, Marilinne Cooper has always enjoyed the escapist pleasure of combining her passions in a good story. When she is not traveling to warmer climates around the world, she lives in the White Mountains of New Hampshire and is also a freelance copywriting professional. To learn more, visit marilinnecooper.com.

ALSO BY MARILINNE COOPER

Night Heron
Butterfly Tattoo
Blue Moon
Double Phoenix
Dead Reckoning
Snake Island
Windfall

Jamaican Draw

Made in the USA
Columbia, SC
16 August 2018